W9-ASH-658

WITHDRAWN

TRAP LANE

*Recent titles by Stella Cameron
from Severn House*

The Alex Duggins series

FOLLY
OUT COMES THE EVIL
MELODY OF MURDER
LIES THAT BIND
WHISPER THE DEAD
TRAP LANE

Other titles

SECOND TO NONE
NO STRANGER
ALL SMILES
SHADOWS

TRAP LANE

Stella Cameron

CRÈME de la CRIME

This first world edition published 2019
in Great Britain and the USA by
Crème de la Crime an imprint of
SEVERN HOUSE PUBLISHERS LTD of
Eardley House, 4 Uxbridge Street, London W8 7SY.
Trade paperback edition first published
in Great Britain and the USA 2020 by
SEVERN HOUSE PUBLISHERS LTD.

British Library Cataloguing in Publication Data
A CIP catalogue record for this title is available from the British Library.

ISBN-13: 978-1-78029-117-8 (cased)
ISBN-13: 978-1-78029-623-4 (trade paper)
ISBN-13: 978-1-4483-0235-2 (e-book)

This is a work of fiction. Names, characters, places and incidents
are either the product of the author's imagination or are used fictitiously.
Except where actual historical events and characters are being described
for the storyline of this novel, all situations in this publication are
fictitious and any resemblance to actual persons, living or dead,
business establishments, events or locales is purely coincidental.

All Severn House titles are printed on acid-free paper.

Severn House Publishers support the Forest Stewardship Council™ [FSC™],
the leading international forest certification organisation.
All our titles that are printed on FSC certified paper carry the FSC logo.

FSC
www.fsc.org

MIX
Paper from
responsible sources
FSC® C013056

Typeset by Palimpsest Book Production Ltd.,
Falkirk, Stirlingshire, Scotland.
Printed and bound in Great Britain by
TJ International, Padstow, Cornwall.

For Jerry

ONE

Absolute stillness waited for Alex Duggins in the kitchens of the Black Dog. Stillness and silence but for an almost sound, like sodden earth's faint sucking after the storm. She closed the door softly and reached hesitantly for the light switches. Two clicks and the early-morning shadows disappeared – but not the silence.

Prickling at her nape, its subtle climb into her hair shocked her. 'Off you go, Bogie,' she said, too loudly. 'Go find your blanket.' *And I will shut out this ridiculous so-called premonition and get on with my day. Premonition of what anyway? It hasn't happened since . . . Shut this out!*

A vehicle rattled into the car park behind the pub. That would be the milk delivery.

Murky as the day's beginning was, complete with drizzle, it wasn't cold. Alex hadn't worn a coat to come from Tony's Range Rover to the building. She took an apron from a hook and slipped it on, then started coffee brewing.

A knock at the front door of the Black Dog jolted her. Tying the apron strings more firmly, she hurried to open up, peering at her watch as she went. Half past five in the morning. Tony had only dropped her off a few minutes ago. Scoot Gammage, the teenager who came in to help at the pub before school, was due soon but always used the back door to the kitchens anyway – just as she did.

Alex unlocked and opened the door. Someone might be hoping to book a room in the inn for the coming night.

A tall woman in a long black raincoat, its hood pulled over her head, stood with her back to Alex who cleared her throat. After a few seconds she said, 'Can I help you?' The raincoat was overkill for the weather.

Turning enough to look over her shoulder, the woman took plenty of time summing up Alex. Narrowed, very dark eyes traveled from head to foot and back. 'I doubt if you can. I'm

Neve Rhys.' *Scottish, but the accent less soft than Hugh's. Skin a milky white. Lines at the corners of her eyes and between her brows but still in her thirties probably.* The derisive curl of her lip was impossible to miss, even in the mean light released by grey clouds that hung like Victorian funeral bunting over trees and hills.

The low, clear voice came again. 'My husband's cousin, Hugh Rhys, runs this place. If you'd go along and tell him I've come, I'll wait here.'

The woman looked away and once more Alex was faced with that blank, black, tall back.

She flipped on more lights. 'Hugh isn't up yet. Please come inside, though, and I'll give him your message.' Even the misty village green across the High Street was still and empty. Not a dog walker in sight yet. Only the first curls of smoke from stone cottage chimneys suggested the village was awakening.

'How do you know he isn't up yet?' the woman asked. 'Who are you?'

If Hugh had more relatives like this it was little wonder he never talked about any of them. 'Alex Duggins. I own the Black Dog. Hugh is my manager. He should be down shortly.'

She stood back while Neve Rhys swung around and came into the restaurant. The inn's seven guest rooms were reached by a staircase on the left, behind a reception desk, while the pub and kitchens took up the rest of the rambling lower floor.

'There's coffee in the kitchen,' Alex said, pointing. 'It'll soon be ready. Through the main bar. Kitchens are at the back, behind the counters. Help yourself. You look a bit chilly and it's warmer in there.'

The stare Alex got suggested the woman either didn't understand the offer, or . . . who knew? An elegant, sharp-boned face didn't move and very dark eyes slid away to look into the distance. Neve Rhys scraped out a chair at a dining-room table and sat down. She pushed the hood away from a closely cropped cap of straight black hair and looked up abruptly. 'I'm tired,' she announced. 'I've done a lot of driving in the past few days. If you don't mind, I'll take a double whiskey and a jug of water. Since I'm family to Hugh, I'm sure that can be managed, even at this hour.'

She crossed her ankles and arms and closed her eyes. Glinting gold hoops shifted gently in her ears. Her left hand revealed a thin band on her ring finger. Her boots, worn over black tights, were laced all the way from their pointed toes and had high, square heels. Again, decidedly wintry for the time of year but Alex felt dowdy beside her, not that she knew if she'd ever be ready for anything approaching Neve's modishly individual look.

A door slammed in the distance and rubbery footsteps made halting progress over wooden floors. Alex watched the passageway from the pub to the restaurant and shortly Scoot Gammage, taller almost every time she saw him, but still thin and with his blond hair as on-end as usual, came hesitantly into the room.

'Morning, Scoot,' she said, raising her brows meaningfully. Scoot was never slow to pick up on an unusual atmosphere. 'Would you mind going up and letting Hugh know his cousin's wife is asking for him?'

He gave Neve a long look and took off for the stairs.

'Now let me see what I can do about that whiskey. We don't carry your family label. Aberlour do? Or Glenfiddich?'

'Whatever.'

Alex turned to leave and Scoot's trainers squealed on the stairs, coming down this time. 'He's coming,' he said, catching up then striding ahead of her. 'I need to get on or I'll be late.'

Alex laughed. 'Not the way you ride that bike of yours.'

In the bar she put a glass of Aberlour and some water on a tray, popped several pastries delivered very early from George's Bakery into the microwave for a few moments, and filled Hugh's large mug with coffee. This she added to the tray and, together with the plate of pastries, retraced her steps toward the restaurant.

She was certain that Hugh had never spoken of his family. There was little she knew about his background and apparently a great deal she did not. He was a quiet man; big, handsome and well-liked, even if he was more of a watcher than a mixer, unless a conversation interested him. Hugh could make people feel comfortable with little more than a smile. Women were visibly intrigued by him.

Would seeing him with someone he'd evidently known a long time – someone with none of his charm as far as Alex could tell – clarify the puzzle of Hugh Rhys at all?

'Well, I'm damned,' she heard him say and he didn't sound pleased, or glad. 'I thought Scoot must have it wrong but it is you. What in God's name are you doing here?'

Not pausing to listen would have taken more control than Alex had. That was a tone of voice she had never heard coming from Hugh.

'It's wonderful to see you, too, laddie,' Neve said, heavily sarcastic. 'I made a difficult drive to this silly little hole of a place to try and do you a good turn. Bear that in mind and we'll get along just fine. You're going to be glad I'm here.'

'An email would have saved us both some irritation. What do you want?'

'Bridge over Troubled Water,' was the first song that came to mind and Alex did her best to hum it loudly as she continued to the restaurant.

She only had moments to observe Neve lounging beside the table and Hugh towering – or looming – over her. The woman appeared smug, pleased with herself perhaps. Hugh's face was rigid, furious.

Alex wished her mother, Lily, were observing this. Lily ran the inn and restaurant, had for years, and she was an excellent interpreter of human interactions.

'This should warm you up,' Alex said brightly, and slid the tray on the table. 'And calm your nerves. What else can I do for you, Neve? If you'd like a room so you can rest, say the word and we'll get you fixed up.'

Neve didn't answer. She put the whiskey in front of her, added a tiny amount of water, then took several sips.

'Thanks, Alex,' Hugh said, his voice expressionless. 'I'm sorry you've been put out. I'll be along to help out shortly. Very shortly.'

A faint smile passed over Neve's features. 'We understand you have a house not far from here, Hugh. Why are you sleeping here?'

'You mean Green Friday? I don't live there. I prefer to be here – but that's irrelevant to you.'

Alex walked away. In the bar, Scoot was brushing the floors but stepped close to her when he could. 'Who's she, then? I mean, what's she here for?' He looked concerned.

'Nothing to do with us,' she said. 'And I don't think Hugh's glad to see her either. But she says she's had a long drive so maybe she's just tired.'

'She's a snooty one,' he responded with a grin. 'Hugh doesn't have a lot of patience with uppity people, so she'd better watch herself.'

'Scoot,' Alex hissed. 'She's family to him so we have to be nice.'

'If he doesn't, why should we? He's not being nice to her – I think he hates her guts.'

'*Scoot!*'

'Right,' he said with his one-sided smile. 'Just sayin'.'

'And from the way you sound these days, you're watching too much TV. I'm surprised Tony's dad allows it.' She grinned at him and gave him a soft punch on the arm. 'Better get on with it or you really will be late.' Scoot and his brother Kyle were wards of Doc James Harrison who had taken them in when their father had been imprisoned. Alex's mother, Lily, was close to James and helped with the boys.

'If you weren't so bloody hard-headed, Hugh Rhys, I wouldn't have had to drive all the way down here to make you see sense.'

Alex and Scoot stared at one another. Raised, Neve Rhys's voice got higher, sharper, and lost its control.

'I thought we'd decided you shouldn't try to change a thing about all the ways I irritate you. You suggest something I should do and for some reason, I always want to either do nothing at all, or something quite different. I haven't changed, Neve. But then, neither have you and that's a pity, not that it matters anymore. We're nothing to each other. When are you driving back?'

'When I bloody well feel like it and that may not be for some time – up to you. Decide to stop being so fucking selfish and think about what's best for the rest of us, why don't you? The sooner you stop driving in your heels just to annoy me, and do what must be done, the sooner we'll never see one another again. There's business to be settled and since you won't come to Scotland and deal with your responsibilities, the only choice was to come to you.'

'How did you find me, anyway?' Hugh said, and Alex didn't think he intended to be drawn into Neve's reasons for coming.

'You must have forgotten we share some friends. You're not as lost as you thought you were. You've had quite the time of it, haven't you? The lovely Sonia still pines over you, or so she tells me on the phone.'

'That's enough,' Hugh snapped. 'Sonia Quillam is a tiny piece of the past to me. And the only reason you'd pretend to be her friend is to find out what she knows . . . about me, that is. She knows nothing. She's out of my life. She's been out of my life for years.'

'That's not what she says. But it doesn't matter. She was never good enough for you and that thing with her was just a rebound anyway. Let's not talk about it. You asked me how I found you and I told you. But watch out for that one, Hugh, she moons over you and that can be dangerous if she decides to hunt you again.'

'I have to start work. Excuse me.'

'Oh, Hugh, don't be like this. It's been a long time. Let's just bury the hatchet and remember the good times. There were lots of those and I think about them if you don't. But we are going to have to do some talking and I think it would be a good idea to get a good start before Perry gets here? It'll take him a day or two.'

'Perry?' Hugh sounded aghast. 'He's coming? What the . . . why? Who will be watching things in Scotland while both of you are trying to twist my arms. In case you've forgotten, my arms aren't easy to twist.'

Neve laughed. 'I haven't forgotten a thing about your arms, Hugh. Or any other part of you.'

Alex glanced at Scoot but he was laying logs in the fire, listening but without noticing the soft suggestion in Neve's voice.

'Anyway,' Neve said, 'since when did you give a damn about the distillery.'

'I know my responsibilities and I attend to them. Now, I'm finished with this conversation.'

This conversation showed a man who was so not the Hugh Alex had come to know. He must recoil from being pushed as he was by his cousin's wife. Alex felt like walking outside. She could take Bogie with her. Rather than letting him go with Tony to the morning clinic at his small veterinary hospital like usual, she had wanted her dog's company and insisted on keeping him with her. Bogie and Tony's dog, Katie, had been asleep in the back of the Range Rover when they'd arrived at the Black Dog and Tony had pushed Alex to leave him there.

She and Tony rarely argued. Perhaps they didn't argue enough. Sometimes she felt she didn't really know him which was ridiculous when they'd been friends since she was a little girl and he started standing up for her in the school playground. And now they were lovers, which was exactly how she liked it.

Enough of that. She wasn't sure what to do next. Daylight had begun to fully bloom even though clouds still billowed in murky grey banks. They needed rain, lashings of rain to seep deep into the dry earth. Full summer would be upon them soon.

Outside it would be fresh, the air nippy but promising warmth later on, piquant with the scents of damp grass and flowers bathed with dew. The freshness wouldn't last long if it turned into another dry hot day.

Alex gathered the last of the discarded newspapers from the day before and looked around, ready to go into the kitchens.

'I need a place to stay,' Neve was saying. 'Green Friday sounds like a good idea.'

'No!'

Hugh refused so harshly, Alex flinched.

'I'm renovating,' he said, but he didn't sound any less angry. 'I don't see any point in you being here, anyway. I mean that. Nothing is going to change.'

'Hugh?' Neve was barely audible. 'I'm so tired. I need to rest and think. Is it all right if I stay here – with you?'

Alex, her ears and eyes open wide, walked toward the kitchens.

'I'll pretend I didn't hear you say that,' Hugh said.

'Why?' Neve said. 'It isn't as if we haven't slept in the same bed before. You sound as if you could use some comforting and I know I could.'

'Go to hell, Neve!'

Alex flinched and held her breath.

'Take a room here,' Hugh said. 'I don't care. You'll do what you want to anyway. Just stay out of my way.'

TWO

A single rider, a thin, hunched, weather-beaten man astride a broad and glossy Welsh cob, clipped downhill toward her, swaying comfortably in his saddle. He tipped his tweed cap with a crop at Alex but made no effort to move aside for her Range Rover. Neither did his smug and bouncing Jack Russell terrier.

'Afternoon, Alex,' Chuck Short called. He smiled and his nut-brown face creased into deep wrinkles. Chuck managed the Derwinter stables. 'It'll be evenin' afore long. It's getting late to start on an outing. You're off your beaten track today.' Leonard and Heather Derwinter's estate covered hundreds of lush acres beyond the Dimple – a shallow valley at the top of the hill that looked down on Folly-on-Weir. Tony Harrison and Alex both owned houses in the Dimple but Alex now lived with Tony and her house was about to go up for sale.

Chuck must have cut across country from the Derwinters' but Alex had never ventured that way in years. Local people tended to keep away from the big estate but she was sure the walkers who invaded the area in weather like this didn't have such scruples.

Pulled as far into the hedgerow as possible on a steep lane she rarely used, Alex leaned out of her window. 'I'm going up to visit Radhika. She works for Tony Harrison at the vet clinic in Folly. She's his assistant. Should have gone to look at her new house weeks ago but you know how that is.'

'Aye. I know who she is, too. We're too busy for what's really important sometimes. She's a pretty thing. Nice, too. Cozy with that detective, isn't she?'

There were few secrets in country communities. 'Bill Lamb?

Yes, you might say that. How are things at the Derwinters? I haven't seen Heather for weeks. That's unusual.' The lovely Mrs Derwinter liked to make splashes in the village of Folly-on-Weir and was almost a regular at the Black Dog, but not recently.

Chuck gave another of his puckish grins. 'I expect she's been busy, too,' he said and urged his horse on. 'There's only the two houses up here. Your Hugh Rhys owns that Green Friday place, so Radhika must have bought the old manor house. Small as far as those places go, but a bit pricey for a vet tech anyway, I should have thought. It'll take a fair bit to fix it up.' He waved goodbye without turning in the saddle.

Smiling to herself, Alex drove back into the lane, her wheels bumping over ruts dried by weeks of sunshine. The sun was going down, turning clear blue skies to dusky mauve. The colors of wild flowers along the verges still popped. After a tense day at the Black Dog, she was glad to escape for a while.

A long time had passed since she'd come this way even though the road below the lane passed both her own house and Tony's.

Local people continued to assume Radhika was dependent on her salary from Tony. Just as well, even if it did make them wonder how she could buy the old house that Alex understood was rapidly being renovated.

Radhika's finances were nobody's business but her own – even if Alex did know about the fortune she'd been left by a friend who had treasured her.

At the entrance to Green Friday, Alex slowed to peer down the long driveway guarded by handsome sycamore trees. A beautiful place, Hugh must consider it a fine investment, but he'd never lived there or even spent a night under its roof as far as she knew. He did rent it if approached by friends. She hadn't been inside it for some time, but it had looked perfect to her, certainly not as if it needed the work Hugh had referred to that morning.

The last time Alex had been at Green Friday was something she tried hard not to remember.

The sight of Hugh's distinctive 1939 BMW Nash – navy-blue and white – parked on the right edge of the driveway surprised her. The car faced out only a short distance from the impressive stone pillars on either side of the entrance gates. The back of the man himself striding toward the house, which she couldn't see from the lane, almost stopped her but she drove on, frowning and wondering why he was there. The pub would be open and he never left the premises during business hours. Not without letting her know, although he didn't have to, not when he would have covered for himself anyway.

He'd been very quiet all day, even for him. Alex's mother, Lily, had settled Neve Rhys into a room at the Black Dog and she hadn't put in another appearance.

A bit further on and Alex saw the slate roofs and grey stone chimneys of Radhika's new home.

She stopped the Range Rover again and idled the engine. In the rearview mirror she saw nothing but the empty, hedge-lined lane and a rapidly falling mauve dusk turning to purple.

Hugh was a mostly solitary man. All she knew about his purchase of a big house on this hill was that he'd come upon it soon after taking the job at the Black Dog – on one of his hikes – and fallen in love with the place. In addition, he now owned some good parcels of the still unimproved surrounding land and continued to ramble there. If he had plans for development he had not mentioned them and Alex would never pry into his private affairs.

Perhaps she should go back and make sure all was well with Hugh.

Prickling cold climbed her spine, echoed on the sides of her face. That made twice in the same day and she hated it.

Movement brought her eyes back to the mirror, but it was only a rabbit bounding up the lane behind her.

Hugh was a big boy and she was being a touchy idiot.

But the insistent cold fingers didn't stop fondling her skin.

Hugh spared only brief glances for the fine golden Cotswold stone façade of Green Friday, or the pyracantha, massed with white flowers, climbing the walls. The tennis courts must need tending and he had no idea about the condition of the swimming pool behind the building. He had come to hate this house. It needed to be sold, or he usually thought it did until he considered having to involve himself with the place again.

The door was unlocked, just as Sonia had said it would be. Hugh let himself in and made sure a good slam would let her know he was there. She wasn't supposed to come near him ever again. He'd warned her he wouldn't be responsible for his actions if she did. She'd called him an hour ago and he had immediately concluded that Neve must have known where Sonia was although he couldn't decide why she wouldn't have told him when she went so far as to ask to stay at the house. He hadn't attempted to challenge her and ask what she was up to, but he wanted to.

He detested the thought of Neve being at the Black Dog, of her sleeping in a room so close to his quarters.

Sonia Quillam had stayed away for a long time but as always, her absolute conviction that no man could remain angry with her had worked its way to the surface again. Her gall in coming here and using a key she should not have infuriated him. She must have kept a key from when she and her family rented Green Friday for a summer. What a disaster that had been.

He heard the sound of her signature backless heels clacking on the stone tiled kitchen floors. The sound carried through the still house like the striking of keys on an ancient typewriter.

It would be a bad idea to confront her without tamping down his anger. She was selfish, vain, sexually obsessed . . . sexy and magnetic. Sonia had made his life hell on too many occasions and whatever she wanted from him now wasn't happening. Hugh took several deep breaths. The silence that fell in the kitchen was not lost on him.

Sonia was waiting for him, arranging herself to best advantage.

The house felt empty. He walked past the curving staircase and unused rooms he hadn't seen since after what he thought of as, The Horror. Gathering dusk through bow windows above drawn draperies turned furnishings cloaked in sheets into shaded memories. Nothing had been changed. Even thinking of coming here to consider making the place over was repugnant.

His pace slowed. He could feel her listening for him, almost hear her breathing – short breaths that caught as she prepared to spin the next lies.

He opened the kitchen door.

'There you are!' Her full voice came at him, fulsome, but squeezed and girlish to gain whatever impression she wanted to give. 'I started to think you wouldn't come. Oh, Hugh. I've missed you so.'

She spread her arms and came toward him, her body as lush as he remembered – all too well – visible inside a near transparent flowered kaftan zipped from hem to between her breasts. She was obviously naked beneath the flimsy material.

Hugh turned away. 'You aren't supposed to be here.'

'Don't treat me like that,' she said, her voice husky now. 'I've had terrible times and you know it. I wouldn't have come if I didn't know you were the only real friend I've ever had. You're the only friend who has been there for me through good times and bad, whether I made mistakes or not. And I know I've made plenty of mistakes.'

'Haven't we all?' He didn't trust himself to look at her again. 'I suppose you kept a key to Green Friday. That doesn't surprise me, but yet again . . . no, you couldn't disappoint me. You don't do anything without calculating how it might benefit you. I don't want to know about your dramas, Sonia, but I do want you to leave. Stay the night and go in the morning.'

'It's Elyan, Hugh. Our son is incarcerated with mad people. A brilliant musician shut away and forgotten. I can't bear it, not alone as I have been. Each time I see him it breaks my heart again.'

Slowly, he faced her. Beautiful, olive-skinned and golden-eyed with rust-blond hair that curled down her back, she didn't need to display a knockout figure as she did tonight. The tearful shine in her eyes, the trembling droop of her full lips, revolted him. 'Liar,' he said, clenching his fists at his sides. 'You haven't seen him. Not once.'

Her mouth sagged, then drew taught. 'How would you know? You won't even acknowledge him.'

'Elyan is not my son, but I am his friend. I see him regularly. He plays the piano in that place every day, did you know that? An old, upright piano. And he gives lessons to other so-called patients. He's finding peace even as he confronts what he became. He never mentions the fabulous career he lost – only the sister who is gone forever and the woman whose life was snuffed out. And he doesn't make excuses, even if we know he wasn't in his right mind.'

Sonia rocked on her flimsy shoes and shook her head in denial. 'Hold me, Hugh. I'm desperate. I need you more than I've ever needed anyone. Take me to bed. Please, darling.'

For just an instant he felt protective, sorry for her. Just an instant. 'I don't know why you wanted me to come here but it doesn't matter,' he told her. 'You told Neve I was here in Folly. How did that happen?'

'She's been nice to me,' Sonia mumbled, wrapping her arms around her small ribcage. 'When she asked, I told her. What was wrong with that? We keep in touch – not all the time, but now and then. She called me in Paris – from Scotland – and said she needed to contact you. You make it so hard for people, Hugh. Why do you hate your own family?'

'And you just decided you ought to pester me in Folly, too?' He extended a hand, warning her not to mess with him. 'Forget I asked. I don't care. You're out of here.'

He'd already had enough. Neve must leave Folly. As usual she had engineered an encounter for some devious reason of her own, and Perry's. 'I have a job and I have to get back.'

'No!' She ran at him and wrapped her arms around his neck. 'For our son's sake I beg you to help me. I'm alone and I don't know what to do.'

Hugh patted Sonia's back as if she were a child. 'Calm down. I take it Percy Quillam is playing the field again. You shouldn't be surprised. That's how you got into your husband's life in the first place. As the mistress of a married man. That's how you got him to marry you. He always played the field and I don't know why you thought you could make him monogamous. Sonia, you're beautiful and talented. You have a voice others only long for. Go back to your career. Sing and build again. You can do it. And we both know, regardless of how much you want to use him as a connection to me, Elyan isn't my son although I wouldn't have minded if he were. I don't know why you came or what you thought you could accomplish here, but it isn't going to work. A DNA examination proved Elyan isn't mine.'

'Percy hates me – he's in Paris conducting – and his beloved agent, Wells, is with him of course.' She reared back, her eyes glittering with tears. 'I'm just his showpiece, someone he likes on his arm. He's punished me for my supposed sins by trying to chain me to him. I came because I need you. Isn't that enough? It used to be.'

'We are history, Sonia.'

'But, Elyan—'

'Isn't my son and you know it. Why do you persist? And you haven't visited him since he was sent away. Not once. What excuse do you have for that?'

She cried, loudly, swiping at tears with both hands. 'I couldn't bear to go there and see him like that.'

'Your husband goes,' he said quietly. 'He's the father. But it's you Elyan wants to see. Sebastian Carstens, faithful piano teacher, still goes. Annie Bell also goes – as often as they'll let her. She still loves him and waits for him, even if it must seem hopeless. I've got to go now.'

THREE

'Hugh will come back to me,' Sonia said to herself, fumbling her way across the bedroom to the bathroom. She had changed into black velvet trousers and an orange silk tunic. 'He wanted to stay with me; I know he did. So stupid. Too proud to give in. But he will.'

She splashed cold water on her face and let it drip onto her tunic. Lights only made this damned house feel bigger and emptier. Barefoot and in near darkness, she stumbled downstairs and into the kitchen.

Low lights beneath the glass-fronted cabinets gave a pale glow that reflected across etchings of grasses swept by wind. Sonia hated those greenish glass doors with their soundless wind and wildness. Even the Aga and dark green appliances made her sick.

The front door knocker, dropped once, sent its iron-hard

sound echoing through the house. Sonia barely breathed, then she ran to answer, her heart pounding. She had known he would regret trying to leave her.

The heavy door swung wide under her urgent wrench.

'Hello, Sonia.'

Annie? Annie Bell – Elyan's Annie?

'I don't blame you for being surprised,' Annie said. 'It's been a long time. I had to see you. I came to Folly a few days ago and I've been hanging around trying to get up the courage to come.'

'Come in.' Sonia stepped back and the girl passed her.

The hair was as thick, curly and shiny auburn as she remembered. Dark, searching eyes. Annie was lovely and Sonia wished her somewhere far from here – now.

She stopped opposite the drawing room. 'Everything is still covered,' she said of the draped furnishings. 'I thought you'd been here for days.'

'Not many,' Sonia said. She hadn't disliked Annie but then, why should she have been particularly interested in her. Elyan had announced their engagement but Sonia had been certain nothing would come of that. Ridiculously unsuitable.

'I'm sorry to drop in on you,' Annie said, 'but the house phone isn't working and I don't know your mobile number.' She smiled, a tremble of her bottom lip betraying just how nervous she was. Her left hand went to her hair and the ring Elyan had given her still shone on her finger.

'How did you know I was here?' Sonia asked.

Annie looked uncomfortable. 'I don't think I'm supposed to say. It doesn't really matter, does it?'

Sonia liked to know all the players in any game, but she said, 'Of course not. How lovely to see you. It's been too long.' Until she knew what was at stake here, she would play her hand carefully. 'Let's sit in the drawing room. It's time I pulled off some of the sheets.'

She pulled off the covers from two chairs and indicated for Annie to sit. The girl was more attractive than she'd remembered. Slender but feminine, her face paler than it should be, the freckles more pronounced than she remembered.

'What can I get you?' Sonia asked. She'd drunk too much wine and keeping her voice steady took an effort.

'Nothing, thank you. I don't want to take up much of your time.' Annie sat in an ivory brocade chair and Sonia took the other one she had stripped of its cover.

A thud reverberated in the near silence and Annie swiveled in her chair to look out into the hall. 'That came from the dining room or the kitchen.'

Sonia struggled to her feet and started forward.

'Did you close the front door?' Annie asked, getting up and passing Sonia before she could get far. 'No, that's it.' She disappeared into the hall and Sonia heard the door shut with a hollow bang.

Annie returned, smiling slightly.

'What's funny?' Sonia asked, afraid her speech was slurred.

'I was just thinking that this isn't an easy house for either of us. Who can blame us for being jumpy. The front door wasn't completely closed. A breeze must have shut a door somewhere else. I would love to talk to you, Sonia. I think it's about something we're both concerned with.'

'Go ahead.' Sonia wanted, more than anything, to think about what she should do next. Hugh was her main concern – and that other diversion she was considering.

'I see Elyan regularly,' Annie said. 'He's brave, but his life is so hard. He accepts that he brought what's happened upon himself, but he's changed so much since he's been at Ashworth. It isn't easy for him there, you know.'

Sonia propped a fist under her chin. 'It's out of my hands. I can't stand the thought of him in that place. I don't understand what they say happened.' She raised her face. 'I've never believed that brilliant, gentle boy could do anyone harm.'

The buzzing in her head sickened Sonia. She put a hand over her eyes.

'Whatever happened,' Annie said, 'I'll never stop loving him and I know you won't either. That's why I came. He needs to know we are all here for him and we'd do anything to ease what's happening.'

Sonia nodded but wished Annie would get to the point without wasting more of the evening.

'Each time I go to see Elyan he asks about you,' Annie said, sitting forward in her chair. 'You're his mother but you haven't been to see him.'

Sonia pressed the corners of her eyes and easily produced rolling tears. 'You don't understand,' she said, her voice breaking. 'I love him so and I can't see him there. It's too painful. All that talent wasted.'

'What's happened has happened,' Annie said. 'The point is that to help him make it through somehow, he needs to know we care about him, deeply. In time he may be released . . . if he gets better. For any hope of that we must support him. I'm here to ask you to see him. Just go up there and visit him. It isn't scary or strange. You'll visit one-on-one. And I know how healing that will be for him.'

She did love Elyan, Sonia thought, a great deal, but some situations were too much for people who were as deeply sensitive as she was. Annie was staring at her, beseeching her with those great, dark eyes. Somehow she had to satisfy the girl without making promises she might not keep.

'I go as often as they'll let me,' Annie said, and tears welled in her eyes. 'I'm not his wife, not a relative. Percy has helped get past that. He sees Elyan regularly even though I know how much it hurts him. I never liked Mr Quillam very much but I've learned to respect him because I think he's really sorry for not being more sensitive to Elyan's needs. And Hugh Rhys goes. I see him there and he comforts me. Elyan loves him and it raises his spirits when he sees him.'

Sonia turned cold. Everyone was a hero, everyone but her. Nobody gave a damn about her needs. She loved people, she was a passionate woman, too – was that a sin? She had her needs and she knew the things she must protect herself from.

'Sonia,' Annie said quietly, 'will you go to see Elyan, for all of us?'

Damn, she had always had to fight for what she wanted and she was fighting again. 'I'll think about it, Annie. I really will. I love my son so dearly. But I want you to see things more clearly and try to understand some of the troubling truths that weigh on me.'

Annie only watched her, the pallor of her skin increasing.

'Percy visits Elyan because he believed this protégé was a

continuation of himself. The maestro produced a virtuoso pianist. And every time he watched Elyan he thought he was watching his own creation. Every accolade Elyan got, Percy snatched as his own.'

'I can't disagree with you,' Annie said. 'I also don't know all the details as well as you must. It seemed that Percy drove Elyan much too hard. But I'm now sure he loves him very much.'

'I wonder if he'd love him so much if he knew the truth,' Sonia snapped, tired of holding back from doing what she needed to do – for herself. She had suffered quite enough.

She felt Annie looking at her and gave her a slight smile.

'What truth?' Annie asked, her voice kept low.

If she hoped to beat them all – and it would be risky regardless – it was time to play her trump card. Sonia stood up and raised her voice. 'Just listen to me.' Her voice, sung or spoken, was a powerful tool. 'Why do you think Hugh Rhys visits Elyan so often?'

Annie still didn't say anything, just watched and waited.

'They all want to pretend it isn't so, but Hugh is Elyan's father. Of course he goes to see him. And he hates Percy. He couldn't bear to think of Percy spending more time with Elyan than he does. Hugh is a jealous man, and I should know.'

Sonia leaned against a counter and used her mobile. It only rang once before she heard the low voice. 'What do you want?'

'I just had an unexpected visitor. I think you know who I mean. We had an agreement that you wouldn't tell anyone I was coming here but you did, didn't you?'

For seconds there was no response. When the voice did come again, boredom dripped. 'Is that all you called for? Whether or not I did whatever you're talking about isn't your business.'

'I feel trapped in this house.' Now she could hear music in the background. 'I'm not good at being alone. Alone I can think of ways to punish people who ignore me.'

'You chose to go there.' The voice became muffled as if the mouthpiece was covered. Who else was there?

'I need to talk to you now,' Sonia said, sniffling. 'Something has happened. If you like I could come to you. Just name the place.'

'You are not learning, are you? Don't push me. You hear? It won't help you. And I want you to stay right where you are.' As always, the threat was implicit.

The phone went dead. Sonia's finger hovered over the keys before she changed her mind about calling back and dropped her mobile into a pocket.

'I hate you,' she muttered.

In one swallow, she finished the glass of Sauvignon Blanc she had poured after Annie left and went to get the bottle from the refrigerator again. She rose to her toes on the cool floor and wobbled as she lifted the bottle to see how much was left. Just an inch in the bottom and she knew she had drunk the rest. So what? She would finish this and start another. Dealing with Annie, with her tears and questions, had been exhausting.

Before the refrigerator could close, a hand passed before her eyes, and clamped over her nose and mouth. The pressure of a body on her back rammed her forward against hard, cold shelves, rattled the contents. Her scream cut off, but not the ragged shudder of her breathing or the surge of burning vomit in her throat. The bottle slipped from her hand to smash on the tiles. Cartons and jars fell. Cold wet liquids splashed over her feet.

He had waited for her.

Did he want to kill her?

It was all black.

For an instant the grip slacked a little. He was adjusting his hold, trying to close the refrigerator door at the same time. She flailed, twisted, grabbed for his face, his head, anything. Flexed muscle in his shoulder pushed her away and drew her tighter against him. He was big. That was all she could tell about him.

Go limp. Drop.

Burning pain stabbed at her feet. They felt slimy and wet. Bleeding. Glass and blood.

Sonia thrust up her arms, punched her fists beneath the arms that held her. She slid to the floor and scrambled, expecting him to fall on her, to shout, but there was no sound from him – until a shuffling like snowshoes on ice.

More silence.

Who was it?

Her lungs filled with rushes of burning air.

Standing again, her bare feet slid on the tiles.

She didn't fall.

Through the door and along the passageway past the downstairs rooms she went. He would catch her, throw her down, beat her, squeeze the life out of her. Sobs grabbed with each breath and no air reached her lungs. Her head pounded.

Now, he would catch her now. *Now! Now!* Thundering in her chest. *Let me go. Someone come. Please come. Stop him.*

The front door was open again. Hadn't she closed it when Annie left? Sliding, slapping her feet down and curling her toes to grip . . . nothing . . . she was outside.

Not just warm. Suffocating. Down the steps, the backs of her ankles scraping stone. *Where are you? You'll get me when you want to. You're watching me, sneering at me. Why? What have I done to you?*

Her feet hit the driveway, the toes curling again, into the gravel. Gravel felt good. Every cutting edge was a pain she hissed at, gasping as she went. But pain meant she was alive.

Sonia wanted to scream. The struggle to keep the noise down bubbled in her throat and mouth. Any loud sound would only let him know exactly where she was.

Running, she left the house behind. Then she reached the trees on the far side of the driveway where they fronted the edge of small but dense woods that stretched away from the line of sycamores, and she knew where to go. Had she heard him fall? Was he unconscious? Yes, he must be or he would have caught her. He was unconscious, and she was free – until he came to and followed her. He would be wilder, more vicious than ever.

Panting, she fumbled for her mobile. The police would come. She hadn't been able to call while she was so close to whoever attacked her, but now she could.

The mobile had been in the right pocket of her trousers. She dug in the left one, too. Again and again she delved deep. Nothing. It must have fallen out. Moving on was essential, and she did, but she couldn't stop the tears.

The woods would hide her. They would also tear her feet apart even more. Bracken, thorny bushes and trailing brambles grew thicker and more tangled with every step she forced through them.

Was she a dreaming fool and he had another plan for her? Did he want her to run?

Where should she go? Once out of the estate grounds and into the lane, downhill was a long way to anything. At the bottom of the lane, the road curved around the hill above that miserable Folly-on-Weir. One way the road went to Folly, the other by some meandering route to a pathetic wide spot in the road called by a name she didn't remember. Uphill there was a house under renovation, and a continuation of the lane to fields she had wandered through once or twice. There was the long back way to the Derwinters and almost opposite, a mostly unused and overgrown route that meandered across the fields to another hill track. No help up there at this time of night.

No way to use a phone . . .

Down to the main road was the only way and then hide in the bushes until she saw a car coming. She would keep going through the trees, working her way toward the hedges that surrounded the estate. She remembered that beyond the hedge there was a steep bank of rough grass along the edge on this side of the lane.

Pausing, rocking from foot to foot and sucking in breaths, Sonia thought she had heard something. Branches snapping? She held her breath to listen. It wasn't there now. Was he coming?

Stumbling on, her feet became first an agony but eventually numb. Roots tripped her. Dragging herself up again and concentrating on the direction she took, she fought her way downhill and toward the lane at the same time. Brambles caught her clothes and she tore them free with bleeding hands.

At last she made out a thinning in the bushes. Cautiously, Sonia parted the hedgerow and staggered through. Clinging to branches at the top of the verge that sloped to the lane, Sonia struggled to let go and slither down. She'd come this far. Now, she would reach the lane and take it down to the road between Underhill and Folly-on-Weir. There, she remembered that other place now. If a car traveling in either direction came by, she could flag it down and at least ask them to call the police? If a car traveled by at all – the place was deserted most of the time. No vehicle had passed out here in the lane. She'd have heard an engine if there was one.

That man had got to the house somehow. He might be in any vehicle driving past but she thought something quite different had happened to him. He could have run away over the hills. She muttered a little prayer that he had.

A car, she couldn't see the make, was parked a few yards ahead against the ragged verge. She could make out it's dark shape. Big. Sonia swallowed hard, stopped, and peered ahead. She thought it might be a BMW but there was little light from a quarter moon. Nothing seemed to move inside the car but that didn't have to mean there was no one inside.

Hands closing on her waist, fingertips digging painfully beneath her ribs, swung her from the ground and threw her, face-first, among sticks and brambles.

Fingers tore at her hair, lifted her head and pushed, pounded her forehead into the jumble. Sonia choked on the blood that flooded from her nose into her throat.

She coughed, retched, and he fell on her, a great dead weight, pushed the air from her lungs.

Steady whining started – low, growing. An engine. Sonia fought to arch her back, to see. A headlight swung across her.

The weight on top of her made sure she couldn't signal. She couldn't shift a muscle. She was trapped against the ground, making certain no passing vehicle saw them.

Dimly, she heard a voice. Once more she attempted to shift. Useless. Her cry was muffled against the earth.

So tired now. So much pain.

Sonia's eyes closed.

FOUR

One look at Hugh and Alex decided small talk would be a bad idea. He hauled out chairs from tables in the saloon bar and thumped them on the wooden floors. From table to table he went, muttering under his breath.

Finally, she said, 'What's wrong, Hugh?'

'If you can't see, I won't bore you with it. Where's Scoot? He's supposed to get in here and do these floors by six in the morning? If he doesn't want the job, I'll find someone who does.'

When she had got back from Radhika's last night, Hugh was tight-lipped but working steadily. His mood had headed downward ever since. She had to think the visit to Green Friday and his temper were connected.

Neve Rhys was apparently in residence although Alex hadn't set eyes on her. Lily said Neve had gone out very early in the morning. There had been a note left saying Perry Rhys, Neve's husband, would arrive in a day or so to stay with her.

'This is Scoot's morning off,' she said quietly. 'He did the floors before he left last night. They look fine to me. Let's have some coffee, Hugh. You sound in as much of a funk as I'm starting to feel.'

'Why are you in a funk? Tony stepping out of line?'

This would be a morning to remember and hope never to repeat. Hugh wasn't a man to make snide digs – or be deliberately annoying. 'No,' she told him, walking past and behind the bar to the kitchen. In fact she was – or had been – in good if slightly anxious spirits since she got up. She had old demons to face but she wasn't unhappy about that – just a little nervous – but glad she'd made up her mind to take an action she should have taken long ago, no matter the result.

Rather than have coffee, she made a pot of tea, expecting Hugh to join her at any moment. He wouldn't feel good about being surly.

He didn't come. She could hear him working with the fireplace in the saloon bar. Even in warm weather they burned a fire in the evenings. The patrons liked it.

A tap sounded at the back door and Sam Brock, the locksmith who worked in several surrounding villages, looked inside. A round-faced man with curly blond hair, he was known to be efficient and honest, if garrulous. 'Alex,' he said. 'I'm looking for Hugh.'

She poured strong tea, added milk and handed him the mug. 'Come on in. I'll round him up.'

'Wait a moment,' Sam said. He grimaced. 'Do you know if there's been any trouble at Green Friday . . . Hugh's place on Trap Lane?'

Apprehension tensed her stomach. 'Trap Lane?' she said. 'I'd forgotten its name.'

'I think that's it,' Sam said.

Alex said, 'I don't think there's anything wrong at Green Friday,' but couldn't get Hugh's visit to the house out of her mind.

'I got worried up there. I was supposed to change all the locks, but I didn't stay. Thought I should have a word with Hugh first. What a place that is.'

'It is something,' Alex said. 'I haven't been there since . . . not in a long time.' She hadn't intended to mention the past.

'I know what you mean,' Sam said. 'A tragedy, that. But it's over now. Or I hope it is.'

Alex swallowed hard. There were places and times you'd rather not revisit. 'Of course, it is. Let me find Hugh for you.'

Leaving Sam in the kitchen, she went through to the main bar, expecting to find Hugh. He wasn't there, but she found him in the restaurant on the other side of the building. 'Hey, Hugh, what's going on?' she said. Bogie had come to sit at Hugh's feet and stare up into the man's face. 'Don't shut me out. You've been there for me when I've needed you. If you've got issues, I'm here.'

'I'm feeling ace,' he said and clamped his mouth shut.

Alex grimaced. 'When did you start with that ace stuff? You feel good – I'm with you. Ace? I don't know about that.'

'I feel shitty. How's that?' He turned away from a window

that looked over the little duck pond. 'I don't know what to say to you, Alex, except I apologize for being a foul-mouthed boor. And I can't explain why right now, OK? When I can, you'll be the first to know. I'm being an ass. Sorry.'

She went to him and gave him a hug around the waist. That on its own was something she'd never done before. 'You are special to me. I know something's bugging you, but I'll wait until you're ready to tell me – or whatever. Sam Brock is in the kitchen. He went up to do something to the locks at Green Friday. Now he's looking for you. I think there was a problem. Why did the locks need to be changed?'

'Oh, God.' Hugh looked down at her, his dark eyes desperate. 'Today? He's supposed to change them all but not until next week. Right, I'd better see him.'

But he didn't move at once.

Alex thought of him walking toward Green Friday last night and looked at the floor. He hadn't mentioned being there, not that he needed to account for his movements.

Abruptly, Hugh turned on his heel and walked away. She followed him across the restaurant, through the archway that led to the short passage that passed the snug, and into the saloon bar. Sam Brock was in the middle of the room, shuffling back and forth.

'All right then, Hugh? I just came down from Green Friday. You asked me to get up there early. I know you said next week but I had some time now. I hope that was all right.'

Hugh gave no response.

Alex made to leave but Hugh turned and said, 'You don't have to go.'

Sam said, 'I was going to start on the front door but it was open so I went inside and called out. No one answered, like. I wasn't sure what to do. I went a bit farther and kept shouting. There wasn't anyone there but there was dried blood on the tiles in the hall. Smears of it. It went all the way to the kitchen. A wine bottle was broken on the floor and there was more blood – a lot more. That's when I stopped. I was going to call the police but I thought I should check to see if anyone was in the house and injured. The whole place was empty. Then I decided you should know before I got the police in.'

Alex gripped the edge of a table and looked at the side of Hugh's rigid face. 'You could have called me from the house,' he said.

'I wanted to get out of there.'

'Right,' Hugh said, suddenly sounding vague. He drummed his fingers on the back of a chair.

'What do you want me to do now?' Sam said.

'We have to call the police,' Hugh said. He looked at Alex. 'What else can we do?'

'I don't know.' She could scarcely breathe.

'Anything else?' Hugh said to Sam.

The man turned crimson. 'I had to check in case I could help someone. In a bedroom there were clothes tossed about. Women's clothes. And there's a car out back. A Mercedes. Kind of dark grey, I think. There were some things scattered on the bed. Lipstick, that kind of stuff. A few pounds. Notes and coins.' He worked something from the front pocket of his overalls. 'And this.'

He gave a couple of photographs to Hugh.

'Holy hell,' Hugh said under his breath.

'What is it?' Alex said. 'What's happened?'

'A piece of history,' he told her, handing over one of the photos. 'Probably taken twenty years ago.'

One picture was of Hugh, probably in his early twenties, his black hair ruffled and longer than Alex had ever seen it, with a very blue sky behind him and scrubby, wind-raked trees on a craggy cliff edge. He was smiling over his shoulder at whoever was taking the picture but looked as if the smile was forced and the photographer had taken him by surprise.

Automatically Alex looked at the back. Written in precise script was 'My Hugh' and nothing more. The other photo was of a thickset man standing in front of a wall painted in bright colors, but in the foreground, the man was badly out of focus. She dropped them both on the table. 'It's too late now but we shouldn't be touching them. Did you pick up anything else, Sam?'

'No. Should you lose those, d'you think, Hugh?' Sam said. 'I don't mean I think you did anything in that house . . . but you know how things can get messed up when the police start in.' He turned red again.

'Thanks for the concern,' Hugh said. 'Even if I thought it was a good idea, it would get out that I'd destroyed evidence.' He glanced at Alex. 'Our local PI will agree with me there, I think.'

'I'm no PI and we don't know anything's happened yet,' Alex said, with more conviction than she felt. 'Should we go to Green Friday with Sam and check around before we call the police? There may be nothing really wrong. Or is that a bad idea?'

'No,' Hugh said. 'Let's do it before we make fools of ourselves with your copper friends.'

Alex picked the photographs up again. She was losing patience with her manager.

'I don't like any of this,' Sam interjected. 'Could be someone hiding out up there – waiting.'

'Don't come then, Sam,' Hugh said. 'Or you, Alex. It'll only take one to deal with it.'

'I'm coming,' Alex said promptly, and Sam fell in with them. 'The photos better go in a plastic bag first. Let's take my vehicle,' she added, certain there was a lot Hugh wasn't saying.

Within the hour the three of them sat on the front steps of Green Friday, waiting for the police. What they'd found inside the house matched Sam's report. Alex took deep breaths, trying to settle the jumpiness in her stomach. She had made sure they did not move or touch anything but it was too late to take back what Sam had already done to the scene and she had a feeling he had likely shifted a few other things.

'Looks like something nasty happened, doesn't it?' Sam said. Repeatedly, he pulled out a carefully ironed and folded white handkerchief and wiped his brow and the palms of his hands. 'I don't understand why we've had so many crimes in the area – killings, I mean.'

'For all we know this goes on everywhere,' Alex said. 'Anyway, we don't know whether or not there's been a killing here. More likely not. I was thinking, though. That wine bottle fell and broke. Why wouldn't it be reasonable for whoever was cut to go looking for help?'

'Why not use the phone?' Hugh said. He'd been silent since they entered the house until now. 'Why not get in a car and go to a hospital? Where's the victim? And there's no sign of anyone, anywhere. We haven't heard about an accident. If someone had walked into Doc James' surgery saying they'd cut themselves badly, or been attacked, we'd probably know about it by now. And if it had been an attack, he'd also call the police immediately.' Hugh didn't sound as if he'd noticed anything untoward at Green Friday when Alex had seen him going there the night before.

Alex sighed. Her lover, Tony Harrison, Doc James Harrison's son and the local vet, had expected to see her around nine for a trip into Gloucester. He asked her to take a few hours off, vaguely talking about buying something to 'zap up' the breakfast room which was really the sitting room but still held on to its old name from before Tony had it almost completely changed.

'Excuse me,' Alex said. 'You've reminded me I need to get in touch with Tony. It'll only take a minute.' She cocked her head but heard no approaching vehicles. 'The police are taking their time.'

'Do it,' Hugh said, feeling his pockets. 'Where's my phone? Damn it, did I leave it inside?' He ran through the door, glancing back at the driveway as he went.

Tony answered at the first ring and Alex told him where she was. True to form, he didn't ask a lot of questions and told her he'd come and get her. She could ask Hugh to drive Sam back down.

When she rang off, Alex wondered how long the police would take to let the three of them go. You never knew which way their thought processes would go. Hugh returned, waving his phone. 'In the kitchen. I'm glad I remembered before the police found it. I looked at the sink. I don't think anyone attempted to wash any cuts there. I don't get that.'

'Tony's coming for me,' Alex told him. 'I forgot we were going to Gloucester. I'll give you my keys and you can drive Sam back to the Dog.' She met Hugh's eyes and tensed again at the anxiety there.

An unmarked car approached down the driveway. A burgundy Kia Optima – spiffy but with the unmistakable feel of a police vehicle.

'Aye-aye,' Sam said. 'Here come the plods, I think. They drive better looking wheels these days.'

'Woman at the wheel,' Hugh said.

'They do have women in the police force,' Alex responded with a grin. 'Who knows what they'll let them do next.'

Hugh raised one brow. 'Scary, if you ask me,' he said.

The car swung to a stop in front of them and Alex almost groaned when Detective Constable Jillian Miller climbed out and walked toward them. The woman's pretty but unfriendly face was tattooed on Alex's memory from two previous cases.

Detective Inspector Bill Lamb, his thick, sandy crewcut unmistakable, strolled to join Miller. He smiled at Alex. She still found it hard to accept the change in his manner over the past year but the man's friendship with Radhika, Tony's assistant, had obviously softened him.

'Detective Sergeant Jillian Miller, and this is my partner Detective Inspector Bill Lamb,' Miller said with aplomb as if she shouldn't have introduced Bill first, or better yet, waited for him to introduce both of them.

'Alex Duggins of the Black Dog,' Hugh said, indicating Alex, and as if Bill didn't already know. 'This is Sam Brock, our local locksmith and I'm Hugh Rhys. I manage the Black Dog for Alex.'

Bill had crossed his arms and looked toward the sky. He lowered his shuttered gaze to Miller – now Sergeant Miller, Alex noted. Did the woman know she irritated her boss?

'Is Dan ill?' Alex said before she plastered on a smile to cover the realization that she shouldn't show any sign of familiarity, especially with Chief Inspector Dan O'Reilly, in front of the touchy Jillian Miller.

'No,' Bill said quickly, although Miller's lips were already parted to make a response. 'But I'll let him tell you all about it when he sees you.'

Miller glared at him. Her long blond hair was worn in braids wound together from her crown to the nape of her neck. Her navy-blue suit fitted an excellent figure perfectly and plain navy pumps showed off a smashing pair of legs. Too bad she wore an almost constantly sour expression.

Hugh cleared his throat. 'Sam came up to do some work for me this morning. I'll show you what he found and you'll understand why he didn't want to get started until he'd talked to me. I can show you around inside.'

'I'd better call for backup, boss,' Miller said. 'These three should be separated, so we'll need help.'

'Excuse me,' Hugh said. 'Alex has an appointment and she only came to give moral support. Tony Harrison's coming to pick her up shortly.'

'Poking her nose in, as usual,' Miller said, not quite quietly enough. 'She'll have to wait just the same.'

'Are you leaving your car for Hugh and his friend, Alex?' Bill said, breaking his silence at last.

'Yes. He'll take it back to the Dog for me.'

'Is there anyone in the house?'

'No,' Alex said. 'Or not that I saw. Sam saw a car out back that doesn't belong to Hugh? That's right, isn't it?' she asked him.

'Dark grey Mercedes, Sam thinks,' Hugh said. 'Not mine.'

'Someone's things are in there,' Sam said. 'All in a bedroom upstairs. And a bottle got broken on the kitchen floor. Glass cuts, too, I should think. There's blood. And in the hallway. Tiles, you know. Everywhere. Hard stuff, those tiles – stone. There were things in the bathroom, the one in the bedroom with the clothes and so on.'

Alex felt disassociated, numb, listening to Sam blurt out every detail he could come up with.

'The front door was open,' Sam went on. 'That's how I knew something might be wrong. I gave it a push and it swung in. I kept shouting but there wasn't any answer. Scared me when I saw the blood, I can tell you that.'

'Understandable,' Hugh said. He must wish Sam would shut up until he was asked some questions.

'And there's the Mercedes out back,' Sam said. 'So they didn't leave in that.'

FIVE

Tony pushed his cappuccino back and forth on the white Formica-topped table. 'What are you thinking?' Alex asked. It could be hard to love a man with a surreal ability to keep his cool. Often, she had no idea what he thought, even about something obviously concerning.

'Nothing revolutionary. Only that you will probably never learn not to rush into potentially dangerous situations. And that if Bill hadn't been there and if he obviously isn't thrilled with his new partner and understandably besotted with Radhika, you would probably still be stuck at Green Friday – or at the station – being asked pointless questions.'

She wrinkled her nose and covered her eyes. A headache bored into her temples. 'At least you said the questions would be pointless. They would, Tony. I don't know anything about what happened and neither do Hugh or Sam.'

'I hope you're right about that.'

She dropped her hand. 'I take that back. I'm not at all sure they shouldn't have asked a lot of pointed questions and been a lot more concerned about what they saw. I think they will be soon. Sam's got nothing to do with what went on in that house and neither do I, but I can't be sure that goes for Hugh.'

As soon as they had reached Gloucester, Tony drove to a Costa Coffee they had been to before. He suggested they needed to catch up on what had happened and Alex agreed; although her stomach jumped around just from trying to make light of the early morning visit to Green Friday.

Tony took a swallow of his cappuccino and grimaced. 'This stuff always tastes bitter to me. I don't know why I order it.' He reached for one of her hands on the table and raised it to his mouth. 'Yes, I do. It gives me energy for a few minutes and I get a bit of a buzz. I'm a druggie, see.' His smile lighted his face, and his dark-blue eyes. Looking at Tony almost always gave Alex a buzz. Public displays of affection weren't like him, but he kept holding her hand and kissing her knuckles. He paused and said, 'Are you going to tell me what you mean about Hugh?'

'I kept thinking about mentioning this before, but I didn't want to start believing it was anything. When I went to see Radhika's house yesterday, I saw Hugh at Green Friday. He'd parked his car facing out of the drive as if he wanted to be able to leave in a hurry. He was going to the house and he didn't see me. I was driving by and I thought about stopping but decided against it. He hasn't said a thing about that visit, not that he had to. It's his business. But he's been in a bad mood ever since. I thought he might say something about being there after Sam came today and we went up there, but not a word, Tony. Do you think that's odd?'

'Not necessarily. If he didn't see anything out of place when he was there last night, why should he think the two things were connected?'

'Whatever happened there was within hours of his visit.' Alex wrapped her spare hand around her mug. 'Either way, I don't see why he wouldn't say everything was all right when he was last at the house. And why was he having all the locks changed?'

Tony thought about that before saying, 'You're logical actually. Why didn't he mention things were OK at Green Friday – when he was there – especially if there's nothing to lose? I don't know about the locks. Puzzling. I want to know more about this Neve, his cousin's wife. It sounds as if there's bad blood there. It's nothing to do with the Green Friday thing, of course. At least it doesn't sound as if it is. But you can't help wondering about the story behind the visit. Hugh's always been so private. He must be fuming about family showing up when he obviously doesn't want much to do with them at the best of times.'

Alex didn't want to think about it all any more – not now. 'Let's try to put it all aside. For a little while. What's this thing you want to buy to make the breakfast room look brilliant?'

He looked at her hand, smoothed the fingers. 'What's your favorite place in your house, or what was your house, or what will soon be the house you used to own?' He grinned, amused by his own word nonsense.

'The conservatory, of course. It was almost enough to make me want to stay there.' Now it was her turn to grin. 'I'd have made you come and live there, of course.'

'But the place is too big. We both agreed.'

'We did. I was only pulling your leg.'

His smile became angelic. 'You can do that anytime you like as long as I can pull yours . . . I'd better behave. Wouldn't want to shock the locals. I want to take you to an outfit that designs conservatories. Blake and Crisswell. They're famous apparently. We're going to build a conservatory at our place. I thought it would work off the breakfast room. I want to see if we can push the fireplace through so we can enjoy it from both sides. And keep the chimney. It draws so well. There's plenty of space for expansion on that side of the house and the place has always been too plain as it stands. A conservatory would add some interest. Good light there, too. Later we'll come up with more changes. You need a studio so you can paint again. I like the tower on Radhika's place, not that we want to end up with something resembling one of King Ludwig's efforts.'

Alex rolled in her lips to stop them from trembling. Tears stung her eyes. This was who he was, a man who always thought of ways to make others happy, especially her. And she had loved her conservatory – in all seasons.

'Hey,' he said quietly, leaning closer. 'Are you going to cry? This is supposed to make you happy.'

'Happy tears. You are so good to me.'

He seemed about to say more but pulled her to her feet. 'Let's go see what Blake and Crisswell have to offer. Then, if I can persuade you, I'm hoping—'

Her mobile rang and she pulled it from her pocket, not quite sure if she was grateful for the interruption or not. She thought she knew what he wanted to suggest. Was she ready now to take that final step – with Tony? He wanted a permanent commitment and most of the time she thought she did, too. Perhaps, once she had confirmed something.

Bill Lamb was calling. 'Hello, Bill? What's up?' she asked. With her eyes on Tony's, she listened, her heart plummeting.

'I don't know anything about those things. You should ask Hugh.' She let him keep talking until she had to break in. 'What do you mean, you can't find him?'

Moments later she disconnected. 'The police want to get in touch with Hugh. Bill made up some hogwash about only needing to verify a few personal details. I think they intend to take him in for questioning. I wanted to ask if they'd found a body but I knew I'd only get shut down.'

'You're making a lot of suppositions, sweetheart.'

'I hope so, but I think that's a pointless hope. Bill says Lily's running things at the Black Dog. Liz Hadley's there, too and they're bringing in extra help. Hugh has dropped out of sight, or that's what Bill said. Lily told him she didn't see Hugh leave.'

'Is Neve Rhys there?' Tony asked. 'They could have gone somewhere to have a private discussion.'

'I don't know. Bill also said the police know Hugh was at Green Friday last night because he was seen there. He was also seen leaving, angry, driving away much too fast is what the witness said. It's not like Bill to be so free with information. I think he was feeling me out to see if I'd drop something useful about Hugh.'

Who had seen him?

SIX

'**A**lex! Am I glad to see you.' Lily Duggins waved her daughter into the empty snug bar and closed the door. 'What's going on? What have you heard? Bill Lamb was in here with that nasty Miller woman. She hardly let him get a sentence out of his mouth. I don't know how he stands her.'

'He probably wouldn't if she were a man. They have to be so careful. You know how that goes.' Alex only wanted to do something constructive – preferably find Hugh and get him to confide in her. 'Tony's gone back to the clinic and taken the dogs with him. We were going to spend the day in Gloucester

but with Hugh AWOL, I thought I'd better get back. Why don't
we all plan on getting together this evening?'

'That's fine, but I need to talk to you now. Bill wanted to
know about Neve Rhys, who she is, why she's here. I told
him we don't know, but he didn't seem to believe me. That
means he'll be back. Miller looked through the guest book
– without asking permission – and asked to see Neve's room.
Of course, I said I couldn't let her do that and fortunately
Bill agreed with me.'

'I'm embarrassed to say I can't stand that woman,' Alex said.
She wasn't about to explain that since Bill Lamb's boss, DCI
Dan O'Reilly, had made it clear on a number of occasions that
he'd like to be more than a friend to Alex, and gossip on the
force potentially rivaled that of the average church altar society,
DC Jillian Miller was fully aware of O'Reilly's feelings for
Alex. And Miller was mad about O'Reilly.

'Listen to them in the bar,' Lily said. 'They've been here
most of the day. You'd think none of them had jobs to go to.'

Voices had become a loud babble in the saloon bar. 'They
don't know anything, do they?' Alex asked. 'How can they?'

Lily, a taller version of her daughter with gray sprinkled
through her dark curls but almost identical, almond-shaped,
green eyes, raised expressive brows in an 'are you kidding?'
signal.

Alex sighed. 'I see. They do know.'

'Even if various coppers hadn't been in and out with inane
questions, someone would have got wind of something being
up. That pushy reporter from Cheltenham was in, the skinny
one with the black-framed glasses like diving goggles. She
can't keep the things on her nose. Now unless someone had
the gall to call her, I wouldn't have the faintest how she . . .
well, of course someone called her. Nothing's actually
happened as far as we know. It's potty. I don't know what's
going on, Alex. Are you going to clue me in so I can at least
fend off questions?'

Alex thought of the visit to Green Friday that morning.
'Mum, has Doc James mentioned anything about a patient
coming in with cuts from broken glass last night or this morning
early?'

'No.' Lily frowned. She and Doc had been close for a long time. 'James doesn't talk about cases, anyway.'

'Of course not. It was just a thought.'

'So what's going on?'

Alex plopped down on one of the tapestry-upholstered banquettes surrounding the little room and her mother pulled out a chair. 'Sometimes it's better not to know things,' Alex said. 'You can't answer questions, then.'

'In other words, don't be nosey? I haven't been called that very often.'

'Sorry.' Alex was annoyed with herself. 'It's already been a weird day and I suppose I'm not holding up perfectly. Sam Brock went to Green Friday first thing this morning to change all the locks – don't ask me why – and came tearing down here to tell Hugh the front door was unlocked and there were smears of dried blood on the floor. The three of us went up there and it was just as he described it. But still no one walking around bleeding or covered with bandages. We called the police and got Bill and Miller. I don't know what's going on there. I was surprised not to see Dan O'Reilly.'

Lily gave her a shrewd glance but didn't make any remarks about wondering if Alex carried a torch for Dan, the way she usually did.

'Well, someone got hurt,' Alex said finally. She frowned and tapped the edge of a beermat against the tabletop. 'I detest saying this, but it's too much of a coincidence that Hugh's dropped out of sight. Unless he dashes in with a perfectly good excuse, that is. For taking off and leaving you to deal with things – without giving you a word of explanation, even a phony one, maybe?'

'That would be a good starting place.' Lily stood up again. 'Is there anything else you know and don't mind sharing?'

'I don't know anything. But Neve Rhys gives me the creeps.'

'There is that. She's an odd one and I don't have the faintest why she's here. She was certainly out of here early this morning.'

'Come on,' Alex said. 'We can't leave Liz on her own in there for too long.'

'Juste Vidal was writing a sermon at St Aldwyn's. I thought to call the rectory and he came over. He's here, collar and all,

helping out in the bar. You can't say this is your average pub.'
Lily smiled.

'I thought when Juste became a curate he wouldn't feel he
should be moonlighting here but he's a very modern man of
God.' Juste had worked at the Black Dog since he was in divinity
school in Cheltenham. 'I understand service attendance blos-
soms when he preaches.' The local girls whispered together
about 'our dreamy Frenchman' and, she knew, plotted ways to
capture his interest. Juste smiled his way through the
attention.

Lily moved toward the door. 'I never expected him to
actually get a position here in Folly but I'm glad he has.'

When she walked into the saloon bar, Alex felt all eyes upon
her. The noise level subsided briefly. 'Afternoon, all,' she said
and hoped her smile didn't look as if it was splitting her face
– the way it felt.

'There's our girl,' Kev Winslet, increasingly beefy, red-faced
gamekeeper at the Derwinter estate, waved his full pint glass
around, slopping beer on the floor. 'Hugh still not shown up,
then? It's starting to feel like another Folly plot in the making.
That scrawny woman from one of the papers was in here already.
Quiet for her, she was. Like she was doing all the listening for
a change. Would that be because this is a really big one and
the coppers have managed to keep schtum?'

'There's nothing to keep schtum about as far as I know,'
Alex said. True, at least until she found out otherwise. She
allowed herself to be pulled aside by Carrie Peale, a potter
with a pottery and tiny showroom in what had been an
outbuilding behind her cottage in Holly Road.

'A word,' Carrie said. 'I came to see if I needed to take
Harvey home.' She indicated her artistically disheveled, rakishly
attractive husband sprawled in a chair cradling a glass of what
was probably whiskey on his flat stomach. A member of a biker
club, regulars at the Black Dog sat with him, leaning forward
and talking earnestly, with the odd poke to Harvey's arm
followed by the pair of them laughing hugely.

'I decided I'd join him.' Carrie raised a glass of beer and
smiled. 'Until I saw he was with his buddy, Saul. But it's been
too interesting around here for me to leave anyway.' Her dark

gray eyes shone. A stocky woman with a wide mouth and a tilted nose, her blond hair bobbed just below her ears, she wore a stained and bleached-out overall and a denim shirt spattered with paint and clay. Her feet were also paint-decorated in their inelegant brown sandals.

'Interesting how?' Alex asked. She liked Carrie and admired her acceptance of a carelessly self-involved husband. He was the brilliant writer yet to be recognized, kept by his 'sturdy potter wife who was lucky to have him'.

'These things will be all over the village very soon,' Carrie said. She repeatedly looked at her husband and his companion. 'Some of them already are. But there's no reason for you to take any flack. The woman detective who was here mentioned you. She said there was a potentially serious case under investigation but although she knew you were a bit of a local celebrity as a so-called PI – her words, not mine – any information should be taken directly to her, not to you. She gave out business cards. Somehow she's got her knickers in a twist when it comes to you.'

'Apparently.' Alex grinned. 'Never mind. What sort of things were being said?'

'Something's happened at a house outside the village. Major Stroud said he'd heard it was on Trap Lane, up past where you live. Said that would be the Manor House or Green Friday. Most likely the latter. He was going on about a death at Green Friday a while back and the house belonging to Hugh. Major Stroud said he thought the police came here looking for Hugh but he isn't here. Kev Winslet talked about how Hugh was always here – which I wouldn't know since I'm usually at the pottery. They were working up a story you might not like, Alex. I thought you'd like to know.'

'Thanks.' She would have heard soon enough and it was better to be prepared. 'Let's hope it all blows over.'

'Absolutely.' Carrie set her glass on a table. She turned a bit pink. 'I did go up there, but I expect you know the police have a crew out searching the hill and woods around Trap Lane. They've taped that off at the bottom. There is talk they're looking for someone who is missing. I don't know for sure how long this person's been gone but it sounded like more than a day or so. Someone was at Green Friday, they say. Staying there and they've left all their things. It doesn't sound good and it's a bad time for Hugh to drop out of the picture.'

The sun had gone out, holed-up between unfurling sheets of grey gauze cloud. And with the sky change came a rising chill that brought goosebumps out on Alex's bare arms.

She had left the Dog shortly after Carrie Peale – who had given up on taking Harvey home when he'd been willingly pulled into a raucous drinking game with the Gentlemen Bikers Club, as Alex now knew these well-heeled people with money to burn called themselves.

Lily, Liz and Juste were well able to manage without her and she would be useless until she followed a strong hunch and tried to find Hugh.

Her vehicle was parked in a field behind a drystone wall. The gate to the field was missing and driving through had been easy. Climbing the hill that paralleled Trap Lane was also easy enough. Her decision not to wear shorts had been a good one. Thick blackberry brambles would have scratched her legs until they looked like used tick-tack-toe boards.

When she reached a ridge, the field swept down steeply, the rough grass scattered with clover and clumps of heather. The air was sweet and heady. If her ribs didn't ache from holding her muscles tense – and she wasn't sick with worry – she might have enjoyed herself.

Climbing in an arc, Alex made her way upward, looking for a vantage point on Trap Lane. She didn't intend to be seen but she did have plans to start searching where she didn't think the police had attempted a sweep yet. If, as she'd been led to believe, they were concentrating on someone having gone downhill to get away from Green Friday – logical enough – but they hadn't found any sign of a person, why shouldn't she follow her hunch and go uphill? Anyone missing for so long must be injured, unconscious, or dead, unless they had managed to get completely away.

Kicking through the clover-laden grass in her hiking boots, she constantly hunted in all directions. Around her neck she carried binoculars – they were better there than in her hands

where they would slow her down. Occasionally she put them
to her eyes and swept the area. Her deepest hope was that Hugh
had already come up to search. There was a lot of ground to
cover but with so few people ever venturing this far, she had a
good hope of finding him if he was there.

From the ridge, Alex saw movement around Green Friday. It
wasn't that far away; policemen and dogs together with an assort-
ment of other coppers, beat their way through the fields. Into the
woods beyond the sycamores lining the driveway at Green Friday,
along hedgerows on Trap Lane, they went. More of them were
farther away on the road between Folly and Underhill.

Men were at work on Radhika's house. They should be
done in no more than a few weeks. Radhika was still spending
her nights at Tony's clinic but she did make use of rooms
that were finished in the corner tower of her new home.
The police must have searched the place and left already,
doubting the workers would have missed a person who
shouldn't be there.

A breeze picked up, tossed the grasses and made miniature
whirlwinds of dusty grit hiding beneath. Alex pressed on,
wanting to keep making a mental map of any route that could
have led uphill. Eventually she should find the area where
Trap Lane petered out and a path led toward an alternate route
downhill. Alex enjoyed feeling at home here. In childhood
she had played over the hills and fields around the villages.
Somewhere was that cart track that led to the Derwinter estate
but anyone going that way on foot, probably in the dark, was
unlikely to get far.

She mused on just how much of this land belonged to Leonard
Derwinter and his overpowering wife, Heather. Likely most of
it. In fact Alex had come to like Heather a lot more as she knew
her better. She had decided much of the bumptious manner
came from insecurity, even if it was well hidden.

Each time she made a visual search in all directions, she
concentrated on looking for a man walking alone. Hugh also
knew and enjoyed these hills. Why wouldn't he choose to come
here after the scene at Green Friday that morning and when he
wanted to get away – and possibly when he was looking for
something or someone?

In the distance, to the south of Folly-on-Weir and visible against a still-blue patch of sky, stood the folly for which the village was named. Tinsdale Tower was its real name but locals had always called it The Tooth for the jagged shape it had acquired with a serious collapse many years earlier.

Gaging that she was coming to Trap Lane, although it would be narrow at this level, Alex started to hike back up the ridge until she could see over the top, then stood very still. Her blood felt as if it had stopped flowing. Not more than yards in front of her and downhill, stood Hugh and her spine started to sweat and prickle. He rested a foot on a rock and slowly studied the hill below. Abruptly, he moved, loping easily over rough ground. And while he wove between hillocks, she stood like a salt pillar. Striding out he went down, cutting toward the direction from which Alex had come. She hoped, desperately, that he wouldn't come upon her Land Rover. Just as quickly she wondered why that should matter, and why she didn't call out to him.

Hugh stopped again, looked around, and turned back abruptly, headed upward again and toward his right as if he, too, were heading for the top of Trap Lane.

Carefully, she went to her knees, eased forward until she lay flat, face down and out of sight.

Why? She wasn't sure, but it seemed important.

After timing five minutes on her watch, Alex eased up to look in the direction Hugh had taken. At first she couldn't see him. Then she picked him out, just below her again and moving fast from the amount of ground he'd already covered.

Why did he go up, then return? He was running, leaping from hillock to hillock . . . running away?

She sat down, cross-legged, and let her head hang forward. The thoughts that crowded her brain sickened her. Without proof, she was convicting a man she'd come to admire of some terrible crime she wasn't even sure had been committed.

What had he been doing up here? And why had he visited Green Friday last evening? And why, most of all, hadn't he mentioned it when the two of them had returned there with Sam, or to the police – or during any of the opportunities he'd had since?

When Alex reached Trap Lane it resembled a path worn by animals or, if it were nearer civilization, children tramping, single-file, along familiar ground. She crossed over, making a mental note to find out exactly where the track that belonged to the Derwinters joined the lane. The track would be lower down but even if it was difficult, someone could have used that to get away. There was the back way from Green Friday that led in the opposite direction but it must be almost completely overgrown by now.

An empty, despondent feeling weighted her but she kept walking. She hadn't really discovered a thing – other than Hugh's whereabouts – and she ought to get back. She couldn't forget her promise to meet with her mother that evening, and Tony was expecting to see her.

The cry of a meadow pipit soared with the bird, high overhead, and eventually slowed when the bird descended like a falling parachute and disappeared from her sight. A few more minutes and Alex would climb down. She'd better be quick about it or she would be added to the 'missing list'.

A small lake, more a pond, all but hid in a wide dip. Shadowed in places by thickets of gorse in full yellow bloom and by bracken and a tier of rhododendron beneath two windblown trees, the breeze sent tiny ripples scurrying across its surface.

If the lake had a name, Alex didn't know it and barely remembered being there before, but she did recall something about it being fed by underground springs and how increased rainfall in winter made it overflow.

At the edge, she stared down. It would be quite unmoving on a still day. Was it deep? She vaguely recalled childhood mutterings about it being very deep but nothing clear. Eerie, she decided, and she didn't like it – and she *had* been there before, as a little girl with a group of children. Alex disliked weakness in herself and branding a small lake creepy was weak.

Tromping along the edge, she searched for anything out of place, anything disturbed. Like signs of digging? She closed her eyes a moment. Why did she invent these disaster scenarios? She scared herself. And no one would bother digging a place to bury a body when they could push it into a lake.

She had set out hoping to locate Hugh and make sure he was

all right. Then she had planned to follow her idea up into the hills beyond Green Friday. Now she'd found a deep pond she'd forgotten existed and was playing with ideas of Hugh tossing a body into the water. Imagination could be helpful, but it could also be a time-waster.

When she saw him, Hugh could have been coming from around here.

What body, Alex? What are you so afraid of? Hugh wouldn't be standing around if he'd just got rid of a body.

Alex had made an almost complete circle around the area when she saw something roll beneath the surface on the far side. Using the binoculars, she located a tangle of thick plants growing from the bank and what looked like a matted tangle of grey wool caught on a stout root. A piece of yellow fabric flapped like a plague flag.

The thing rolled again, slowly from side-to-side, heavy and mostly under the water so she caught only glimpses of more colors. And she set off, making sure her mobile was in her pocket just in case – and feeling silly.

Her phone rang and Alex jumped hard enough to grind her teeth together. Looking across the pond, she answered, already seeing Tony's number. 'Hello,' she said, shaking. 'Tony?'

She was giving in to dread. 'You never get used to shocks,' she muttered.

'Alex? What did you say?'

'Nothing.' She'd spoken aloud, darn it. 'Just muttering to myself. I'm up in the hills behind Trap Lane. Behind Green Friday and Radhika's place, actually. After Trap Lane completely peters out. We came up here as kids. Or I think I did.'

'We did – you said you were shocked.' When Tony dealt with trouble, his voice went flat. He was much tougher than he seemed.

'Um . . . not really.' That wouldn't cut it and she was digging in deeper. 'I came up here to look around for anything the police might have missed. I don't think they've even been up here yet. They're too busy with the obvious route for someone to go – down to the road. OK, I did say something. I think I said you never get used to shocks and I think I just had another one. But I'll deal with it. I'm going to check something out, then I'll meet you wherever you decide. There, you get to be the boss. I'm mellowing.'

'Alex, I don't get put off that easily. You've had a shock. What kind of shock?'

'Probably nothing. Just let me get down the hill again and I'll explain. I'm being stupid.'

He was silent for a moment. 'The police are still at Green Friday. Can you see them from where you are?'

'Yes.' Alex cleared her throat. 'What does it matter?'

'I think I'll give Bill Lamb a call and ask him to get someone up there with you.'

'You will not!'

'One more chance, Alex, and then I'm going to race up there. You matter too much to me to let you go off on a tangent doing things you shouldn't be doing alone. Just tell me what's going on?'

'I feel ridiculous, that's what's going on. I scared myself over nothing and decided there could be a body in a pond up here. I vaguely remember it's always been here – the pond that is. Fed by underground springs or something. Where shall I meet you?'

'Right where you are. I know exactly where it is. We called that pond Dozemary like the Excalibur pool or some such thing. The older kids did. You were a bit younger. It's damn deep so be careful.' He rang off and wouldn't answer when she tried to call back.

Hurrying at first, then slowing to a reluctant pace, Alex made her way to the edge of the pond again. The yellow ribbon, if that's what it was, still flipped in the breeze and a log, a bag of rubbish, whatever, continued to roll, just showing above the water.

Tony would get here quickly. He knew the area and he was used to hiking over these hills with his dog, Katie – and with Bogie now. Hiking wasn't Alex's favorite pastime.

She kept her eyes averted from the yellow ribbon. What a fool she was going to feel.

Now. She would go and check it out immediately. Marching along, whacking shrubs and bushes aside as she got closer, Alex made up her mind to stand firm and unafraid, no matter what she found. She was glad that once between the shrubs and the pool, she was more-or-less hidden.

When she reached the right spot, she paused. Even through long, swaying grass she could see the yellow ribbon, and the loose knot that had slipped free from what she'd taken to be a mass of gray wool, not tangled hair. But it really was tangled hair pulled back behind a head. Her heart thundered; a whole percussion section of a large orchestra threatened to split open her chest and she felt so sick she slapped a hand over her mouth.

To the very edge she went and crouched. She took hold of a shoulder inside a multi-colored tapestry coat of some kind and heaved to try turning the body over. It was a body. And by now it was a very dead body.

Alex couldn't roll it, but, reaching her hands into the water, she turned the head to the side and looked at the face. Nothing to do for this man now. Clouded eyes were sightless, covered with a gummy, pale substance. The face, slack, grey and marred by small, gaping wounds, had started to bloat up and pieces of weed together with crawling things, already clung to skin and flesh, turned thick by immersion.

Alex pushed backward, tried to stand, and vomited. Her head felt so light, so filled with skittering, scrabbling stuff. The field and sky spun before her. Again she tried to stand but fell flat on her back instead and stayed there.

'Alex!' She heard Tony's voice – not too close – but she couldn't respond yet. Her mouth tasted foul and she fancied she had drunk the water around the body. Perhaps she'd been trying to drain the pool to get him out.

She was losing her mind.

Retching repeatedly, struggling to clear away the horrible imaginings, Alex tried to call Tony's name. She couldn't.

'Alex! Answer me, for God's sake. Where are you?'

She struggled to her feet and saw him, breaking through the trees, then running when he sighted her. Even sick with disgust as she was, she registered how important she was to him.

Once more she flopped down, cracking the bottom of her spine on a rock. It didn't matter. 'Tony,' she cried. 'I'm over here. Come over here.'

He reached her and fell to his knees, took her face in his hands and stared at her. 'You're ill. Why didn't you tell me?' He held her against him so hard she could scarcely take a breath.

'Listen to me,' she told him, her voice a husky whisper. 'He's there in the water. Caught on roots at the bank. Look. We have to do something.'

Without letting her go, Tony turned aside, and Alex felt the moment when he saw the body. Then he did let her go, putting himself between her and the corpse.

In only moments, he looked at her over his shoulder. 'I think it's Percy Quillam, Sonia Quillam's husband.' He sat on the grass, hands hanging between his knees. 'I'm pretty sure it's him. Before I call Lamb, I want to ask you something. We need to get it straight. The police have a priority on tracing the Mercedes at Green Friday. LeJuan Harding told me. Only it was gone by the time the police searched the place this morning. And they didn't find keys, or a phone or wallet. No personal stuff or ID. Is there any reason to question any of that?'

LeJuan was Detective Chief Inspector Dan O'Reilly's very good-looking black sergeant. Good-looking, charming and too free with information among friends of which Tony and Alex were two.

'Sam said the car was there when he got to the house,' she said. 'I had no reason to doubt him. He also said there were things scattered on the bed in that bedroom. Who knows what was among them? I didn't see the car but I didn't look for it. I assume it was on that gravel outside the kitchens. If there were keys on the bed when Sam was there and they weren't there later, they must have been taken while we were sitting on the front steps, waiting. The police didn't say anything. Not about the car or any keys, now I think about it.' Alex couldn't wrap her brain around this. 'Things could have been taken between Sam leaving Green Friday and the three of us going up there together.'

'LeJuan's tracking down who dealt with the possessions on the bed,' Tony said. 'Not his job but he and Dan have been pulled into this in some way. He didn't mention a car at all.'

'You mean the car *wasn't* there . . . when wasn't it there? When was it taken?'

'Like you just suggested, sweetheart, it may not have been there by the time the police arrived. Not the car or the keys. I don't know how it could happen but it looks as if someone drove the car out of there.'

'Do you think it was Percy Quillam's car?' Alex said, her eyes drawn in the direction of the pond. As far as she knew, Percy and Sonia were still married, even though their son, Elyan, the prodigy who had been their reason to live, was now in a mental institution – a prison for the mentally ill.

Tony shoved his hands in his pockets and shrugged. 'Who knows? It would seem the Mercedes must have gone missing before the search. No one saw it driven away. Whoever took it knows their way around here. That's assuming there ever was a vehicle there.'

'Sam wouldn't make it up,' Alex insisted.

Tony frowned at her. 'Is there another way out of the estate? If that car was driven down the drive this morning, it would have been seen. Are you sure it was still there when you and Hugh went back?'

Alex thought about it. 'I just accepted that it was.' Her heart thumped. 'I don't really know. I didn't look for it. Tony, there is another way out. You can park by some outbuildings behind the house, on the far side of the swimming pool, I think, and use a track through the fields – in the opposite direction from Trap Lane. But not many people would know about it. I remembered it earlier while I was walking. It must be an overgrown mess by now.'

'I can think of a few who definitely would know about it,' Tony said.

Alex looked away. She still hadn't told anyone except Tony, who hadn't taken her very seriously, that she had seen Hugh at Green Friday, and that she doubted he had any idea he'd been seen, by her or Bill's second, still anonymous witness.

'The things left in that bedroom weren't Percy's,' Alex said. 'Lipstick and so on. It could be that Bill's witness and the missing woman are the same person.'

SEVEN

SOCO had erected their white tent, and lamps that turned encroaching dusk into a murky curtain behind the pitiless lights. The technicians said little but worked intently gathering specimens Tony either couldn't see or didn't see as anything of importance. These they put into bags, labeled and dropped into brown paper sacks.

After reams of photos, and video film taken *in situ*, the crime scene manager ordered Percy's body to be taken by stretcher into the luminous tent. Dark shapes moved inside, adjusting equipment, starting to photograph again. Tape wrapped around trees, bushes, or pegs driven into the ground where there was nothing else available, marked off the whole area.

Bill Lamb, with Jillian Miller and a group of other officers had arrived. Tony realized most had already been at Green Friday. They had gathered on the hillside quickly. Everyone was still watching for Molly Lewis, the forensic pathologist.

'I don't know why they don't fire Dr Lewis,' Miller said, supposedly quietly to Bill. 'She wastes a lot of valuable time.'

He repeatedly pushed his fingers through his crewcut sandy hair. Tony admired how he kept his expression blank. 'Because she's damned good,' he told Miller. 'The best. Let's chat about this later. In the meantime, keep schtum.'

Tony felt a spark of shameful satisfaction thinking that perhaps the upstart detective sergeant might get a tongue whipping.

The shame wouldn't last . . .

A chill had crept in. Alex had accepted a SOCO suit to keep her warmer and looked even more diminutive in the white gear that was puffy all over and rucked around her ankles.

'Bill,' Tony said to his former enemy who had miraculously turned into a pleasant enough companion. 'Could I ask you something?'

'Sure, not much to do but wait anyway.' He followed Tony but turned back when Jillian Miller tagged on behind. 'Stick around here and watch for Dr Lewis, please, Miller. And give me a jingle on my mobile when you see her.'

Tony didn't wait to see how that went down. A few yards away, the two men stood close together. 'None of my business, but you know how we are around here – at least Alex and me. Bloody nuisance to you, I'm sure, but bear with me.' He noted that Alex had not followed them. Finding Quillam had shocked her even more than he would have expected and she seemed disoriented.

'Sometimes I wish I could totally agree with what you've just suggested,' Bill said, 'but I can't. You two have been damned useful on too many occasions.'

Tony didn't comment on the unexpected compliment – the change in Bill's attitude could so easily reverse. 'Sam Brock told Alex and Hugh about a Mercedes being parked at Green Friday when he was looking around. That was just before he went to the Black Dog to get Hugh. If the car was gone when you looked, that wasn't much of a window of time.'

'I'm very aware of that,' Bill said and expelled a hard breath. 'Information does get around here. By the way, since it's starting to look as if there could be a connection to one of his old cases, Dan's joining us with some psychologist who is worming his way into a lot of situations in the area. The man has some theory about copycat or linked murders. Been looking into unsolved cases. The volume of murders in this area has noses wiggling even though they've all been solved and there were different perpetrators in each one. Apparently he's out to prove we've messed up somewhere. He'll probably be a pain in the ass but the chief constable is enamored of him, so we have to put up with it. LeJuan Harding is Dan's new sergeant – that's just information in case you didn't know. But this Dr Leon Wolf is likely to rub a few of us the wrong way. So try to keep you and Alex in the background.'

'I had heard about LeJuan's reassignment but nothing about this Dr Wolf,' Tony said, suffering an overwhelming longing to grab Alex and leave this lot behind them.

'Good. You're right about the car. And if Sam Brock did see it there, we don't have the faintest who took it. Tony, I don't think Hugh's been completely forthcoming. I don't expect you to say more than you feel like saying.' He paused, looking hopeful, and after an instant gave a one-sided smile. 'We will have to take him in for questioning. It would be best if Alex didn't raise any fuss about that.'

'Damn, what a mess,' Tony said. 'But I get you and so will Alex. She's a wise woman.'

Bill gave him a completely wide smile. 'Not that you're at all biased where Alex is concerned. Most of the time I agree with you, by the way. Here comes Molly Lewis. Someone will have driven her as far up as possible. She doesn't like driving herself these days.' He glanced away.

Even in poor light Tony recognized Molly Lewis's short, bright, blond hair as she climbed toward them with a uniformed officer.

The next thing he had to do, Tony decided, was get Alex on her own and ask what she wanted to do about Hugh being at Green Friday the night she went to Radhika's. She wouldn't want to say anything that would add to police suspicion of Hugh, but if he continued to say nothing, Alex might have to tell them everything.

Bill took the lead, joining up with Miller on the way to meet Molly Lewis. She had gone directly toward the pond and Tony could see a powerful torch beam bobbing.

'Wait up.' Alex jogged beside him and they went on together. 'I like Molly but if I never had to see her like this again it would be too soon. Why is she going to the pond?'

'Probably to see where the body was found.'

'Right.' Alex sounded vague. 'What did Bill say? He's being too pleasant these days. I keep waiting for him to blow up and be his usual sarcastic self.'

'I think it's Radhika's influence. She wouldn't be impressed if he didn't treat you well, and for Bill, she is the all-seeing sun.' He put an arm around her shoulders. 'Let's go home if they'll let us. It's been a long, nasty day.'

'I know. But I can't just go. Tony, I'm so worried about Hugh I don't know what to do. The police haven't said anything else about him. I haven't had a chance to tell you, but he was up here before I found the body. He didn't see me but he was just staring around. Then he ran off. If I call and ask if he's at the Dog they'll figure out I don't know where he is either. I don't want to say or do anything that draws attention to what's going on.'

'We'd better talk but not here.' There was nothing to gain by continuing to keep quiet and possibly a lot to lose. 'I'm going to find out how long we have to stay.'

She slid her hand into his and they crossed the rough ground toward Bill who was now in the company of several officers and the crime scene manager, Werner Berg. They heard Dr Molly Lewis from yards away. She sounded furious.

'What were you thinking of, Werner?' Her voice grated. 'You know how I like to do things.'

'Yes, marm,' Werner said, dragging on a cigarette. 'I thought it was best to get things moving given the cause of death.'

'Which is?' Molly said.

Werner smirked, accustomed to Molly's little catch-out tricks. 'I should have said, possible, of course.' His German accent remained heavy. 'With water there is so much that can interfere. And the body had clearly been there for hours. I knew you would consider every moment important.'

She narrowed her eyes at him, pinched her lips together and pushed past on her way to the tent. 'Not as if I might like to see the position of the body when it was found, hm? I hope you have taken scrapings of everything it may have touched, and samples of the water. Tomorrow morning divers must go down.'

Tony shuddered at the thought. As kids, the potential depth of the pool had been a subject of much conjecture. The thing looked obsidian and bottomless.

'Affirmative to the scrapings,' Werner remarked. 'It's very deep in there, marm. Could have a couple of feet of mud on the bottom. Or a lot more. Perhaps we should wait and see if we really need divers. It would be too bad to lose a man for nothing.'

Without warning, Molly stumbled sideways and Werner caught her arm firmly. He said not a word but when Molly tried to pull away, he held on, transferred one arm across her back, and ushered her rapidly into the tent.

Bill looked back at Tony who frowned but said nothing. The

pathologist seemed unsteady and he wasn't sure he bought the rumor that she drank too much. He wondered if she had been checked by a doctor – this wasn't the first time Tony had seen her appear shaky or even disoriented.

'I don't think Molly drinks too much,' Alex said quietly. 'She could be ill but doctors are the worst for looking after their own health.'

'You stole my thoughts,' he said. 'And I think Werner knows something about it, not that he's the type to share any information about a friend. She is a friend of his, I can tell that, despite the snarling she sends his way. Anyway, I say we see if we can get in there and listen. What about you?'

'All right. It doesn't sound like the best way to spend an hour or so but we're at least on the fringes of all this, whether we like it or not. Listen hard, Tony. You're better at this part than I am.'

A wiry little female constable in uniform stopped them at the opening to the tent. 'Sorry, sir,' she said to Tony. 'May I see your warrant card?' She smiled apologetically at Alex, and Tony could see her making a mental note to wear a Tyvek suit in future, whenever she wanted to go where she shouldn't.

'I found the body,' he said – only the mildest stretch. 'We're with Detective Inspector Lamb.'

'And you're SOCO, ma'am?' the officer asked Alex.

'They lent me a suit to keep me warm,' she said, barely above a whisper.

'Then I'll have to ask you both to wait until someone comes out to verify who you are. Sorry about that. Would you wait on the other side of the tapes, please? I can't leave my post at the moment.'

Quelling an urge to laugh, Tony led Alex away. Automatically they set off down the hill. 'Did you bring your vehicle?' Alex asked. 'Mine's in a field somewhere over there.' She gave a vague wave.

'I parked in Trap Lane near Green Friday. That's closer. Shall we go that way and get your Range Rover later?'

'Yes,' she said and started to run. 'Later or maybe never. I don't care – I want to get out of here.'

He pulled her to a stop. 'We'd better walk, not run, or one

of us will break something in the dark. Damn, why didn't I think to take the torch out of my car?'

'We've got to find Hugh,' Alex said. She clutched Tony's arm with both of her hands. 'He hasn't done anything wrong. We both know that. But he could get into a lot of trouble if the police start looking for him more seriously and he's keeping out of sight. Why would he do that anyway? And why wouldn't he be open about everything?'

'Listen to me.' He glanced over his shoulder. Alex was asking him to reassure her, but that wasn't on the cards, not now. 'The police are looking for him – very seriously. They're going to take him in for questioning. Bill told you someone reported seeing Hugh leaving Green Friday the same night you saw him there.'

'I don't understand who that could have been. Tony, what if we took Hugh to our place, until this calms down, and they work out what really happened?'

'Good God, Alex.' He turned away from her. If not for some weak moonlight, they would be in total darkness – appropriate, he decided. 'You don't mean that.'

He saw her bow her head. 'I don't know if I do or not.'

'You saw him on this hill before you found Quillam's body. And something about him worried you. How do you know he wasn't aware of that body and where it was?'

'Why would Hugh behave like this? If he knows anything about what happened he should already have told the police.' Her voice rose. 'We don't know Percy didn't just fall in. Nobody said a word about a weapon. Could Percy swim? I don't know, do you?'

'The wounds on the face were made by something, Alex. We don't know what other injuries there are yet. If we want to get ourselves into the biggest mess of our lives, all we have to do is harbor a potential criminal.'

The instant the words were out of his mouth he regretted them.

'Hugh is our friend. He's been with us through thick and thin. He is not a criminal, potential or otherwise. I'm going to find my Range Rover.'

'Sweetheart,' he said, his throat tight, 'please don't do that to me. I'm trying to be rational. I have to put you and your safety and reputation first. And mine. Of course, I'm sure Hugh is a good and honorable man but we're in a hard place right now. Would you at least help me figure out the best way through all this?'

'I just want to find him – and talk to him.'

'Of course.' But she'd passed on a chance earlier – because she must have felt unsure about him. 'OK, let's get going. Hold my hand, please.'

She stepped close to him, looking up in the darkness, and he thought she might be close to tears. 'I know I'm not always easy but I can't even start to explain what happens to me when I feel things so . . . protective and angry at the same time.'

Tony gave her a hug. 'Could be you're hard not to love just because you're the way you are. Ever think of that? Let's go. Just stay with me and concentrate on where you put your feet.'

They made good progress even if they stumbled and repeatedly wandered from the route he thought he knew so well.

Each breath was sweet and cool. Too bad those breaths didn't quiet his mind. Not a cloud touched the darkened sky, while a thin moon hung like a comma without a sentence to punctuate.

Without warning, Alex yanked on his arm and stopped them both.

'Are you OK?'

She didn't answer at once, then sucked in a breath. 'Voices,' she whispered, too loudly. 'You hear that?'

He did. From farther down and to their left. The direction toward Green Friday. 'Doesn't sound like anyone's worried. Just carry on the way we are.'

'Someone's coming,' he heard a man say. 'Hold still. Hello, anyone there?' the same voice rose.

'Alex Duggins and Tony Harrison,' Tony replied, raising his own voice. 'On our way back to get my Range Rover by Green Friday. Who are you?'

'Dan O'Reilly,' another and familiar voice called. A torch beam flashed upward and swept across them. 'I see you. Stay put and we'll come to you. Dr Wolf and Hugh Rhys are with me.'

Alex leaned close to him and he put an arm around her

shoulder. 'It'll be OK,' he murmured. 'Wouldn't have expected this trio.'

'I don't understand,' Alex whispered.

The torch bobbled closer and the three men were visible as shapes moving behind the illumination. Then they were there, in front of Alex and Tony, calm and pleasant as if meeting on a hill, in the darkness, and heading toward the place where a man had been found dead was usual. Perhaps they didn't know about the death. But that was a ridiculous idea.

'Hey, Dan – Hugh,' Tony said, looking at the third man whom he saw only as solid and of medium height.

'This is Dr Leon Wolf,' Dan said. 'He's a psychologist working with us on a series of cases. Hello, Alex. I should probably say the suit doesn't become you, but I'd be lying.'

Tony set his jaw. Some things never changed, including the way Dan O'Reilly felt about Alex, damn him. Dan stepped close enough to give her a quick hug and touch her face. 'Good to see you,' he said and there was no doubt he meant it.

'Good to see you, Dan,' Alex said, but she leaned closer to Tony.

'Do you know what's happened up here?' Tony said, looking directly at Hugh. 'A drowning in that pond. Of course, you know. Messy business. Alex and I found the body some hours ago. We finally got to leave.'

'My God,' Hugh said, staring upward. 'I heard someone was found but had no idea you were involved. We're headed up there now – or Dan and Dr Wolf are. I offered to show them the way. Do you know who it is?'

'As far as we know there hasn't been an official identification yet,' Tony said, squeezing Alex's hand, hoping she understood that it was better for them to reveal nothing, to leave it to the authorities.

'Hugh,' Alex said quietly, 'why are you here? How did you meet up with Dan, and . . . and . . .?' she raised a hand vaguely in the direction of the doctor who didn't speak.

'I went to Green Friday to check the place out more thoroughly – with all the talk about someone missing and the police still being there – and I ran into Dan,' Hugh said. He scrubbed at his face, turned his back, turned to face them again.

'I haven't been sensible. I should have gone straight to the police when I knew there was something wrong. I didn't and now I won't blame them for thinking I may have had something to do with whatever happened at Green Friday.'

Illuminated by his own torchlight, Dan's expression didn't change, but he studied Hugh intensely.

'What do you think happened?' Tony said. He couldn't help himself.

'Perhaps we'll know soon enough now,' Hugh said, glancing up the hill. 'Unless the killer is too clever and very few are.'

Had anyone mentioned murder to Hugh, Tony wondered.

EIGHT

Tony parked behind the Black Dog and turned off the engine. 'I thought we'd walk to Harriet and Mary's from here,' he said.

Alex's mind wouldn't leave Hugh and the case but she tried to concentrate. Harriet and Mary Burke, the septuagenarian sisters who lived above their tea shop, Leaves of Comfort, phoned while Alex and Tony were still making their way back to the Range Rover. They had already left Dan, Hugh and the strange doctor to climb the rest of the way to the death scene.

'You've been quiet,' Tony said. 'Is there anything you want to say before we go to see them?'

'I'm not sure. They're usually here at the Dog by now. Harriet sounded upset . . . or perhaps, anxious more than upset. She said she wanted you to take a look at Lillie Belle but I don't think that's what's really on her mind.'

'So you already said,' Tony said, turning toward her. 'What else are you thinking?'

'Well, I already said it really.' Alex couldn't sort out her thoughts from her feelings. 'It's Hugh who is completely confusing me. He obviously has no idea we know he's hiding something. What he said tonight about not going to the police when he should have – that could mean anything or nothing.

He went up to Green Friday with Sam and me and didn't call the police first? Hugh could say that's what he meant. Until he finds out he was seen last night, he could think he can pretend he was never there before today. If I could only figure out how to make him open up. Why don't I tell him I saw him?'

'We'll have to come back for the dogs after we see Harriet and Mary,' Tony said, not looking at her anymore.

Alex pulled her heels onto the seat, wrapped her arms around her shins and studied him in the shadows. The vehicle was warm inside, yet she shivered. 'What does coming back for the dogs have to do with anything? We always come back for them. Why don't you tell me what *you're* thinking?'

'Because you won't like it.'

'Try me. You'll tell me in the end, so you might as well get on with it.' She rested her chin on her knees. 'I can be so pushy, I make myself sick sometimes.'

His laugh diffused some of the tension. 'I'm not touching that,' he said. 'We can't be sure Hugh hasn't done something wrong. Even very wrong. He's a great guy, at least that's what we think, and we've known him a long time. Or a fairly long time. But what do we really know about him? Why did he show up in Folly and interview for the Black Dog job when he'd never managed a pub before?'

'He had plenty of previous business experience. He ran a successful whiskey distillery. I'd never managed a pub and I bought one,' Alex said, starting to simmer.

'You've never mentioned why he left the distillery. Bit of a comedown – and I don't mean to be rude. And it's none of my business. But Lily worked at the Black Dog for years and you'd been around the place since you were a baby. You knew what you were doing.'

'I don't know why he decided to change his occupation,' Alex said. This was getting them nowhere. 'I didn't ask because he impressed me and I'll always be glad I followed my instincts.' Please don't let anything make her change her mind. 'I think Hugh and Neve have slept together.' She sucked in a breath through her teeth. 'I shouldn't have said that.'

Tony leaned down until Alex looked at him. 'OK, your turn again. What makes you think that?'

'Darn my flapping mouth. The day she came, I heard Neve suggest she share Hugh's room. At least that's what it seemed like. I couldn't see his reaction, but he sounded furious when she reminded him that it wouldn't be the first time. But I don't really know what she meant by that, do I?'

'I think you do. OK, sweetheart, out we get. We'll see what the sisters are dying to tell us and I'll take a look at the pup.'

'Any thoughts about who the missing woman is, Tony?'

He paused. 'I've wondered . . . hell, what do I know?'

'Tell me.'

'It's only because she's the first one who comes to mind, but I've wondered about Sonia Quillam. She and Hugh have some history and she tried to attach herself to him when all the trouble happened with her family.'

'I don't think that's one bit off base,' Alex told him. 'I'm wondering the same thing. If she was at Green Friday, he could have gone to see her. Who knows what might have happened? They seemed like oil and water.'

'She's also the one woman we know Hugh was involved with.' Tony turned his face away and was quiet for a moment. 'I don't think we should be giving any opinions on this, do you?'

'No! We could make trouble where there isn't any. Let's get to the sisters, shall we?'

As they walked to the forecourt of the pub a line of powerful motorcycles roared in to park, one and two deep along the grass verge. The Gentlemen Bikers were a noisy bunch but they spent freely and were pleasant enough. At least they were fairly well behaved.

Coming down the path with several others Carrie Peale's husband, Harvey, laughed as loudly as the others and swung his own crash helmet over one arm. He saluted Tony and Alex on his way past.

'Odd fellow,' Tony said. 'Bit of a chameleon.'

Alex muttered agreement and, arm-in-arm, they carried on. The walk to Leaves of Comfort, on Pond Street, took them past cottage gardens thick with flushes of roses. Creamy clematis, luminous in the near darkness, climbed in mounds over door canopies. Lavish scents saturated the evening.

A single weak streetlight shed a bluish nimbus.

Alex held Tony's arm tighter and closed her eyes a moment, reluctant to let the peaceful moment pass. She had to. 'Hugh's explanation of how he came to be with Dan and that psychologist today didn't wash. I believe he met them deliberately.'

'Meaning?'

'Don't you think it looks good for him if he had a friendly encounter with Dan and volunteered to walk them up to the pond? If he were trying to avoid police questioning, he wouldn't do that. Or he might be trying to plant the idea that he wouldn't be likely to seek them out if he had any reason to feel guilty.'

The warm windows of Leaves of Comfort lay ahead. Tony pulled Alex to a stop. 'I thought of that, too. Wouldn't you like to know a lot more about Hugh? I've never thought of him as avoiding questions but I'm wondering if he's so good at the persona he wears that we buy it without question.'

'Then why doesn't he just cut and run?' Alex shook her head. 'If there's any reason why he could end up in big trouble here, why not get out while he can? And he could probably do it. As you've mentioned more than once, he's wealthy, so money isn't a problem. Lease a private jet and go anywhere he wants to until everything blows over. That or never come back at all. You can bet he's got funds outside the UK.'

She could almost feel and hear Tony thinking that over before he said, 'He won't do it. I don't know why – or not yet – but he won't run.'

'That's what you want to believe.'

'Yes, I do. But I'm not happy about the way I feel. He's going to shock the hell out of us, I can feel it. The question is, will we come to hate him?'

From the instant Alex and Tony climbed the stairs inside Leaves of Comfort and walked through the door, the Burke sisters' rosy-colored upstairs living room felt wrong.

Rather than sitting in her big, overstuffed, chintz chair, Harriet stood, a lamp with a deep pink silk shade turning her fine white hair into a blush aura. Her smile looked forced.

'Hello, ladies,' Tony said, frowning. 'Sorry if we've kept you waiting. It's been quite a day.'

Mary, also standing, gripped her walker and nodded at Tony and Alex, whose stomach began revolving. She needed to practice managing that one of these days. Mary wore her hair in a bun with an ivory Spanish comb holding her wispy waves back. Both women had powdered their noses but their naturally pink complexions were too pale and they darted glances at one another every few seconds.

'Sit down,' Harriet said at last. 'Lillie Belle's under the weather. I'm wondering if some more of her teeth need to come out.'

'I'll take a look.' Tony made a move to lift the elderly Maltese from her cushion. 'She has very few teeth left.' The little dog's long, pink tongue lolled from the side of her mouth and she looked up at Tony with adoring black eyes that shone with health. The sisters had adopted her a few months ago after her owner died.

'Let me hold her,' Alex said and Tony put the dog in her arms.

'The teeth can wait,' Mary said, much too quickly. 'Sit. We haven't seen the two of you for a chat for far too long.'

Harriet cleared her throat. She turned awkwardly, facing them with her back to the kitchen and one of the two tiny bedrooms. 'Mary's right,' she said. 'It's been too long.' With her right forefinger, she made an elaborate pointing motion that seemed to indicate something behind her.

Alex looked from one to the other of the three doors in the room, other than the one that led up from the tea rooms below. Harriet raised her eyebrows and gave a single nod.

Someone was here, in one of the rooms.

Listening hard, Alex sat on the lumpy, rose, velvet-covered couch reserved for visitors and kept on straining to hear. These old buildings had thick walls meant to keep out cold in winter and heat in summer. They also rendered rooms almost soundproof.

'What am I thinking of?' Harriet suddenly announced. 'I haven't offered you anything. Have you had dinner?'

They hadn't but Alex quickly said, 'We've been nibbling all day. I don't think we need anything.' She was starving now that she thought about it.

'I know what you won't say no to,' Mary said, a little color returning to her cheeks. 'Harriet, you know what to give them. And those cheese balls. The ones in a tin. This is the perfect time for them. There's a box of Turkish Delight in the cupboard over the stove, too.'

Harriet hurried away, clearly grateful to do something, anything. Alex met Tony's eyes but he gave a slight shake of his head. He read her too well. He would know that she was thinking of asking what was going on.

Then Alex heard it – a hiccup and a loud sniffle. It came from the bedroom beside the kitchen.

Mary took a deep breath and stared at the worn, rose-covered carpet. It was soft and beautiful but had definitely served a number of owners well. 'It's warm,' she said, still not looking at them. 'I hate these days when opening windows doesn't do a thing.'

They all made noises of agreement and the moments stretched.

The kitchen door opened and Harriet backed out. She faced them triumphantly with a silver tray bearing sherry glasses and a bottle of the ladies' favorite Harvey's Bristol Cream. She set this on a small antique mahogany table polished to a mirror shine. 'Do the honors, please, Tony,' she said, sounding much more normal. The Turkish Delight, pink and white and smothered with powdered sugar made a small mountain on a glass plate beside a bowl of what had to be the cheese balls. The latter resembled miniature footballs wrapped in yellow wafer. 'There,' Harriet said. 'A bit like Christmas.' She laughed but the laughter faded away and she all but downed the glass of sherry Tony gave her.

In a stage whisper, Mary said, 'Harriet will tell you what's going on. Stay by her, but don't look as if you're telling secrets in case . . .' She looked at one of the bedroom doors.

'What?' Alex said.

Mary put a finger to her lips. 'Hush. Go by Tony and let Harriet explain. I'll get it all wrong. And don't fall over Max or Oliver – they get so angry if you do.'

Grey tabby Oliver and one-eyed, orange Max slept peacefully on either side of the hearth, far away from Alex. She put the sleepy little dog on the couch and went to stand beside Tony.

They both bent close to Harriet who looked quickly over her shoulder but didn't say anything.

At last Alex said quietly, 'I heard someone in your bedroom.'

'Nothing feels right,' Harriet whispered. 'She was crying after they left. Sobbing so hard we made her come up and lie down. When she fell asleep we called you but you took so long . . . well, if she was awake now, she'd come out, wouldn't she?'

Tony leaned closer. 'Who? Harriet, please explain while you can.'

However long that's likely to take.

'Those people . . . we had never seen them before . . . they walked into the tea rooms late. She had stayed on to talk to Mary and me but she saw those two and looked shocked. She stared at them and they moved to her table. They talked to her, or the woman did. The man didn't say much. We overheard some of it – not everything – but bits and pieces.'

'Mm.' The sisters, Alex thought, had a way of overhearing all manner of things.

'We don't think it would do to press Annie. She's too fragile. We think she trusted us once and she could trust us again – all of us. Then it will be easier for her to confide in us. But something is definitely very wrong.'

'Harriet . . .?' Tony hesitated.

'Annie, who?' Alex asked.

'I don't remember her last name. She was . . . she still refers to herself as Elyan Quillam's fiancée even though he's in jail, a psychiatric place. He may never get out.'

NINE

'It's been too long,' Detective Chief Inspector Dan O'Reilly said. 'I mean it's been too long since we had a chance to talk about anything but business and not much of that since the shake-up.'

'Right,' Bill Lamb agreed. He'd told Jillian Miller to drive the psychologist back to Gloucester and return in the morning.

Both he and Dan had taken rooms at the Black Dog. They had a good excuse for staying – in addition to wanting an opportunity for some personal talk.

Hugh had come back with them. Keeping an eye on him was another reason for sticking around.

'Your old room,' Bill said, glancing around. The breeze coming through open windows was warmer than when they'd last been here. He sat on a newly installed easy chair, but Dan had passed up the straight-back in favor of lounging on the bed. 'I'm across the hall from you. Hugh's rooms are at the end. We can hope to hear him if he decides to do a moon-light flit.'

'Let's have some of that Aberlour,' Dan said. 'I've developed a taste for it. We may have to lay in a few more bottles by the time we're finished with the latest Folly fiasco. Anything to do with the Quillams is likely to turn into almighty chaos.'

'I think it defies reason that Percy Quillam raised his head here again – not that it lasted for long.' Bill picked up the bottle of honey-colored Aberlour. 'At least the body would be hard not to identify. Just about everyone who sees it knows it's him. Fingerprints won't be as easy as they should be after hours in the water, but they'll get to them. Then there's the clothes – Percy certainly had his own style. Tracking down why he came is at the top of my priority list.'

'Too bad this isn't prime door-to-door territory,' Dan commented. 'I still believe in good old-fashioned legwork but you're most likely going to have to go pretty far afield with this one.'

'I've got someone finding out Percy's last known location. We're starting with his professional bookings. And I'm praying he's been busy recently.'

Dan rubbed at the old scar on his jaw and nodded. 'Good move,' he said. The scar was from a knife wound he'd suffered on a night when his wife and son were home alone, and he'd been barely in time to intercept a thug who had broken into his house, bent on revenge against him. That night had been the start of the final rift in his marriage.

'I had a chat with LeJuan.' Bill didn't like the distant expression he sometimes saw in Dan's eyes. 'He's very happy with his new situation. How do you think it's going for the two of you?'

'He's a good man,' Dan said of his sergeant, the replacement for Bill Lamb after his promotion to inspector. 'I'm glad he was available. Neither of us is keen on playing babysitter to Dr Leon Wolf, though. The man thinks our only job should be to help him make fools of us.'

'What good will that do him?' Bill asked.

Dan grimaced. 'It's hard to know for sure but he's too chummy with the chief constable. At first I wondered if we were supposed to feel threatened and improve our slapdash ways. I don't really think so now. Wolf has something in mind that will benefit him. Let's hope he's not writing an exposé of some sort on police work.'

'I hope he stays away from me,' Bill responded. He had used water glasses for the whiskey and grinned when Dan gave the large pour a skeptical eye. 'Let's ask Hugh about them carrying Aberlour here. He's the resident whiskey expert, even if he doesn't drink much of it.'

'I'd like to try Birnam Bricht, the stuff his distillery produces. Pretty rarified, I'm told. That's all part of the Hugh Rhys mystery, too.'

'Yep, he's a mystery all right. You haven't told me why you came here this time, Dan?'

'Supposedly to see if you wanted a hand. The suggestion – if you can call it that – came down from the big boss. The doc is far too interested in the Folly cases for me to believe that, though. You can bet Wolf asked for it to be suggested that I come. He knows way too much not to have studied everything that's gone down here before – closely.'

'Shit,' Bill said with feeling. 'That's all I need. How would you feel about giving LeJuan lookout duty? He'd make a good job of keeping an eye on our friend. I don't like the idea of him reporting every move we make to the chief constable.'

'That would have to be carefully done,' Dan said. 'I can't drop LeJuan into a situation where he draws the wrong kind of notice. Let me see what I can do. I admit that Percy Quillam, deceased, is a complication I couldn't have expected. But it does make a connection to my old case.'

'It might mean all this will unravel easily,' Bill said. 'But I'm not holding my breath. It's too bad Dr Molly wouldn't give an opinion about the wounds on Quillam's face and neck. His hands, too.'

'Forensics will turn up some useful yay or nay responses in a hurry. If Percy's blood type matches samples from Green Friday you'll be off and running.'

Bill had other, less optimistic thoughts. 'Unless Percy's taken to leaving women's clothing and personal possessions around, we're still looking for a woman. A woman who may be alive or dead. If it's the latter she's also a missing woman. No ID found – nothing. They've taken the house apart. I thought the locksmith who found the house open and walked around inside was telling us there were all kinds of things on that bed but he's backtracked a bit. That or he thinks he may get caught out in exaggeration. At first he said there was money, bills and coins. We are doing another search but so far that wasn't found by our people. I believe there was definitely a car and that was gone. Brock – that's the locksmith – is sure it was a dark gray, late model Mercedes.

'We don't know if or how someone got in without being seen and took both the car – and any of the other normal things that would identify the owner.'

'And it could have been the woman herself who did that,' Dan put in. 'Doesn't that seem most likely? That's what I think. And Radhika's the only neighbor?'

'Yes. When she's there. She spends nights at Tony's clinic. Sleeps upstairs. Only the tower is finished at the new house – more or less. She likes to hang out there and meditate or read. She's been trying to persuade Alex to paint in the top room because the light's so good and Alex hasn't been painting for ages – it worries Tony and he's talked to Radhika about it. Radhika was there last night. I'm not sure how late she stayed but I intend to ask if she'll keep away while all this is going on – just to be safe. Given the time frame she wouldn't have seen anything, though. We've talked to the people working on Radhika's place but again, they didn't see suspicious movement, or not that they remember.'

'And we know who else was there last night, before we got

anything on it – according to Chuck Short,' Dan said. 'He works for the Derwinters. Stables manager, I think.'

'That's who he is,' Bill said. 'I don't think I heard what he had to say.'

'Alex went up to Radhika's for dinner. She and Chuck spoke when she was on her way up Trap Lane.'

'I'm damned,' Bill said. 'How did you find that out?'

'LeJuan's a favorite with the Burke sisters. They told him.'

'But neither Alex nor Tony mentioned it. Bloody suspicious if you ask me. They should have made sure I knew and they'll be explaining why they didn't.'

'Sorry not to pass it along earlier. I assumed you knew.'

Bill seethed. He poured another slug of Aberlour and took a healthy swallow. 'Too bad Hugh showed up at Green Friday all innocence and helpfulness this evening. If he hadn't I'd have had him brought right in for questioning. What the hell, this way we can give him a little space to make some mistakes.

'I need to nail Tony and Alex. I'll keep it friendly specu-lation as long as I can but get at anything they might be hiding. The anonymous caller we got said Hugh was seen leaving Green Friday last night. I think he knows exactly who was there – who the missing person is. Maybe Tony and Alex do, too – or think they do. They could be protecting Hugh. They've been tight a long time.'

Dan grunted. 'Sound like good moves. You and Radhika are still an item, then?' he asked mildly.

'More so,' Bill told him. He didn't like discussing the relation-ship but he wasn't about to lie about something so important to him. 'I won't say we aren't still feeling our way, but we both intend to be together permanently.'

Dan looked into his whiskey, brooding, Bill thought. 'You're a lucky bugger,' Dan said. 'She's terrific.'

'Yes, she is.' And he wanted the subject to close there. 'When's that boy of yours coming back from Ireland?'

'Calum? In a week or so, if his mother doesn't pull another stunt on me. How about Simon?' Bill also had one son from a defunct marriage.

'I see him every other weekend, or I try to. Really good kid,

Dan. Not spending more time with him is my only regret about the marriage failure, not that Charlene isn't a good woman.'

Bill's mobile rang. A tech from the lab in Gloucester apologized for calling so late. The woman spoke succinctly but said plenty and he could feel his pulse speeding up.

'Well, that tells us something,' he said when the call finished. 'No blood match between the body and what was in the house, but they found orange silk fibers in the woods beside the driveway – with definite traces of the blood in the kitchen and hall. Another search in the morning. Dogs again.'

Dan sat up and poured more Aberlour for each of them.

'We really won't be surprised if the car turns out to be a rental – Chuck Short remembered a sticker on a bumper he thought was for a rental place, but not what was on it. There aren't many rental agencies around the Cotswolds but we'll get them checked out, at the same time as we get an alert to all outfits around airports. We'll find it. That's all for now – unless any other techs decide to work all night.'

'Oh, you're not referring to the Mercedes,' Dan said. 'What car? Where?'

Bill used his glass and extended fingers for emphasis. 'This was this morning before we were called. A car was seen coming from the direction of Green Friday. Short said he doesn't know one car from another, but it looked new and expensive. He was heading up Trap Lane on horseback – about mid-morning – and this car passed him. Chuck uses a track from the top of the Trap Lane hill to the Derwinters'. He said it's convenient for the stables up there and he likes to ride in peace. After the car passed him, he looked back to see who was driving but couldn't. He did see what he said was a rental sticker.'

'That's a lot better than nothing,' Dan said. 'Someone could have been driving from Green Friday. Too bad he didn't recognize a make.'

'Alex and Tony are in this up to their ears as usual,' Bill said, trying to sound casual. 'You do wonder how they happen to show up on every one of these cases, and, come to that, why the damned cases keep showing up around here.'

Dan punched up the pillows on his bed and settled, although Bill saw tautness in his former boss's body. 'The only weird thing is that there's been a string of these events here. And that Alex walks into them. But it's a small place so there aren't that many people likely to end up in the middle of a problem – they tend to turn a blind eye. And she's a very observant woman – Tony's no slouch but I think he mostly follows in her footsteps to keep an eye on her.'

'Right.'

He waited for Dan to say more but he stayed silent.

Bill outwaited him and Dan eventually cleared his throat. 'Any thoughts about Hugh Rhys?'

That was more like it. 'Yeah. He wanted to run into us today. Don't ask me why but we'll find out.'

'We're on the same wavelength.' Dan lifted his head to swallow whiskey, then closed his eyes as he settled again. 'Maybe you should get some sleep. I don't expect we'll hear anything else from Gloucester tonight.'

A door slamming below made sure they were both wide awake. The only light on in the room was beside Dan's bed and he switched it off. At the same time he put his iPod on low. The smart bastard thought of everything, Bill thought, smiling in the gloom. He set his glass quietly aside.

Voices, faint but unmistakable, followed, then steps on the stairs – only one set. He wondered if it was the mysterious Neve Rhys whom they had yet to set eyes on.

Light footsteps passed outside the door and carried on to the end. There was a faint tap on a door. Dammit, he wanted to see through the wall, see who was out there.

The tap-tapping came again and a while later a surprised mutter, deep, a man's voice, and what sounded like a woman's muffled response – then nothing else but a door closing.

Silence hung in Dan's room for as long as Bill could take it before he got up and went to the bed. 'What the hell?' he said, knowing the noise from the iPod covered him.

'Damned if I know,' Dan responded. 'Except I think Hugh just let a woman into his room and he wasn't expecting her.'

'We're on the same page. And whoever is still downstairs is either waiting for a reaction or . . . I don't know, but I'm going down to find out who it is. Could be nothing or something but I hate to pass up an opportunity to find out.'

'Do it,' Dan said. 'I bet you it's Neve Rhys. See you in the morning unless you need me earlier.'

Bill left the room quietly, knowing Dan wouldn't attempt to sleep until he was sure there wouldn't be action tonight.

A single light was on inside the front door but following low voices to the snug didn't take skill. Bill put a knuckle to a glass panel in the door and walked in.

Alex and Tony sat, side-by-side, on a banquette. They appeared rumpled and worried and gave Bill a startled look when they saw him.

'Good evening,' he said, attempting a casual approach he'd never achieved particularly well. 'I've been upstairs in my room and I thought I heard voices down here. I hoped it was you, Alex, and I get both of you. A bonus.' He cringed at his own phony effort.

'Was there something you wanted?' Alex turned those upslanting green eyes on him. Sleepy and concerned as she obviously was, he almost understood what a hold those eyes might have on Dan – even though he also knew the man needed to stop punishing himself and find another focus for his attention.

'You know how it is when your mind won't turn off,' Bill said. 'You must be thinking about everything you've dealt with today, too – how could you not? Any thoughts you believe could be useful?'

Tony settled a hand on Alex's and squeezed. 'Lots of thoughts,' he said. 'No conclusions.'

'I thought you two spent your nights at Tony's now. Or so the scuttlebutt goes.' He smiled but they didn't seem to relax even a fraction.

'We do,' Alex said. She turned her attention on Tony who ran his spare hand through his hair. 'We had to stop by for a bit.'

He'd be within his rights to ask a bald 'why?' to that, Bill thought, but he didn't want to risk turning off any communication.

'Anything I can do to help?'

They both stared at him. He didn't blame them for looking confused. What were they supposed to say to that?

'Will they really send a diver into the pond tomorrow?' Tony said. 'You know how stupid kids will take risks. When I was still in school a boy who was a really good swimmer went in to try to find out how deep it was. He almost drowned. A couple of others went in and dragged him out. He wasn't going to make it all the way back on his own. We actually did CPR on him and a bunch of water came out when we did that holding up by the waist thing. It was horrible.'

'I heard about that,' Alex said. 'I'd forgotten it.'

Did Tony not want anyone to go in because he was afraid for their safety, or because he didn't want them to find something he'd rather they not find? 'He went down without equipment, but he made it out. Thanks to you kids. And he lived?' asked Bill.

'Yes, he lived.' Alex pressed her thumb knuckles into her eyes. 'And later he said he never found the bottom. A diver shouldn't go in there.'

Tony raised his eyebrows at Bill but didn't add anything to the conversation.

Heavy footsteps pounded toward the snug and the door flew open. 'What the hell were you two thinking of?' Hugh just about shouted, before he saw Bill.

'Natty duds,' Bill said of Hugh's striped sleep shorts and black hoody with frayed cuffs and bottom. The man had enviably muscular legs.

'We phoned because we wanted to have a word with you,' Alex said and Bill noted how Tony's mouth dropped slightly open. 'Sorry we woke you up.'

The lady was almost a talented liar only it would be hard not to wonder when exactly they called Hugh, and why he hadn't done a better job of getting some clothes on after what Bill figured would be at least a twenty-minute time lapse if the call had been made right before he arrived in the snug. And where was the advance guard who went to his room?

Alex raised her hands and let them fall in her lap. 'I give up. I've made a complete mess of this. Where's Annie now?'

'That's probably the best decision you've made tonight,' Hugh said. 'Some corners are so tight there's no way out other than to be honest. But thank you for trying to save us all. Annie is upstairs in my room. She's exhausted and I'm no shrink but she seems close to some sort of breakdown. Why you let her come to my rooms like that I don't know. Some people would have a good time making something of it.'

'There's no one here but us and we knew she'd be safe with you.'

'Dan's upstairs,' Bill said. He was overdue to say something around here.

'Annie wouldn't listen to us,' Tony said. 'We tried everything to make her wait until tomorrow to see you, but she wouldn't have any of it. As far as she's concerned, you're the only one who can be trusted to help her. She was coming here with or without us so we just tagged along. Better we were here than she was alone – not that we thought you were a danger to her – as Alex already said.' He cast his eyes to the ceiling.

'Sheesh,' Hugh said, pulling a chair forward and sitting. 'I know that. She's beside herself. Over the top. I made her lie down and she seemed to pass out in seconds. What the hell are we going to do?'

'Get Doc James over here,' Alex said.

'Exactly,' Tony agreed. 'And ask your mother if she will come and help us. Lily is always the rock.'

Bill reached for his mobile but Alex had already started using hers.

Hugh looked like hell. He hunched over with his elbows on his knees and his fingers driven into his thick, currently wild hair. 'Do you remember who she is, Bill?' he muttered. 'Annie Bell? You would have seen her during the case at Green Friday.'

It would have been easier if no one had asked and he could have found out from records of the Elyan Quillam case. 'Not really.' He shouldn't be getting any deeper into this discussion.

'She's Elyan Quillam's fiancée of almost three years. He's probably never getting out of a secure forensic psychiatric hospital at Ashworth as far as I can tell, but she's not about to give up on him. She blames Percy. But so do I. The man pushed him so hard from when he was a little kid – and all the way up until the disaster when Elyan snapped. He was a prodigy and that was that. Practice, practice, practice. The boy loved the piano but he wanted to live as well . . . did you ever hear him play jazz the way he did at the Black Dog on occasion?' Bill shook his head, no.

Hugh sighed. 'Percy wouldn't have that. Or he wouldn't have it other than the way he, Percy, allowed it. He was a pig to the boy. Everyone he touched, he hurt. I didn't know most of this until Elyan was locked up. I still visit him and bit-by-bit he's told me.'

'And you believe his story about Percy?' Bill asked. He knew he was in dangerous territory, and with witnesses.

'I do.'

'Did you kill Percy Quillam?'

Hugh looked at him, his dark eyes narrowed. 'There's no doubt that body is Percy Quillam's? I didn't see it, remember?'

'None. And my question stands.'

The Scottish accent that was unexpected with Hugh's Welsh name snapped out, crisp and sharp, 'Will you believe me if I tell you, no?' He waited while Bill stared back and said nothing. 'I didn't think so. That's for you to find out, then.'

TEN

'She's still asleep, James,' Lily whispered. She got up from a chair beside Hugh's bed where Annie Bell lay beneath a quilt. The room was cool but she looked feverish with her auburn hair a tangle around her flushed face.

Doc James Harrison came into the bedroom and closed the door to the hallway quietly behind him. He went into the combination office and sitting room that had been converted from a second, smaller bedroom adjoining Hugh's. He indicated for Lily to follow him. The two of them had been very close for years and Lily spent a good deal of time at Doc's home which was also where teenagers Scoot and Kyle Gammage continued to live while their father was absent from their lives. Doc James and Lily had become the boys' stand-in parents and so far the arrangement had been good for all of them.

'Any developments?' Lily asked James, all but shutting the door between the two rooms. She stood with her back to the window, leaning against the sill. Her spine ached from napping on the side of the bed where Annie slept. 'Alex thinks the police are going to take Hugh in for questioning this morning.'

James and Tony were obviously father and son, both tall, good looking and curly haired, although James' curls had been white for years and he'd formerly been dark-haired, whereas Tony's coloring was lighter. They both had dark-blue eyes.

'Tell me how you are first,' James said.

'A bit stiff.' Lily smiled at him. 'I'm too accustomed to a comfortable bed. Annie doesn't seem well to me. You didn't say much when you examined her last night.'

'That was perfunctory,' he said. 'She's an essentially healthy young woman, as far as I can tell, but she's exhausted and probably emotionally compromised. She should be examined more thoroughly by her own doctor. I understand from Tony that she talked quite expansively to Harriet and Mary Burke at their tea rooms, but clammed up when he and Alex showed up there. We can't help her if she won't let us but I'm hoping that will change.

'Did I tell you I got the white handkerchief wave out of the sisters' windows when I passed Leaves of Comfort earlier?'

'Earlier?' Lily said. He had so much more energy than she did. 'No you didn't tell me. It's only eight thirty now.'

'Harriet flagged me in to give me a brief rundown. I don't think we've got a lot of time to get our ducks in a row – or at least to try to work out what we're dealing with. Not if we're going to help Hugh. Harriet let me know that one of her scouts saw Dan and Bill leave here before seven this morning.'

'Darn, I wonder if they had breakfast?'

'Lily, my love, we don't care about their breakfast today. We care that they were picked up by LeJuan Harding and set off out of Folly, so we can hope they're on their way back to Gloucester and we've got some time to get together with Hugh. If necessary we're going to hammer some information out of him.' He frowned. 'Do you know if Neve Rhys came back last night?'

'She didn't but she hasn't checked out. Her things are still in her room. I don't know if both of them are there, though. She said her husband would be joining her but there's been no sign of him yet.'

'We're getting together at my house later this morning,' James said. 'We can all make it there by the back way and hope not to be seen. I've talked to Hugh. He'll be coming down from Tony and Alex's – thank God he agreed to spend what was left of the night there. He knows where our spare key is so he'll let himself in.'

'I'll stay here. It's more important for Alex to be there with all of you. Liz Hadley comes in this morning. Scoot is an angel. He did the fireplace as well as setting up as much as he could before he went to school. Carrie Peale – our village potter – has been putting in a few hours and she'll come in, too. I think she's finding it hard to make ends meet with just the pottery and a husband who does little else but drink, ride around on the back of his friend's motorbike, and talk about his future literary stardom.'

James opened his briefcase and pulled out several pieces of printer paper. 'This is information on Quillam's concert schedule. I'm sure the police already have it. He's supposed to be in Paris – in the middle of an engagement. Supposedly it's been announced that he's ill and there's a stand-in everyone is raving about.'

Lily crossed her arms. 'This is only getting nastier. Lies, lies and more lies. Mr Quillam couldn't be more ill than he is now, could he? Those people in Paris probably have no idea he's lying in a morgue. But someone must be speaking for him over there – telling them he's ill. Whoever that is would know something's gone very wrong, surely.'

'Tony's seeing what if anything he can find out about that. The news will have it all out there today but the police won't be giving away any of the details we'd like. I'd better get going. When Annie wakes up try to have her stay in bed. She needs her own things. Those can be brought from wherever they are. I assume she has a car.'

'We don't know,' Lily said. 'I'll get back to you as soon as I have any information. James, what if the police come looking for Hugh?' Tiredness was overtaking her and anxiety about what would happen next only made it worse.

'Tell them you'll ask him to contact them – when you speak to him,' James said.

'I don't think they'll accept that. Especially not from me . . . or any of us. They could insist on knowing how I'll go about finding him. If they think I know where he is . . . that scares me.'

The door to the bedroom swung open wider and Annie stood there, her clothing rumpled. 'What's wrong?' she said, her hand at her throat. 'What do you mean? Hugh hasn't done anything, so the police don't want to talk to him.'

'It's just that Hugh knows all the people involved in what's been going on here pretty well,' Doc said. 'Lily's quieter than most of us – thank goodness she is – so she doesn't like dealing with the police.'

'Don't worry about it, Lily,' she said. She put a shaky hand to her mouth and started chewing a thumbnail. 'Hugh always knows how to deal with people.'

Burford was a pretty town; old, picturesque and slathered with tourists all day, every day at this time of the year. Nevertheless, once away from the famous and steep main road that poured down from the wolds to the Windrush valley, terraces of stone cottages reminded you of the way the place must have looked a century and more earlier.

Alex knew she was out of her depth. She slipped past bursting flower baskets hanging from walls, climbing roses, wisteria, every possible flower that might bloom now and they all bloomed with an almost overwhelming fervor. What did she think she was doing here in the early morning – trailing Detective Sergeant Jillian Miller as she studied numbers outside front doors? At least Miller was so intent on reaching her target that a novice boy scout could probably have followed her without being seen.

Dodging into doorways, behind bushes and into narrow alleys felt ridiculous but what choice did she have? She'd stayed out of the way while Hugh got ready to leave Tony's house, assuming he would go straight to Doc's. A couple of minutes after he drove away in the Subaru he used to run around the area, the car Alex recognized as Bill Lamb's followed. She didn't know Miller was driving until she saw her get out in Burford. Alex had tucked the Range Rover into the forecourt of a butcher's shop and set off at a trot.

Miller stopped in front of a short row of houses with a board
outside advertising holiday rents. There were three houses with
curly stucco rooflines atop flat fronts. One pink house, one
yellow, and one green. The window at the very top suggested
a fourth and very small floor. The detective sergeant breezed on
past but quickly turned down a tiny alleyway toward the back
of the buildings.

Loaded with guilt, Alex phoned Tony and started talking
before he got past his first question about where the hell she
was. 'In Burford,' she said. 'Hugh left right after you. I was
looking out of the window and saw Jillian Miller drive after
him. Thank goodness I was ready to go. I couldn't understand
why Hugh didn't suggest we drive to Doc's together, but now
I know. He had somewhere else in mind.

'Wait . . . Miller just went behind a row of houses and I
think Hugh must be inside one of them although I can't see
his car anywhere. Since Miller was following him it must
be around, or she wouldn't have stopped. Got to go or I'll
lose her, if I haven't already.

'Yes, I know you don't like me doing this, but it seemed like
the only thing to do. Hugh's being ambushed and I'll at least
be able to break things up with one of my brilliant excuses for
him being here.'

She had started to jog and turned in at the alley in time to
see Miller make a sharp left behind the pastel houses.

'Sorry, Tony. Gotta go. Tell everyone to hang in and I'll be
there as soon as I can – hopefully with Hugh in tow. Maybe I
can head Miller off . . . yes, I'm interfering with the law. Hugh
is my friend and until I know he's guilty of something, I'll
stand up for him. Get the sisters to tell everything they heard
at the tea rooms when Annie was there. Bye.'

She was in time to see Miller open a rotting wooden gate
and slip through. This was the middle house.

Alex stopped. She looked at her mobile and punched in a
contact. If she had really been thinking she'd have done this
before, probably as soon as she saw Miller following Hugh.

'Alex?' he answered. 'Sorry I'm going to be late. I've got
an unexpected meeting but I'll get there as soon as I can. You've
got plenty to discuss—'

'Just get out of that house, Hugh. Detective Sergeant Jillian Miller is looking for a back way in – probably to spy on you or whatever. Just get out.'

'Good God.' He spoke to someone else but what he said was very unclear. 'Right, on my way, Alex. We'll talk about why you followed instead of calling me when I see you. Thank you, anyway.'

'Where's your car?' She wanted to snap back that he wasn't in a position to be snarky. 'Do you need a lift?'

'No, thanks. See you at Doc's – I hope. Please keep on trusting me. I know it must be looking bad – suspicious – but it will all work out. I'm out of the house and on my way. You'd better be on yours.'

Alex backtracked to the street but saw no sign of Hugh or his black Subaru Outback. She ran for her own vehicle and drove too fast to get out of Burford and on her way back to Folly by winding, little used roads through mostly deserted fields.

Parked behind Doc's house, she went through the back gate, let herself in by a side door to which she had a key and hurried through the mud and laundry rooms, following the rise and fall of voices. She found her people gathered in the little used sitting room, seated around a low, ebony and brass table where empty cups and saucers, plates, and the remnants of croissants, meant someone – probably Harriet – had provided a late breakfast.

Alex dropped onto a sofa beside Tony. 'Hugh's on his way. He should have been here before me but I'm past trying to make reason of anything he does. Where's Annie?'

'Sleeping,' Doc said. 'I gave her another sedative. She's exhausted and needs complete rest for a day or two. She's been staying in Stow-on-the-Wold. She's got a Mini – which used to belong to Elyan Quillam – parked behind the Black Dog. Convenient since her things were in it.'

'Shouldn't she be here?' Tony said.

'No,' Mary Burke said. Lillie Belle, the tiny Maltese with her long pink tongue, watched from Mary's lap with inquisitive black button eyes. 'We don't need Annie here. Not if you want us to be able to talk freely about what was said at Leaves of Comfort. You didn't get her to tell you anything, did you? And you tried.'

Always blunt. 'That's right,' Alex agreed. 'I was hoping Hugh would be here by now, but we'd better get on with it. Tell us what you heard, ladies.' She held up a hand. 'Why isn't my mum here?'

'She thought she ought to run the pub,' Doc said, straight-faced. 'Or that someone should.'

Alex nodded, yes. There was too much to think about.

Harriet looked at Mary who indicated for her to continue. 'The woman who moved to Annie's table after we closed behaved like she must be a friend. Annie looked confused, but I don't think she knew what to say and she's too polite to tell someone to go away. I got the definite impression she'd seen the woman before. I don't know about the man.'

'Time she learned the difference between friend and foe,' Mary said tartly.

Harriet frowned. 'Too few people have manners these days,' she said. 'The man who was with the woman just sat there and looked at the tablecloth. He kept running a fingernail along the embroidery. I wanted to smack his hand.'

Alex hid a smile. Harriet never forgot her priorities.

'The woman said she knew all about Elyan Quillam and what a horrible childhood he'd had. She told Annie someone should have taken Elyan away from his father because the way he was made to work at the piano was child abuse.'

'It probably could be,' Doc said. 'Not that I'd know in this case. Brilliant pianist. Wicked waste.'

'Quite,' Harriet agreed. 'That's when the woman started talking about Hugh and saying he was dangerous and Annie shouldn't have anything to do with him. She insisted Hugh had enemies and he wouldn't stop at anything to make sure they didn't get in his way.'

Alex and Tony looked at one another. Alex didn't say that it sounded as if Harriet, and probably Mary, had overheard just about every word spoken at that tea table. But she didn't know what to make of the reported conversation or what was said about Hugh. It all seemed unbelievable.

'What did these people look like?' Alex asked. 'You're sure you never saw them before?'

Mary slowly shook her head. 'I'm sure. The woman was a

bit theatrical. Short dark hair. Very pale skin and her eyes looked black.'

'Tall,' Harriet said. 'He was nice enough looking but she used up all the attention.'

'Oh,' Alex said, and swallowed. If Hugh or her mother were there they'd both know who the sisters had seen. Alex hesitated to blurt it out unless she was absolutely sure. She was sure but she still couldn't say the name.

'Isn't this something the police should be hearing?' Doc said. 'They'll have to know it all sooner or later and the less we hold things back, the less likely we are to venture into dangerous waters. They won't like us keeping information from them.'

'They haven't asked us questions that would lead to this,' Alex said. Or the right questions, she thought. There were a number of ways to avoid the truth and she was guilty of at least one or two of them right now. In addition to not mentioning Hugh and his car at Green Friday the previous evening, she hadn't revealed to the police how she'd seen him on the hillside near the pond, or his strange behavior there.

'So we're keeping our mouths shut when we have information the police will need? They need it now. We're obstructing them.'

'Damn it, Dad, you're so bloody reasonable.' Tony spoke through his teeth and Alex shifted back on her seat. 'If they're so brilliant, they'll find their own information.'

Doc's expression hardened. 'I think a lot of us know we can hide facts for a while but they tend to come out eventually and when they do, we've only made them worse by making them more mysterious – and potentially more dangerous if something happens that might have been averted.'

He and Tony looked at one another, unflinching. Alex had never seen them so openly at odds toward one another. She could have sworn there was a subtext in what they said but it made no sense to her.

The sisters sat, their backs rigid, hands in their laps – or in Mary's case, on the dog in her lap.

Mary cleared her throat. 'Toward the end, the woman leaned close to Annie and spoke in her ear. She took hold of Annie's hands as if she was holding her there. We couldn't hear a word but Annie looked dreadful. She closed her eyes and I think she was already starting to cry. We thought afterward that the couple was trying to turn Annie against Hugh and that they hoped she would be on their side in something they had planned, only the woman saw me and it must have been obvious I was listening because she got up to leave. The man took a while to get the message – he looked blank – then he followed without a word. That's when we took Annie upstairs and she broke down. So we made her stay quiet on her own and called you, Alex and Tony.'

'She wasn't happy about it when she saw us,' Tony said. 'Did she say anything else about why she's here in Folly or why she wanted to see Hugh?'

'No, but there's something else – two things.' Harriet stood up, her lips sucked in. She walked to the window and pulled a curtain aside. 'It's going to rain.'

'What else?' Doc pressed quietly.

'I don't think I should tell you.'

Alex rubbed at her face. You couldn't force someone to tell you something, but Harriet wouldn't have mentioned whatever this was if she were not longing to unburden herself.

Doc sat quietly, waiting, and Mary tutted. 'Harriet, we have to say. It could be dangerous or wrong not to.

'As long as we all keep Annie safe until this is all over, it won't be. But she should tell these things herself. She hasn't even told us any real details, remember, and from the way she clammed up, she was already wishing she hadn't said anything at all.'

'All right.' Harriet returned to her seat and sat with a thump. 'We aren't sure she wasn't rambling. This is probably nothing, but she said she wished she could ask Zack about it. We thought that was the name. She put a hand over her mouth. I felt terrible for her. She was running a fever, but then Annie said she thinks Elyan doesn't love her anymore. That's what she said. Then – just as she was falling asleep she said something else – but we weren't sure what it was and we couldn't ask again.'

'You couldn't make it out at all?' Alex could hardly contain herself. 'What do you think she said. Do you have any idea?'

Harriet let out a long sigh. 'We're not sure. But it could have been that Elyan might be ill again . . .' She looked at Mary, who nodded. 'Or that he could kill again.'

ELEVEN

'I'll leave you to close,' Molly Lewis said to an assistant, as she stepped back from the stainless steel table where Percy Quillam's corpse lay, the torso still open.

Bill lifted his mask enough to push more wintergreen gum into his mouth and followed Molly, stripping off garb as he went and tossing it into a hamper. Like Molly, he scrubbed his hands at a deep sink. Even minus any of Quillam's bodily fluids on him, he felt the need to scrub hard and long. No matter how many post-mortems he attended, he still felt vaguely sick at some points and his throat wanted to shut. He was glad to see how well Jillian Miller did, even if she usually disappeared once she got out of the morgue.

Miller had arrived late and with an infuriating smirk on her face. Bill had no doubt he would be hearing the reason for that shortly.

They convened in Molly's small office where she maintained a miraculously clear desktop. She motioned for the pair of them to sit and flipped on a giant screen.

'You understand that anything I tell you now is preliminary,' she said without looking at them. 'These are teaching films, not that you need them. They just make it easier for me to point out what I mean. Lungs of a suspected drowning subject who did drown.' She indicated films on the left of the screen. 'And here, the lungs of a suspected drowning subject who did not drown. Percy Quillam's lungs resemble these and his films will be similar. He did not breathe underwater, breathe in water, or die under the water.

'There are events called dry drownings but given what else we now assume, that does not apply here. There are signs of violence to the corpse – I would have expected more – but petechiae or small hemorrhages, in the eyes in this case, point to strangulation and there are signs of pressure – bruising – on the neck. I believe these are from manual constriction although they are only present at the front which could almost mean they happened during an attempt to lift or pull him back. There are numerous cuts and abrasions on the neck and arms – on the shoulders – but no defensive signs that I can see. However, the deceased had cardiac issues and almost certainly suffered cardiac arrest. Further examination will clarify that, but I think we can take this to the bank. Had the cardiac event happened under different conditions he might not have died. Compromised cardiac elements added to some extreme stress made the difference – probably. This type of thing happens all the time and is not particularly significant, but under the circumstances . . .' She spread her hands.

'He was murdered,' Bill said. 'By strangulation. And put in the water to make it appear he'd drowned.'

'That fits with my conclusions – more or less,' Molly agreed. 'Although strangulation isn't a positive. The abrasions are a puzzle but we're on our way to solving that. I have to wonder if death happened before the attacker intended – or if death occurred without it being immediately noticed. Did the attacker only expect the deceased to be incapacitated enough to go under water, without much fight, and drown? Did he even realize the body had caught on those roots and remained barely submerged and coming up entirely when it rolled? It's reasonable to set the time of death during darkness but I still doubt that theory. I'm only the forensic pathologist here but I think perhaps the attacker ran away and ran fast once he thought his deed was done. Forgive me if I sound a little Shakespearean.'

Bill studied her. 'There's something else, isn't there?' She avoided meeting his eyes and rubbed a forefinger slowly up and down the edge of a folder.

Molly glanced at him and then away again. 'Yes, there is. Unfortunate on our part but these things can happen in the best of times. It may not change anything substantially, other than . . . give me time, Bill. I'll get back to you as soon as I can.'

TWELVE

Tony leaned across the bar and spoke close to Alex's ear. 'I'm damned, me darlin',' he said. 'Is that who I think it is?'

'I think it is. Yes. Hugh asked if it was all right for him to take the first hour or so off but he didn't say why – or where he was going. Then those two showed up and sat themselves right there. I think we're looking at people who don't know everything we know. Or at least they think we don't know anything. I'm not sure I just said what I meant. Hugh joined them as soon as they got here. I wish I thought I could ask him to take me into his confidence.'

'I understand the way you feel,' Tony said. 'It might even have been a good idea but if it wasn't, we'd have lost any chance of him coming to us if and when he's ready.'

Alex gripped the edge of the bar. 'You're right.' She pulled a beer for a man in motorcycle leathers and passed it across the counter. He drank it down in an open-throated swallow, nodded and walked away.

'Ever wish you got a steady stream of customers like that?' Tony asked, grinning. 'No need to ask how his mother is or if his cousin's over shingles. Nothing.'

'No, thank you.' Alex swiped a cloth across the counter. 'And even if you are fond of your quiet spaces, you'd miss the little dramas in here.'

'Mmm.' He supposed he might. 'Have you had any more ideas about why Hugh was in Burford this morning? You said he sounded defensive when you phoned him.'

'It's a complete puzzle to me. I expected him to talk to me about it when I saw him earlier but he didn't say a word – unless his grim mood was supposed to be expressive, which it was.

'And last night when he was at our house, he didn't bring up anything Annie might have said. I thought it was because there was nothing much to talk about. But after hearing the sisters today, surely Annie said something to him, don't you think?'

What did he think? 'Maybe yes, maybe no. She was in a state. Hugh said she seemed out of it, but if he weren't avoiding any conversation with us we could ask about it.'

They were going to have to take most of this to the police and they'd still look like obstructionists for not contacting them sooner.

The Black Dog had barely opened and the first few customers, most regulars, had come in with their orders. Colonel Stroud's tightly clipped grey mustache was already tipped with foam from the single beer he drank to begin his evening. Afterward he shifted to whiskey and rarely left the premises until his gait became decidedly unsteady. Kev Winslet, the florid and rotund gamekeeper for the Derwinter estate, rocked on his heels as he drained the end of his second pint. He liked to get a head of steam on fast, did Kev.

The two men stood together but stared silently past one another in the customary rumination stage of the evening.

'Do we know the man I just served?' Alex said, looking beyond him. 'Nice looking in a way although I don't like the sideways stares he gives. He's watchful – or maybe just shy. Don't turn around.' She stopped him as he would have done just that.

'No. I could have seen him before, but I don't remember him. At least, without taking another look, I don't.'

'Oh, forget it, he's Harvey's friend – unlikely friend.' She glanced at Carrie Peale who was working at the bar this evening and not looking happy. 'I know Carrie doesn't like Harvey being here, drinking all the time. Poor woman is in a bad place, I think.'

Tony took advantage of a new group of customers at the counter to turn around and face the room. He rested his elbows on the counter and casually surveyed the crowd – he hoped he looked casual. The man in question, average height, blond and well-built, had a forearm on Harvey's shoulder while the latter chuckled at whatever the biker said into his ear.

The table tucked into a bay window, where Hugh sat, captured Tony's attention again. He turned back to Alex. 'That is Neve Rhys with Hugh, right?' he asked.

'Yes, and I believe the man with them is Perry Rhys, her husband. Mum said she got a call this afternoon to say he was definitely joining Neve later today.' She passed a customer's change across the counter and smiled her thanks. 'He's Hugh's cousin. The coloring's similar but Perry doesn't look like him, does he? Do we think they're the ones who spoke to Annie at Leaves of Comfort?'

'I'd say so,' Tony said. He studied the body language of the threesome. Hugh had his back to them. 'The sisters should be in shortly and we'll know the answer to that then, as soon as they see each other. From the look of things, Hugh doesn't like either of those two. Or if he does, there's some other reason he wishes they'd evaporate. He still doesn't know the sisters have seen them before, does he?'

'No,' Alex said sharply. She braced her weight against the counter. 'I'd forgotten he wasn't at your father's house for the meeting. I can't get my mind off what happened with Hugh and Sergeant Miller in Burford this morning.'

'I don't like the way any of this is going,' Tony said. 'Jillian Miller must have had a good reason to follow him like that.'

Alex couldn't take her eyes away from Hugh's table. 'Look how the woman stabs the table with her finger. They want something from him. They're trying to make him agree with some point or points. She's a dramatic one, isn't she? When you can, take a look at her hands. She uses them like laser pointers. It's a shame her fingernails don't light up.' She gave a short laugh.

'Why would they meet here?' Tony asked. He couldn't see it. So public. 'Unless this is the only way Hugh would do it at all.'

'I can't think what would make him decide that.'

'Safer? Easier to keep things under control with them?'

Alex frowned. 'Sounds unpleasant. Do you want a drink?'

He shook his head, no. 'Not yet.'

'Hugh knows how the noise works in here,' Alex said thoughtfully. 'You're overlooked but not easily overheard unless you shout. The other voices make sure of that. Neve keeps looking around. I think she's nervous. Perry's got those puppy dog eyes. Sad and thoughtful but you get the impression his mind is somewhere else. No, he doesn't look at all happy. I don't think it was Hugh's idea for them to meet in here, though.'

'If Annie comes down, the shit . . . Sorry. But it would hit the fan.'

'Unless it was another couple who went to see her at the tea rooms.' Alex stiffened. 'It wasn't another couple. Don't turn around now but Harriet and Mary just came in and almost fell over one another when they saw the Rhyses.'

Tony glanced over his shoulder to see the sisters' progress across the room to their reserved table by the fire. Harriet pulled Mary's tartan shopping cart in which Max, their one-eyed orange tabby cat, traveled, supposedly because he couldn't be left at home with the other cat, Oliver. Lillie Belle was tucked inside her blanket.

The two ladies pinned their attention ahead and settled at their table where Katie and Bogie waited on blankets by the fire. Rather than lean close and talk, both women sat quite still as if they were waiting for something.

'Give me two glasses of Harvey's Bristol Cream, please,' Tony said. 'The occasion may call for more than a thimbleful. Use small wine glasses, not sherry glasses, and I'll take half a pint of shandy.'

'Shandy? Good grief, Tony. When did—'

'Since I don't want to look as if I'm not having anything even though I really don't need anything. This could be a long, or at least a difficult night.' Lemonade and beer, mixed, wasn't his favorite but it was innocuous and passed for light beer. Alex put the drinks on a tray and he pulled it toward him. 'Have you thought what happens if Dan and Bill walk in? They are staying tonight?'

She grimaced. 'Yes. And Hugh knows that. He also knows they've been trying to reach him again. What is he thinking of, just showing up and sitting there like that?'

'I'm starting to wonder if that's the problem – he's not thinking.' He regretted the words as soon as they left his mouth. 'I don't mean it to sound like that. It could be that he's got something on his mind that we don't have a clue about.'

'Right. Like he wants Bill or Dan to find him here with Perry and Neve. Don't ask me why that would be, though – but he didn't have to meet them here.'

Carrying the tray, Tony went to the Burke sisters' table. 'May

I join you?' he asked quietly. 'I think we've got something to talk about.'

Harriet pulled a chair back for him. 'So that is the Rhys couple, I take it?' At Tony's nod she continued, 'Does Hugh know they talked to Annie?' She studiously avoided looking toward the window. 'They obviously don't know Annie's here at the Black Dog, though, or they wouldn't have come. Or, I don't think they would.'

'I don't think Hugh knows the Rhys couple spoke with Annie,' Tony said, knowing he couldn't be certain. 'He would have if he hadn't been absent this morning. Those two could think they said enough to keep her quiet around him. They're bound to run into her and it's likely to be soon. Doc James is having her rest upstairs so I don't suppose we'll see her down here tonight. They've moved her to Alex's room. She talked to Hugh, though, on their own, remember. Who knows what she said then? Could be she mentioned them coming to your place and making accusations about him.'

Mary looked at him through her thick-lensed glasses, her eyes huge and distorted. 'Harriet and I wondered if Annie came to us to ask advice on finding a place to live here. We'll do that if she still wants to once she leaves the Black Dog, but she shouldn't want to be here where she lost her hopes for love with the man she loved. I'm so sad for Annie. Everything she dreamed of is destroyed and she isn't trying to start over. I understand how it is when you love someone so much – I was there once, so long ago it seems like another era – but her life must not stop at twenty-three. I think that's how old she is. She doesn't seem to think about a future at all.'

'Ladies, please think about what I'm going to say to you.' He drank some of the lemonade-laced beer and winced. 'You said she sounded afraid of something to do with Elyan. That's a riddle all by itself. I know you want her to explain this herself but I'm not sure she will. I'm not even sure she would say it to you again. Doc and Lily say she's not very well.'

'I know.' Harriet studied her fingernails. 'Mary and I talked about this during the afternoon. We're hoping you and Alex will help us decide what to do about it. Annie was distraught after those people got through with her and I think she just spilled things out. She wouldn't repeat it and she wasn't making any sense. But something was said that made her desperate and afraid. That's it . . .' She looked at her sister. 'Mary, those people frightened her. Why would they do that? It needs to be brought out into the open – for Annie's sake.'

Tony looked into the fire. His old dog, Katie, came, rested her gray-blond head on his lap and looked into his face. He scratched beneath her chin while he thought.

'I wonder if we should get some official advice,' he said finally. 'Bill Lamb's all right. I know he can be brusque but—'

'Radhika loves him,' Mary broke in. 'You know perfectly well she wouldn't if he weren't a good man.'

There wasn't a soul in Folly – as far as Tony knew – who didn't think his assistant was wonderful, including him. 'You're right. What if we ask Radhika's opinion first?' That was a cop-out and he knew it, but he was only human.

'Indeed,' Harriet said. 'What a wonderful idea and I just know Radhika will talk to Bill about it. She would break the ice and make everything so much easier. But she'd say if she didn't think it was a good idea to go to Bill – until we know more.'

Tony barely contained a laugh. He wasn't the only one capable of looking for an easier way out.

The urge to laugh faded abruptly. Through the passageway from the restaurant and inn came Bill Lamb with Jillian Miller. Tony turned to see Alex but two groups of noisy men dressed to ride had come in and both Alex and Carrie Peale were too busy pulling pints to notice drama elsewhere.

Bill approached Hugh and tapped his shoulder. He paid no attention to Perry or Neve.

'Oh, good gracious,' Harriet said. 'Do you know where Radhika is, Tony?'

'She's sleeping at the clinic during the week at the moment,' he said. 'On weekends she spends time at her new house. It's only partly finished. Anyway, Bill doesn't want her at Trap Lane again until this case is solved. She's probably at the clinic now. Why?'

'I'm going to call her and ask her to come over,' Harriet said. 'I'll do it from the kitchens. I'll explain why to her. I think

Hugh's in a muddle. He needs time to sort himself out. We need an intervention.'

'I think it's a bit late for that,' Tony said.

Bill Lamb closed the door to the interview room. The thin file in his hands was more because he was expected to have one than anything else.

'Would you like coffee or tea?' he asked Hugh Rhys – seated across the table from Jillian Miller. This was not an interview he expected to enjoy. 'It's all pretty bad but it's wet.'

'Nothing, thanks.' Hugh's tone was neutral. He didn't look angry and certainly not scared or confused.

Bill had his own styrofoam cup of black coffee.

Miller appeared nervous enough for all of them. Interviews were not her strong suit yet and might never be but at least she tended to say too little rather than too much.

'If it's OK we'll be recording this interview,' Bill said and nodded to Miller to start the machine. 'Just a formality. For your benefit as much as ours. You understand you're not under arrest?'

'Yes.' Hugh's dark eyes didn't flicker.

'We've asked if you want your solicitor present and you've declined. Have you changed your mind, Mr Rhys?'

'No.'

Sliding into his chair beside Miller, Bill put his cup on the table and opened the folder with its few forms inside. These he read through, more slowly than necessary. Miller had provided him with a notepad and he pulled it toward him while she went through the preliminaries for the recording.

He was warm and stood up to remove his jacket. 'It's hot in here. This room is always warm. It's supposed to be air-conditioned but you wouldn't know it. Windows would probably help.'

Hugh made none of the frequent thin and nervous jokes about potentially escaping through a window.

No windows, slightly shiny yellow walls, metal chairs and a yellow Formica-topped table – and this was considered the best of the interview rooms. Bill had not thought about the institutional scent of disinfectant, unfortunate air-freshener and sweat for some time but with Hugh already looking completely out-of-place, Bill smelled it all sharply.

Seated again, he picked up a pen. 'You didn't have anything to say on the way here to Gloucester. Do you know why we brought you?'

'No.'

'I'll get to that right away, then. You were seen leaving the house, Green Friday in Trap Lane, Folly-on-Weir, on the twelfth of this month. Early in the evening.'

For the first time there was a slip in Hugh's perfect composure. He looked away for a moment.

'On the morning of the thirteenth,' Bill continued, 'you called us to the same house.'

It didn't take long to run through the details of the encounter with Hugh, Alex and Sam Brock, the locksmith, or to go over what had been found inside the house.

Throughout, Hugh looked directly at him, his expression solemn but giving nothing away.

'You went into the house before calling us?' Bill asked. He knew the answer but there was more that he doubted he knew at all.

'We all did,' Hugh said. 'It was the natural thing to do. Sam had been there earlier to do some work for me. He came down to the Black Dog and told us there was blood and broken glass on the kitchen floor. More blood in the hall. And clothing strewn around in a bedroom.'

'You looked at all these areas?' Bill asked.

'I looked all over the house.'

Bill glanced at the top sheet in the file. 'And you can confirm that all the things Sam mentioned were there?'

Hugh leaned back in his chair, frowning. 'I don't think I can be sure. I didn't look closely – there was just a pile of things on the bed and I wanted to make sure there wasn't anyone hurt somewhere.'

'Reasonable,' Bill said. 'Sam told us there was a Mercedes parked out back. Did you look at that?'

'No. Vehicles are sometimes parked up beside some outbuildings. Beyond the swimming pool.'

This had never seemed like a man who would play word

games, but Bill decided he'd started playing one now. 'Didn't Sam say he saw the Mercedes from a window in the house?' He ran a finger down one of the computer-generated forms. 'Says so here.'

'I didn't see a car from any window.'

Bill made another note. 'Would it be possible to see vehicles by the outbuildings from the house?'

'I . . .' Hugh frowned and paused. 'Possibly from upstairs although I'm not sure which rooms.'

'What were you doing at Green Friday on the twelfth?'

Moments passed in silence before Hugh said, 'I own the house. I was checking on it.'

A flicker of anger irritated Bill. Would he be irritated if he were getting this runaround from a stranger? 'You parked your car close to the front gates, facing out. Did you want to be sure you could leave in a hurry?'

'Yes. I wanted to get back to work quickly.'

Bill turned a little toward Miller, indicating she should take over for a while. She needed the practice and he wished he were somewhere else.

'Six of one, half a dozen of the other,' Miller said, and her voice cracked. Her cheeks turned pink. 'You had to turn your car to leave, what did it matter when you did that?'

Hugh looked amused. 'How right you are, sergeant. I hate to be late – I get tetchy, so I suppose I was guilty of faulty logic.'

Miller looked pleased with herself. 'Why didn't you mention being there on the twelfth when you called us in on the thirteenth?'

'To say what? There was nothing to tell you.'

Bill pushed to his feet and started to pace. He owed any interview skills he had to Dan O'Reilly who was brilliant. 'How long were you at the house that night?'

'As long as it took.' Hugh ran both hands through his hair. 'OK, let's stop this. Or I should say, I'm going to stop this. Not that I'm guilty of anything illegal.'

Bill sat again.

'Would you like something to drink now,' Miller said, and Bill had the urge to stand on the pointed toe of one of her high-heeled shoes. Had she forgotten that the last thing to do at a moment like this was stop the flow?

'Coffee, please,' Hugh said. He looked increasingly worn. 'Cream, no sugar. Thank you.'

Miller popped up and sashayed to the door. Looking back, she said, 'You, guv? You must be hungry. Shall I check the cafeteria for a sandwich?'

'Just water, thanks.' What a difference it would make to have someone like LeJuan with him, but it was up to him to help Miller grow into her new position.

Once she was gone, he scooted close to the table and propped his elbows. 'Why not tell me anything you think would help, Hugh?' No harm in loosening up a bit. It might even help.

'Do you remember Sonia Quillam?' Hugh said. 'Percy's wife and Elyan's mother. She called me from Green Friday that day – the twelfth – asked me to go and see her. She and her family had stayed there that time when there was so much trouble.'

'I remember. It would be hard to forget. Tragedy on top of tragedy, that was.'

'Yes. It still is. I see Elyan. His father did too. I can't imagine what he will make of this death. Sonia never went to see him – she told me she couldn't face it. Annie Bell was engaged to Elyan and I think she still is – hopeless as that is, but she sees Elyan whenever it's allowed. It all got so twisted. Did you ever hear Elyan play?'

Evidently Hugh didn't recall asking the same question before. 'No, but Dan did. He said Elyan played some jazz. Seems unreal now.' Enough of that.

Hugh only nodded and frowned. 'The Quillams had stayed at Green Friday for some weeks before everything went sideways. You know all about that. Anyway, Sonia must have kept a key and she went there sometime before the twelfth without letting me know or asking if it was OK. I wasn't happy. I went to see her as she asked. It wasn't pleasant. I left telling her to be out of there by morning. And that was that. She didn't contact me again, thank God.'

'Do you remember what she was wearing.'

'Yes.' The man's mouth twisted down at the corners. 'A flowery kaftan, flowing thing made of some sort of thin stuff.

Backless high-heeled sandals. She always wore those. She'd been drinking, I think.'

'Always wore backless sandals? You sound as if you're well acquainted with her.'

'I was at one time. Not now – not for a long time. She liked those sandals.' At that moment he appeared distant.

'Sounds as if you may have been close.'

'We were, as I've already said, but that's history. I wasn't in the best place at the time and I was young. She was even younger. She met and married Quillam. She was becoming a noted soprano and he took her under his wing.'

The temptation to mention that it sounded as if Percy had taken her under more than his wing was strong – and inappropriate. 'So that was it? You never rekindled the relationship?'

'She married Quillam. End of story. And now it's history, but I've already said that twice.'

'How was she when you left that night?'

'Angry.'

'Why?' He wanted this over, if only for tonight. At least they had a probable identity for their missing person.

'She had some idea of getting back together. I wasn't interested – never have been since we broke up. That's all I can tell you. I could hate her, but I don't. She deserves more pity than hate. But she did a lot of damage to the people around her.'

Miller knocked and came in with coffee and water. Hugh drank his coffee, grimacing.

'I warned you it was bad,' Bill said. 'Sonia Quillam doesn't appear to have been seen since you left her.'

'I don't know anything about that.' Hugh let his head hang back and sighed. 'I don't want any harm to come to Sonia, but she knows whatever we had was over a very long time ago. She also knows that I'm aware she uses men when she needs something from them and always has.'

'It doesn't look good that you avoided mentioning your encounter with Sonia Quillam. You see that?'

'I do. But when I left her, she was alive and well. Angry, tipsy but fine. I just had to get away. I'd been through the act before and it never ended well. Easier to get out of there. And before you ask again in some different way, I didn't want to discuss that night because this is just what I was afraid of – that someone would blow the event out of proportion and start accusing me of something. I don't know where Sonia is but if I had to guess I'd say she's found herself a safe place to be with someone who will be only too glad to have her. She's a beautiful woman and there is no shortage of men happy to settle for that – even if it's only skin deep.'

Bill considered what he was about to say and decided, *what the hell*. 'You hate her, don't you?'

'I hate what she's done to some people. Do I hate her? No, that's a very big word and I save it for more capably hateful people. Sonia is not a great intellect.'

'Why did you go to Burford this morning, Mr Rhys?' Miller snapped out baldly and in opposition to the way she and Bill had agreed to handle the matter. Bill was angry she hadn't let him know her intentions beforehand. She continued, 'I'm sure you remember entering a house there on Hollows Lane. Middle house of a terrace of three. Your behavior, getting there in a hurry, and appearing to be surreptitious about entering the building, was suspicious. I doubt you'd deny you hoped you wouldn't be seen. Why don't you explain what that was all about?'

While Hugh frowned, Bill seethed. He tried to catch Miller's eye, but she avoided looking at him.

'Could you be more specific?' Hugh asked. He pushed his cold coffee away.

'I don't have to be,' Miller said. 'I ask the questions.'

'Right,' Hugh said, sitting even straighter. 'And I asked for clarification. I was there, yes. I'm free to go where I like, when I like and since no charges have been made against me, I surely have the right to understand any of your questions. Do you know where you're going with this?'

The bright flush on Miller's cheeks further annoyed Bill. He stepped in while she was still formulating a response. 'You were there. Thank you for that.'

'And you left in a hurry as if someone warned you to get out.' Miller blustered now. 'Was that because you were doing something you shouldn't be doing?'

A head was going to roll. This would get them nowhere.

Finally, Miller glanced at him with a triumphant little smile as if she were pulling off a brilliant coup. He shook his head faintly.

'We'll get back to this,' he said. 'Your friends held a gathering at Dr James Harrison's home today. Weren't you invited to that?'

'Is there anything you don't know?' Hugh said. 'There was a meeting, yes. I was not there, yes.' He relaxed his posture and Bill decided the man thought they were on a fishing expedition – which they were. That could always be a good idea if it was handled properly.

A tap on the door preceded the welcome appearance of Detective Constable Longlegs Liberty – who was aptly nicknamed – someone else Bill had, at least in part, inherited from Dan O'Reilly. This was a capable, useful officer. Longlegs inclined his head and Bill excused himself.

'Won't take a minute, guv, but I thought you'd want to see this.' With a gloved hand he opened a brown bag and took an evidence bag from inside. 'These were found in a charcoal grill near Green Friday. There's a little park there with barbeques. Someone was in too much of a hurry trying to get rid of these.'

He pulled out two scraps of orange silk with curled and singed edges. 'This matches the bits found in the woods beside the driveway at Green Friday. Looks like a buttonhole here.' He reached in again. 'We haven't identified the rest at all yet.'

A strip of mostly melted black cloth, and another orange fragment. 'Good work,' Bill said. 'I hope we'll get some identification on these very shortly.'

THIRTEEN

The rain started around midnight. Not the kind that pattered softly on the windows and lulled you to sleep, but a battering downpour on the slate roof tiles of Tony's house, punctuated by thunder and lightning of the variety that ripped the skies apart, sending flaring darts through the slatted shades and across the bedroom.

The latest salvo startled Alex and she rolled toward Tony. She liked storms but this one seemed to vibrate through her. She had been awake for ages, staring at the illuminated face of her bedside clock.

There was too much to think about and she had that wideawake sensation that meant sleep wouldn't return easily.

Hugh had come back from Gloucester not long before closing and started working immediately. He said little. Once the last customers had left, he suggested Alex call it a day – his smile didn't warm her one bit but Tony said the idea sounded good to him. It had been a long day, he said.

Alex rested a hand between Tony's shoulder blades. He hadn't been relaxed since he'd left the Burke sisters' table to come behind the bar and tell her Hugh had left with Bill and Miller. He had looked at her frequently which unnerved her. She had come close to asking him why he was watching her, but for once managed to keep quiet.

He wasn't asleep either.

The muscles in his back were taut and he was all but holding his breath. Breathing shallowly, anyway. She swallowed hard. For the first time in a while the back of her neck prickled. He was upset about something but not telling her about it. Tony was usually open with his feelings.

Probably worried about Hugh the way she was. That was natural.

Lightning cracked again. For an instant she saw the shadow of an old beech tree waver against the window shades. Thunder came close behind, rumbling across the sky.

He knew she wasn't sleeping.

'Are you OK, Tony?' She rubbed his back again.

No answer. Pretending sleep was an even stranger piece of behavior from Dr Harrison.

'OK, that's it.' She propped herself up on one elbow and pulled at his shoulder until he rolled onto his back. 'What's going on with you? We're both worried about Hugh – among other things. Do you know something I don't know?'

He pulled her face onto his chest. 'Go to sleep. We're likely to have another unpleasant day tomorrow. You need your rest.'

Sleep wasn't likely to come as long as his warm skin was

against hers. 'That's not an answer. Hugh didn't talk about what happened in Gloucester. Not to me. Did he tell you anything?'

'No, sweetheart. I'd have told you if he had. We'll have to let him decide if he wants to tell us anything but that's going to depend on . . . damn it. It's impossible to completely shut out any thought that in some way he may have been involved in what's happened. I just can't make myself see him as a killer.'

'Don't,' she said, holding on to him. 'It's unbearable. Neve and Perry Rhys looked shocked, didn't they? Or at least Neve did. After Hugh left with Bill. Perry just looked bemused. They just stayed there, staring at each other. I think they were waiting for him. I don't know what time they went upstairs but Hugh didn't say a word to either of them when he got back.'

'I noticed. But I don't think I can warm up to that twosome no matter how decent they turn out to be. In fact Neve disturbs me and Perry seems as close to unresponsive as a living man gets.'

Alex laughed, she couldn't help it. 'That's horrible, but it's funny. His face hardly moves.'

Tony reached out and turned on the bedside lamp.

Alex hid her eyes against his shoulder. 'Turn it off,' she begged.

'Nope. I want to see you. Since you initiated this chat, I'm going to participate. Did you know the Derwinters are expecting a baby?'

She raised her face. 'Gosh, no. Heather pregnant? Now that's an odd thought. She'll probably deliver on horseback.' Heather was rarely out of riding clothes.

'You haven't seen her since she's been pregnant?'

'No. Don't you think I'd have mentioned it?' This wasn't a conversation she wanted to have, not now and possibly not ever. 'I'm glad for them. It's unexpected but I bet they'll be adoring parents.'

Tony slid away from her and sat on the edge of the bed, hunched, his head in his hands. 'Heather saw you in Cheltenham a couple of weeks ago.'

'I didn't see her, Tony. Does this matter? How do you know she saw me, anyway. Did she make a point of telling you? If she did, it's strange, isn't it?'

'Depends.'

Alex felt vaguely sick. The room was stuffy, and her face was hot. 'What's the matter with you? You're scaring me. Not scaring, worrying. Tell me, please.'

'Are you pregnant?'

The thump in her chest had to be her heart trying to jump out. If she were able to think of a response, it wouldn't be possible to speak. Her throat had zipped shut.

'Heather stopped by Leaves of Comfort,' Tony said. 'Evidently she's got a sudden urge to knit and wanted some help from the sisters.'

'OK. Heather knitting is something else I can't imagine but it would be a reasonable thing to do.'

'Are you?' Tony repeated. 'And if you are, why haven't you told me?' He looked back at her and she couldn't tell if he was angry or close to some sort of panic.

'Alex?' His voice rose and she jumped.

'This is cruel,' she told him. 'Are you getting around to telling me Heather saw me and thought I was pregnant? That's ridiculous. And hurtful, frankly, that you'd believe for one minute I wouldn't tell you. I'll have to talk to her and find out what her motive was.'

'Don't do that. She's probably a bit highly strung at the moment.'

She looked at him, disbelieving what she'd just heard. 'Right, Tony. Hysterical on occasion, too, don't you think? I don't believe this.'

'She said she saw you at the clinic where she goes for her check-ups and just assumed.' He turned and put an arm around her. 'Sorry, old thing, dopey of me to take any notice but the sisters were agog, thrilled at the possibility. They're the ones Heather shared her little story with.'

So that was it. 'Unfortunately, Heather isn't very observant apparently. There's also a fertility clinic in the same facility. I decided to get checked out. I wanted to be sure the trauma of losing a baby the way I did hadn't done more damage than they told me at the time. That seemed a fair thing to do for both of us. I would just rather not have told you about it, or not yet.'

An urge to get up and go to her own house came and left rapidly. She wasn't a child and it wasn't Tony's fault if people in the village gossiped, although Heather Derwinter should know better. And her own house had been closed up for a couple of months which wouldn't make it particularly welcoming.

Alex rolled away, pulled up the covers and closed her eyes.

'You're doing this clinic thing because you want us to have a child?' Tony said. He sounded strange, but she wasn't giving him an easy break. He needed to learn to think before he waded in. 'Alex. Oh, hell, what a fool I can be.'

'Can't we all?' That wasn't giving in, it was being grown up. 'And yes, that's why I'm going. No big deal.' To her it was an enormous deal but she wasn't about to say so.

'Um, could we . . .?'

Scratching at the door preceded it opening enough to let Bogie in. He came uncertainly to the bed and stood with one paw held questioningly in the air. If dogs cried, his tears would be dripping.

'Hi boy,' Alex said. How did dogs know when you needed comfort? 'Good boy.'

His tail wagged. He leapt onto the bed and lay beside Alex.

'Little opportunist,' Tony muttered. 'Well, I'm not stopping now. I know better than to overdo things, but would you come with me to buy a ring? We could call it a promise of a promise ring, if you like. Or a hope ring. Or a ring of potential. Just let me put the bloody thing on your finger before I go mad.'

She hid her face in her pillow. This was one of those times when she was going to cry soon.

'Alex?' He shook her. 'Don't you go to sleep on me.'

'All right, we'll get a ring.' She turned on her back. 'Just don't talk about anything else yet. People will start muttering, but we aren't kids and we'll do what we want to do, when we want to do it.'

'You've got it, sweetheart.' Tony assisted Bogie from the bed and planted an elbow either side of Alex's head. 'In the morning it's back to horrible reality. Things are going to get nastier and we both know it. But for now we'll do what we want to do, when and how we want to do it.'

* * *

Knocking on the front door, distant but insistent, woke Tony. He still held Alex and across her shoulders he saw the clock read almost six in the morning.

More knocking. Louder this time.

He carefully pulled his arm free, but Alex sat up and stared at him, wide-eyed. 'What is it?' she whispered hoarsely.

Tony flung from the bed, pulled on tracksuit bottoms and ran for the stairs. The visitor was giving the door an even less polite hammering.

'Hold your horses,' Tony said and he threw open the door – and immediately thought that he should at least have asked who was there. 'Radhika? What are you doing here? Get inside, now.'

'Good morning, Tony.' Radhika's turquoise and gold sari was all the more brilliant in the gray and damp early morning. She smiled, intriguing to look at as always, but he could see concern in her dark eyes, feel it in the stiff way she stood.

'Come in,' he insisted, taking her elbow this time. He avoided the temptation to mention that he wouldn't have expected so fierce a banging on the door from her. She wore a fringed silk shawl over her sari but couldn't be warm, and she carried a plastic shopping bag decorated with mallard ducks. 'Now we get fog on top of the rain. Drizzle really, I suppose. Into the kitchen and I'll make some coffee.' He was aware of being shirtless. 'I'm sure you haven't eaten, either.'

'Radhika!' Alex came downstairs, barefoot, wearing jeans and a red T-shirt and carrying a sweatshirt for him. She tossed it to him and didn't appear remotely self-conscious that Radhika had come. He tended to feel his assistant was very reserved, old-fashioned, even.

'Oh, good,' she said. 'I hoped I would find you both here. I must talk to you.'

So much for old-fashioned.

'It's chilly in here,' Alex said, darting ahead and turning on the oven. She opened the door. 'Sit here. The temperature really dropped in the night. I've turned up the heat in the house but it'll take a few minutes. This will help.' She placed a chair not far from the oven and shepherded Radhika to sit there.

Tony busied himself with coffee, knowing that Radhika enjoyed a cup of very strong coffee in the morning – frequently more than one cup.

Radhika sat quite still and kept silent until they each had a cup and sat together in the warmth of the oven. She smiled then and said, 'Almost like home when my mother and father and I sat like this in the morning. People do not think of India being cold, but in some parts there are extremes.' She flexed a thin hand, curved the fingers back from the palm and stared at the perfectly oval nails. 'I prefer it here now.'

She was stalling. The thought surprised Tony since Radhika was a straightforward woman. The duck bag leaned against her legs and she touched it from time to time.

They drank their coffee in silence.

Radhika cleared her throat and looked up at them from beneath long lashes. 'I do not know how to start. Forgive me, please.'

'Of course.' Alex gave him a helpless glance.

'It was by chance that I saw Kyle Gammage this morning. I like to look at the stream in front of the clinic and I couldn't sleep so I had pulled the curtain aside to see out. He had put his bicycle down against the bank and was walking back and forth. He looked so worried.'

Immediately, Tony shifted in his chair. That must have been some time ago and Kyle should still have been in his bed at Tony's father's house.

'He wanted to talk to me but was nervous I would be cross. I think, if I had not seen and called to him, he would have left again. He had thought of going to Underhill, to that cottage where the Gammages lived, to hide these things he worried about.'

Alex scooted her chair close to Radhika. 'Please tell us what's happened. We'll work it out together. Where is Kyle?'

'He is at the clinic until it's time to go to school. Doc James is out on a call and Scoot will be on his way to the Black Dog to work there. Kyle is fine. I have food at the clinic.' She looked at Tony. 'You are so kind to let me stay there until my house is finished.'

'Kind?' he said explosively, throwing up his hands. 'Taking

advantage, you mean. I get round the clock coverage for our patients and you know I don't like any of them alone in the night. I usually feel I must go and check on them.'

Alex laughed. 'He does. But you know that.'

'I shall still visit them at night when I move to Trap Lane,' Radhika said, seriously. She looked away and Tony heard her swallow.

'Please, Radhika,' Alex said. 'What did Kyle want?'

She let out a long breath and pushed back her sari scarf. 'On the morning when Alex and the locksmith went to Green Friday with Hugh, there were two photographs in the bedroom at that house.'

Tony frowned at Alex who flushed. 'Yes,' she said very quietly.

'You left them at the Black Dog in a plastic bag, Alex,' Radhika said. 'So Kyle told me.'

'That's true.

'Scoot was worried in case you should not have taken them from Green Friday.'

Tony closed his eyes and waited.

'I shouldn't have been so careless with them. I forgot all about it. Then I couldn't find them when I got back so I thought the bag must have been thrown in the rubbish. I couldn't find it.'

'But you didn't tell Bill you'd taken them?' Tony said. Pain niggled behind his eyes. 'You still haven't mentioned it to him?'

'So much has been going on ever since. And actually, I didn't take them. It was Sam who brought them from Green Friday to show Hugh. I didn't think about them again.' She stood up abruptly. 'Well, not much. And then I did forget until now. What difference does it make? They were just an old picture of Hugh on a clifftop or something, and a grainy photo of someone we didn't know.'

'They were with the possessions of the person they haven't found,' Radhika murmured. 'On the bed in the bedroom. Scoot told Kyle he heard they had been there.'

'Good grief, Alex – you took them?' What would make her do a thing like that?

'No. I already explained how I had them. But I didn't make sure the police got them and I know that was a mistake. Or I do now. When I got around to thinking about it I was afraid the police could make something of it and tie the missing woman to Hugh. She still hasn't been found.'

'Who is this woman?' Tony asked. 'Has everyone but me known there was a missing woman. First Percy Quillam's found dead, now a woman is missing? We can't keep things from the police at a time like this. Or any time, come to that. They'll have to know about these photos now.'

Radhika took two photos from her duck bag, the one of Hugh on top. 'There is writing on the back of this one.' She turned it over. 'It says, "My Hugh". Such a handsome man. He was younger, I think. Doesn't it seem strange that the photographs should be left by the person who took other things?'

'How do you know that?' Tony asked.

'Scoot said that Sam the locksmith talked about it. He should not be repeating these things, of course. The media will report them and any advantage will be lost. Isn't that so, Alex?'

'It could be. Sometimes little things mentioned help bring in information – especially about a missing person.'

'Bill's still staying at the Black Dog?' Tony asked Alex who nodded, yes. 'I doubt if he's left for the day yet. I think we should ask him to talk with us. If he doesn't think it's important, fine. But he should know. Don't you think so, Radhika.'

'Yes, of course,' she said softly.

'Why wouldn't you want to tell him?' Alex asked. 'I'm the one he's likely to be angry with, not you.'

'Bill is not an angry man. But I have been foolish. I saw her.'

Tony frowned at Alex who shrugged. 'Who did you see?'

'I should have told Bill at once but I know how much Hugh means to you and I didn't say anything in case it . . . I should just have spoken up. What do I know about anything anyway?'

'Radhika . . .?'

'After you left my house, I saw the woman who was staying at Green Friday.'

FOURTEEN

'You want us out of your hair, don't you?' Neve said. She paused to look back at Hugh. 'Wouldn't that make your life simpler?' Perry walked beside her toward the pond in the middle of Folly's village green. They had left the Black Dog as soon as Lily got in. The morning was cool and still damp from last night's storm.

Hugh slowed down and let them draw ahead. He didn't want to be with them, ever. Most of all he didn't want to be anywhere near his cousin's wife. Perry hadn't been such a bad stick until she got her claws into him.

'Come on,' Neve called, wearing the enigmatic smile he'd come to detest. 'The walk was your idea, Hugh. Let's get this done, shall we? You can't avoid the inevitable, although you always were one to run away from anything you didn't want to deal with.'

As usual, she tried to goad him into losing his temper. Given that on the one occasion when she had been successful in riling him his reaction had been anything but what she wanted, she must have some motive he couldn't guess. He laughed aloud and they both turned around to stare at him. Hugh spread his hands in supplication and walked on. No, he had not become a man for whom anger triggered surrender . . . unlike Perry.

'When are you going to tell us what the police wanted you for yesterday – when they interrupted us for the second time in a day?' Spiteful replaced enigmatic in Neve's half-smile. She tipped her face up and looked at him through glittering narrowed eyes. 'I bet you'd have been happy to get away from our discussion in Burford if it had been anyone other than the police tailing you. Are they on to you, Hugh? Or perhaps I should ask what you've done this time. Run out of clever ways to cover up for yourself, have you?'

She sounded disturbed, bizarre, but this wasn't the first time he had thought Neve's jealousy of and hatred for him came from a kind of craziness. Unlike with Perry, she had never been able to pester Hugh into giving her what she wanted.

'I no longer discuss my private life with you, Neve. You're a stranger to me, thank God.'

Perry took two steps toward him. 'We don't do this anymore, kiddies,' he said, and his face was a cold mask. 'The fighting's over, remember? We agreed a long time ago that there's only the business between the three of us. That's the only reason I'm here. I didn't want to come – I'm needed at the distillery.'

'Perry,' Hugh said, and it cost him too much to keep his voice level. 'You can still speak after all. Good. You never used to be so quiet, cousin. In fact you were the noisy one.'

'Right,' Perry said, smiling slightly, his shoulders dropping a fraction as if he felt the tension passing. 'If I remember rightly, that housekeeper of your mother's used to look at you and say, "Still waters run deep". I got, "Empty vessels make the most noise".'

'Violet had a saying for just about every occasion,' Hugh said. As he drew level, he looked sideways at Perry. 'She was good to both of us. We had a lucky life growing up.'

'Yes, we did.'

'I think I'm going to get sick,' Neve said. 'You sound soft, Perry, but then, you were the gentle one, too, weren't you? And even though I didn't live in the big house, I saw enough of it. Enough I knew the atmosphere in that place might give me a nose bleed.'

'I remember Violet finding you a woolen cap with strings and crocheted flowers over the ears when you came without a hat,' Perry said to her, still smiling. 'It was the color of Colman's Mustard. She tied it on and you were as pleased as punch. You must have been about five.'

She glared at her husband. 'Are we done with memory lane? I probably didn't have a hat because I didn't have a mother or anyone else to take care of me. Now, Hugh, all we want from you is a fair hearing. You're not a completely stupid man when it comes to business. Agree to the sale and you need never see us again . . . well, perhaps for document signing, but—'

'You wouldn't be needed for anything to do with the business, Neve,' Hugh remarked. 'Sometimes I think you forget your place.'

'Over there,' Perry said, quickening his strides. 'One of the benches under the trees. I'm tired and we need a little privacy – and less sniping.'

Neve's face had turned a rare shade of red. She didn't usually blush. She was angry, and Hugh waited for her next salvo.

'How's your dad?' he asked her. 'Walter's a good man. He did his best for you.' He didn't add that he did if he wasn't drunk.

'I don't know how you have the nerve to ask,' Neve said. 'You made sure he got pushed out of his job even though he was the best master distiller you were ever likely to have.'

He didn't argue. Neve had been born late in her parents' lives and her father doted on her, even more so after her mother died, but he never got the hang of staying sober. David Rhys, Hugh's father, had kept Walter Beath on, but when Hugh had needed, at least for a couple of years after his father's death, to take over the distillery and learn the business – hands-on – the man's behavior became insufferable. He had made the hard and unwelcome job Hugh had been forced to do appalling. Hugh had let Walter go.

'Walter agreed it was time to retire,' Perry said mildly, as if he'd forgotten Hugh had given the man no choice but to 'retire'.

'We're not here to discuss that,' Neve said. She reached the bench and sat close to one end.

Perry sat next to her leaving plenty of room for Hugh. Hugh remained standing.

'This conversation could be a better idea than I'd thought,' he said. 'Let's deal with the issue logically, sensibly. Selling Birnam Bricht to the South African consortium will accomplish what, and for whom?'

'We are in the drivers' seat – at the moment,' Neve said quickly. 'There will never be a better time to sell. We stand to make the kind of return we could only have dreamed of in your father's day and if we don't strike now, the opportunity will never come around again.'

Damn, you are not only a selfish, money-grubbing bitch, you are insulting. You have the gall to assume I'm the malleable dreamer you once knew. 'Crap,' he said with feeling. 'That's crap and you know it.'

'Steady on,' Perry said, his Scots accent growing thicker. He paused, blinking, before adding, 'There's no call to speak to Neve that way and I'll not have it.'

Neve crossed her arms and looked into the distance.

'Really?' Hugh said. 'There will never be a better time to sell? How do either of you know that? How does anyone know that? What's the hurry, Neve? Are you and Perry having money problems – again – and you need a big infusion of cash?'

'Sonovabitch!' Neve shot to her feet. 'We keep the company running while you flit about down here with the Sassenachs, sucking up and making another fortune out of buying up what they're too thick to hold on to. And then you accuse us of . . . You know damn well we've put body and soul into Birnam Bricht. You owe us. Now it's time to pay up and let us follow some of our dreams. It's not always just about you.'

He considered for long enough to make them restless. The night and early morning of wild rain was finally giving way to a soft day. A pale sun didn't bring a lot of heat, but it flaked the pond with silver and the diving and flapping ducks were having a great time. Three willow trees behind them dipped and swished in a careless breeze. Hugh closed his eyes and wished he were alone, or more honestly, he wished Perry and Neve were anywhere but sitting on a bench in front of him.

'Perry's been running things without you, Hugh,' Neve said. 'He hasn't needed you and he hasn't complained about shouldering the responsibility. But it's coming to an end and soon. Look, there's an easy way out. Come to an agreement with us about your share and we'll make the decisions without you. That, or for God's sake, stop dilly-dallying around and let's sell while the selling's good.'

'Have the horses been kind to you these last couple of years, Perry?' Hugh said. He didn't like himself for dropping the question like that and wouldn't have done it if Neve weren't doing what she always did, trying to make sure that whatever happened she came out smelling like a rose and to hell with anyone else.

Perry gave Hugh a confused look.

'He doesn't have time for the races,' Neve said. Her eyes turned hard and if he'd had any doubt she hated him, it would have dissipated then. 'You dig at him, but he's saved your rear end. He's picked up the pieces you didn't want to deal with. Why would you not want to sell? Tell me that. You'll make plenty.'

'And your interests are entirely altruistic? My, you're a changed woman.'

'We'd not see what you would out of the sale,' she snapped. 'And even if we do make a goodly sum – we'll have earned it. You don't even know a thing about the day-to-day running of the business.'

He laughed, dropped his head back and laughed louder.

'Shut up, you idiot,' she said. 'You could always be such a fool. And this time you can't laugh your way out of what we want now because you don't have the upper hand anymore.'

He'd been about to enlighten them about what he knew of the business. They obviously had never considered that he took a deep interest and examined every communication from the company solicitors and accountants. He had bided his time deciding when and how he was going to step in and remove acting control from Perry. It would have to happen while making sure that his mother, living in Paris with her sister, wasn't senselessly shocked. And the faithful employees of the distillery out of jobs with a closed distillery behind them all because Perry and Neve steadily drained assets from the business. Things were far from going under yet and he intended to make sure they didn't even get close, but the process was going to be tricky.

'Look,' Perry said. He stretched his arms along the back of the bench and Hugh realized how thin he'd become. 'Look, I will never forget how your father and mother took me in after my parents were killed. How could I? But I know Uncle David wanted to provide for me because he told me and the way he left his holdings proved it. I may not have your flair, Hugh, but a solid and knowledgeable plodder can do very well. That's what I am and I want the best for Birnam Bricht.'

Hugh believed him, but he also knew Neve, as Perry's heir,

would come into his share should anything happen to him. In moments when his fears got away from him, Hugh wondered how hard Neve would find it to bleed Perry's holdings dry. If Perry's share became unencumbered, what would Neve be capable of to get her hands on it and leave him. After all, it wouldn't be the first time she'd left a man when she thought there could be a bigger prize on the horizon.

He smiled at Perry. 'I know you want the best for the distillery,' he said. 'That's the main reason I'm not comfortable with this proposed acquisition. I think it's attractive on its face because the money looks huge. I don't think it's a fair offer – or I won't until we've given them more time to show us how much they really want us.'

'No!' Neve said. 'No, Hugh. You aren't in the business in a real sense. You don't see what goes on. It's going to get harder to keep up with competition and before we know it, someone else in the running will get this offer and take it. Waiting is too risky.'

Ignoring Neve, Hugh said, 'Perry, I'm not ready.' He stuffed his hands in his pockets to conceal curled fingers. Neve's desperation told him he was right to stand firm. 'But I'd like you and I to discuss it all further. And I am fully aware of the day-to-day running of the company. I'm aware of everything and it's probably time for me to take a more active role. No, I'm not moving back to Scotland or usurping your position there, but I hold a considerable majority and I will exercise that. I'll also exercise my mother's portion.

'Please hang in with me. I'm very invested and nothing's changed. I've got to get back to the pub before the mid-morning rush. Can we talk later?'

'Yes, of course,' Perry said, and Hugh thought the man was relieved.

'I didn't want to do this,' Neve said, standing up and moving in closer to Hugh. 'Your business is your business but when it looks like getting in the way of what we need to do, it's mine, too. I've been trying to reach Sonia Quillam. She's not answering her mobile. She's not back in London or Paris. And without drawing attention to you I can't make an all-out effort to find her.

'The police aren't saying a lot but we know Percy Quillam was found dead somewhere off Trap Lane above Green Friday. It's not news to you that Sonia and I keep in touch. After all, we have something in common.'

'Why do you keep in touch?' he asked, standing his ground but with a tightening of his scalp. 'Sonia can't mean anything to you.'

'As I said, we have something in common. We were catching up while she was in Paris with Percy and she told me she was coming here to see you. That's how I found out where to find you, and what you've been doing here. She's been staying at Green Friday but now she's gone. You had to know she was there. She told me that when you were together in London, short time though it was, you had sex like rabbits. She laughed a lot about that – said you like it rough.'

She wanted him to ask again what she had in common with Sonia and she wanted him – desperately – to get angry. He didn't do either.

'I wasn't going to press this, but who is your accomplice, the person who tipped you off about the police being after you in Burford yesterday?' This was Neve at her triumphant worst. 'Where is Sonia, Hugh?'

FIFTEEN

Alex didn't look any more comfortable than Bill Lamb felt. She hovered in the doorway from a comfortable sitting room into a kitchen where he could see brass pots and pans hanging from a ceiling rack. He had not been in Tony Harrison's house for a long time and then only briefly. It was the kind of warm, well-furnished home he'd like himself.

Lush gardens came up to the windows on the far side of the kitchen and while Bill looked, Tony Harrison, with Radhika in front of him, came from outside through a sliding glass door. They walked directly into the sitting room and whatever uncertain thing Bill had been feeling about seeing her in this setting ebbed at the sight of Radhika's smile.

'Hello, Bill,' she said. 'Tony and Alex have a beautiful garden.'

Automatically, he held an arm out to her and she walked into his hug. Over her head he couldn't miss the smile that passed between Alex and Tony. The time for pretending he and Radhika weren't seriously involved was completely over. He kissed her forehead.

'The new house will need a lot of work in the gardens,' she said. 'But there will be plenty of time for that.'

'Yes,' was all he could think of to say. They had many decisions to make and gardening was way down the list of concerns, at least for him.

Radhika moved away from him and sat on a striped brocade couch. She grew quite still and looked at the floor.

'Bill got here as quickly as he could,' Alex said in a rush. 'I think a lot is starting to break in his case, so he's been very busy.'

Radhika nodded and gave him another smile. 'He works so hard.'

'It took a while for your message to catch up with me,' he said. 'The officer who took your call said you want to tell me something, but you wouldn't say what it was about.'

'It could be nothing,' she said. He was struck afresh by what a fragile figure she made even though he knew she detested giving that impression.

'We should leave you to it,' Tony said.

'No!' Radhika's sari scarf slipped from her head and her eyes became huge. She blinked rapidly. 'I think we are all . . . I would feel better if we sat as friends. Of course, if I must go to the police station to tell it, I understand.' She started to get up.

'Sit down, please, Radhika,' he told her, suppressing a grin. Always proper and willing to do what was right, she could still amuse him with her very serious demeanor. 'Let's do what you suggest. I'm beat anyway. It can't be that serious.'

'I'll make tea,' Alex said. She all but jogged into the kitchen.

Bill took off his jacket and settled into a chair with his feet outstretched. Tony joined Radhika on the couch.

'I'm probably not supposed to ask,' Tony said, 'but there hasn't been much reported on Percy Quillam. There must have been a post-mortem by now.'

'Under the circumstances, yes. It doesn't always happen so quickly unless there's a question of foul play.'

'Murder?' Radhika said. 'For certain? I did hear suicide mentioned. Such a sad, difficult thing to deal with for his family.'

Bill didn't remind her that Percy's only daughter was dead, his only son in a psychiatric prison facility and his wife yet to be located. 'The pathologist's findings haven't been made public yet,' he said.

'Mm.' Tony hiked an ankle onto the opposite knee and looked thoughtful.

'What does that mean?' Alex asked, coming in with a tray of mugs. 'Mm usually means something.'

'Just having my own thoughts,' Tony said and again Bill saw a look pass between the two.

They would know soon enough. He was surprised the word wasn't out already. 'Percy Quillam was murdered. It'll be all over the press at any moment.'

Alex finished passing out tea, set the tray aside without picking up her own mug and stood with her arms folded. 'How long had he been dead when I found him?' she asked, and he could see what was on her mind.

'He'd been there long enough for the killer to be well away.' He had yet to read the final post-mortem report or speak in greater depth with Molly Lewis – the essential details had been given to him on the phone. 'But we will know much more later.' He concentrated on Radhika, wishing they were speaking alone and not understanding why she wanted Tony and Alex with her.

'You must have contacted people about Percy Quillam,' Alex said. 'Do you know where Sonia is yet? There's talk around the village that she's now considered a missing person.'

Bill considered how much he could say. 'We haven't found Sonia. Percy's agent – I think you'll remember Wells Giglio – he's coming in from Paris. He was expecting Percy to return there.'

'So, he knew Percy had come back to the UK,' Alex said.

'We heard that he was ill in Paris but that must have been made up for convenience.'

'Perhaps he knew Sonia was here,' Radhika said, glancing at Bill, as if asking for approval, he decided. 'He could have come to see her.'

'Well, possibly.' She was repeating remarks already made between his team members. Giglio was flying into Gatwick tomorrow. He said he intended to find accommodations near Green Friday, 'In case Sonia returns,' he'd said. On the phone, the man sounded as if he were crying.

'Perhaps we should open our other house,' Alex said. 'Lime Tree Lodge. We haven't started getting it ready to put on the market yet and it looks as if we may need additional comfortable places to put people. They can't all stay at the Black Dog – even if that was a good idea which it isn't with you there, Bill – and perhaps someone else from the police.'

Like Dan? Too bad you're fond of him but not fond enough to want him as more than a friend. He misses you, Alex. 'Could be a good idea,' he said. And he had not failed to notice Alex referring to her house as 'our other house'. Things were finally moving with these two.

'Will you set up an incident room in the parish hall?' Alex asked. 'Gosh, I can't believe this is happening again.'

'Possibly the parish hall. As to the other.' He shrugged. 'We are a society of our times and they're complex. And let's not forget that this time the players have some definite connections to an old case in the area.' He knew he got too comfortable with these people, perhaps talked too freely.

Without warning, Radhika got to her feet and stood in front of him. The anguish on her face shocked him.

'No,' she said when he went to get up. 'Please, stay there. I'll speak fast and get this to you. I have been very foolish, Bill. There are photographs I have brought to give you, but it is not that. It is the woman. I saw her.' She put a hand over her mouth.

He got up and took her by the arms. 'Calm down, please. Nothing is so bad it should make you suffer, Radhika.'

'It isn't,' Tony broke in. 'Here are the photos.' He came and thrust them into Bill's hands.

'Hugh?' He turned the first one over and saw the words, 'My Hugh' on the back. Damn it, he should have had this when they interviewed the man, but there would be a next time.

The blurred second photo was of a man in front of a multi-colored wall of some kind. It would have to be dealt with by the lab and, he hoped, turned into something useful.

'I'm the one who made a stupid mistake,' Alex said. 'They were found by Sam Brock among that woman's things at Green Friday. He gave them to me and I should have turned them over to you, but I put them down at the Black Dog, couldn't find them afterward and thought they had been thrown away.

'Scoot Gammage had picked them up and been nervous it could spell trouble for Hugh. His brother, Kyle, took them to Radhika this morning. He works at the clinic after school some days and trusts her. He was really scared they'd get into trouble.'

'I told him it would be all right,' Radhika all but whispered.

'OK,' he said, glancing at Alex. Now he had a second apparently guilt-ridden woman on his hands. 'We'll get all this sorted and recorded properly.' And they might have to have a more formal discussion since Alex's explanation was more than sketchy.

'Please let me tell you,' Radhika said, looking up at him. 'As you know, the tower at the Trap Lane house is finished. I like to look out of the window at the top because I can see so far and it makes me happy.

'On the day Alex came to visit me and see the house, she left when it was getting quite dark. There are no lights in the lane and it winds so she didn't stay too long. I watched the headlights of her car when she started driving down.

'I can see Green Friday, the house – where the driveway widens there, and the steps. My tower is closer to Green Friday than you might think. There is a light that comes on over the front door when it gets dark. A woman came there – from inside – and she looked wild. She walked, then she ran a step, and stumbled and kept going. She may have been without shoes. I didn't see her for long at all. Perhaps only seconds. But I should have made sure she was all right, only I judged her. I thought she was drunk and perhaps not behaving well, so I turned away.

'Bill, could she have been the woman who is missing?'

Shit, who knew what another human being would think of or do in any situation? 'I don't know, my love, I don't know. Can you tell me anything about her, anything at all? How big she might have been? How old? What she was wearing?' He decided not to mention the anonymous call by someone claiming to have seen Hugh in the driveway at Green Friday.

Radhika was pale beneath her golden skin. She repeatedly shook her head, no, then said, 'I cannot be sure, Bill. I am so sorry. She was not old. Long, bright hair but I couldn't see her face. She wore something very rich. Like the color of ripe persimmons, I thought.'

SIXTEEN

The back door into the Black Dog kitchens swung shut behind Alex. The first things she heard were a woman's rich, low voice singing 'Trouble Town', and the piano. Something completely unexpected, especially at lunch time.

She almost left, but leaned against the door instead. Elyan Quillam and his sister, Laura, had been on her mind together with an overwhelming sadness at what had befallen that family. The last thing she wanted to hear was a woman singing an evocative, bluesy song to the piano. She had such a clear memory of Annie Bell singing Jazz while Elyan, the brilliant classical pianist, bowed over the keys to play that same piano with so much skill and glee.

She looked down into Bogie's shiny black eyes. He had some grey on his muzzle now. 'You look distinguished, boy,' she told him lightly and bent to scratch him between his twitching ears. He hovered just long enough not to be rude, or so she told herself, then shot off into the bar and his favorite spot by the fireplace.

Alex sighed. *Pull yourself together. Scoot and Kyle need reassurance, you need to check on Annie, and make sure Radhika*

*isn't beating herself up for whatever she thinks she did wrong
. . . and call the clinic in Cheltenham.* She bit her lip.

And who the hell was on the piano that had been turned to
the wall and covered for such a long time?

'Hey, stranger.' Hugh came from the bar into the kitchen
looking and sounding breezier than he had in days. 'I thought
you must have taken the day off.'

'Nope.' She almost told him she'd been talking with Bill
Lamb but thought better of it. 'Who's playing the piano? I
thought we had it covered up.'

'We did – in the uproom.' The uproom as it had been dubbed,
was a step higher than the rest of the bar with wooden tables
and high-backed bench seats where some customers liked to
have a meal in the early evening. 'It's OK, isn't it? We used
to have someone in to play and sing up there. Could be time to
start that again. Makes a change and people like it.'

'You know why we stopped, Hugh. We weren't in the mood
after the Quillam fiasco.'

'Right, but we move on. That's Carrie. Who knew she had a
good voice.'

'Carrie?' Alex frowned. 'Our Carrie Peale? You're joking.'

'That's who it is. She came in, turned the piano around on
her own as if it were a wheeled suitcase – a small one at that
– and started in. She's good. But she's mad as hell, Alex, and
I think that's why she's doing it. Letting off steam. She works
hard while Harvey swills beer, rides around on his friend's
motorbike, and talks about himself.'

Alex recognized the sound of two hands crashing down on
the piano keys and went into the bar.

In her paint-and-clay daubed overalls and worn-out sandals,
Carrie Peale came to the counter. 'Afternoon, Alex,' she said.
'Do you have any tea?'

'Of course.' Alex smiled. 'Half a mo'.' She popped back to
the kitchen, surprised not to find Hugh still there, and was
grateful a teapot under a cozy felt piping hot and smelled fresh.

She took a cup back to Carrie who had the fingers of one
hand over her mouth.

'Funny you should come in today,' Alex said. 'I've been
thinking about asking you to make me some mugs with the name

of the pub on them. Perhaps with a black dog like the one on our sign.'

That got her a curious gaze and a long silence, but Carrie dropped her hand.

'Of course,' Alex said finally, 'that may not be your kind of thing. I know you like making one offs, but—'

'I'll be glad to,' Carrie said hurriedly. 'I'll bring in some samples. What color do you think? All the same, right?'

'I think so – but why don't we have different shapes? Whatever catches your fancy. I plan to have the sign out front repainted. It's faded. I think the black dog would look good against a deep sky blue, don't you? The mugs could be fired in the same colors. I'll sell them here – people like that sort of thing – but we'll settle on a price up front.'

'I like those colors, but you're only doing this to help me.' Carrie turned her face away.

There were times when protest only proved the issue. 'Partly,' Alex admitted. 'Partly because I think it's a good idea that would be good for both of us. I'd put up a sign that pub mugs are coming and they're from your pottery. Will you definitely do it?' Sometimes you had to push a point quickly.

Carrie wrinkled her upturned nose for a moment, then said, 'Yes, I will. It could get the odd looker into my pottery and I can use anything on two feet that breathes and can buy. Sounds awful, but since we're being honest . . .'

'Sounds sensible to me,' Alex said.

The bar was mostly empty, but Harvey Peale and the fellow from the Gentlemen Bikers he hung around with sat nearby with half-empty pint glasses and completely empty shots. They had pushed aside plates with remnants of chips and crumbs from pies. Harvey was less loquacious than usual, at least when he was drinking, and his companion spoke to him earnestly.

'He's in here all the time now,' Carrie said without turning around. 'Harvey never stops talking about him. Loads of money, so he says, loudly. Saul. One of those city types who rides around on a great big expensive cycle pretending to be a biker. He's been holding forth that Harvey needs to get completely away, somewhere he can devote all his emotional energy to his writing.'

Alex didn't know how to respond.

'He's even offered to pay for a retreat place where Harvey can write without responsibilities.' Her crooked little smile turned Alex's heart. 'That's pretty rich, don't you think?'

The sight of Annie coming through from the restaurant and looking completely recovered grabbed all her attention. She waved and Annie waved back but turned to wait for Hugh to catch up with her.

Without being sure why, Alex balled a tight fist hard on the counter. Her forehead tensed. Annie was smiling widely at Hugh who crinkled his eyes at her.

Oh, my God. What am I looking at?

Carrie followed Alex's gaze. 'Oh, my,' she whispered. 'Looks as if Hugh's finally got a woman in his life. About time.'

Short of explaining Annie's history, Alex could only keep her mouth closed and try to set her thoughts on neutral. As usual, she'd jumped to a bewildering conclusion. But the two of them did look at each other with more than casual warmth.

Hugh approached the counter with Annie's hand looped under his forearm. She truly didn't look like the same person Alex and Tony had brought here so recently. Her auburn hair shone in waves past her shoulders. Her pale skin appeared translucent and healthy and her big, dark eyes shone – on Hugh.

'Hello, Alex,' Annie said. 'Thank you for putting up with me cluttering up the place. I don't know what kind of bug hit me, but I feel so much better. Hello,' she said to Carrie. 'I'm Annie Bell. I'm here on holiday but I've been to Folly a lot and I love the place.'

'Carrie Peale. I'm a local potter.' Her interest in Annie was evident. 'We've been here less than a year. Sounds as if you've been ill. I hope you're better.'

'A potter? How wonderful. Here in Folly? I'll come and look at what you make. Pottery makes such lovely gifts.'

Hugh slipped free of Annie and joined Alex behind the counter. 'I insisted Annie come down,' he said quietly. 'She can't hang around upstairs all the time. Did I hear you're going to use some of your house for friends who need a place to stay? Could Annie stay there for a week or so? I don't know when Green Friday will be available again.'

And Alex couldn't imagine Annie wanting to go anywhere near Green Friday after what had happened there. 'I have mentioned using the house if necessary,' she said. 'She doesn't want to stay on here?'

'I don't think it's a good idea,' Hugh said, glancing away.

'Well . . . how long will she be in Folly? I don't really know why she came.'

'She told me she likes the people here and I get the feeling she's pretty lonely. So far she hasn't opened up to me completely but I think there's a lot she hasn't told me. You and I should talk about that. Her parents wanted her to cut any ties to Elyan so she cut ties with them – or that's how she's putting it. She even mentioned wanting to live here in Folly.'

Alex waited for him to meet her eyes. 'Hugh, what would she do in Folly? Does she have independent means? I don't get this.'

'Neither do I,' he said. 'I think we should let her work these things out. She's old enough to make up her own mind.'

'Well, look who we have here.' Smiling, Hugh braced himself on the edge of the counter. 'Harriet and Mary. They're not usually middle-of-the-day visitors.'

The sisters came in through the main door to the pub, Harriet pulling Mary's tartan-covered shopping cart that would contain Max the cat, while Alex knew a little blanket bundle in Mary's walker basket held the elderly Maltese, Lillie Belle.

Harriet gave a waggle-fingered wave and they progressed to their table beside the fire and an ecstatic Bogie.

'Let's talk about Annie's plans a bit later,' Alex said to Hugh. Carrie and Annie were talking animatedly. 'Is she all right, do you think? She doesn't seem hyper to you?'

'Not really. Just more like she used to be when I first met her – vivacious – except she needs friends around her. She really is on her own. She's got some notions I don't understand. It's almost as if someone's been deliberately planting negative ideas in her head. We could help her here.'

Alex didn't trust herself to look at him too directly. All she said was, 'Hm.' What Annie needed was to at least make a start on letting go of the past and getting back to the normal life someone in their early twenties might lead.

And for herself, Alex desperately wanted to get rid of her fears about Hugh. For Hugh. He had some involvement with whatever happened at Green Friday that night. It could well be innocent of any wrongdoing, but she would be a fool not to wonder.

Harvey Peale's friend, Saul, got up from their table and approached Annie and Carrie. He smiled at Annie and spoke in low tones, evidently turning on charm, before leading them both away from the counter. Annie seemed unphased, pleased even, but Carrie's suspicion showed. The two women sat with Harvey while Saul remained standing.

When she realized her mouth was open, Alex shut it firmly. The actions of adults were their business.

'I'll go and see what Harriet and Mary would like,' she said. 'They might go for a steak and kidney pie.'

But she didn't leave the spot where she stood. Instead she grasped Hugh's shirtsleeve and stopped breathing. He followed her gaze and drew in a deep breath. 'What does he want? He looks as if he's ready to blow.'

Wells Giglio was Percy Quillam's agent; had been Elyan Quillam's agent also. An eccentrically dressed man given to drama, he emoted in a dramatically Latin manner and Alex would have preferred never to be in his company again.

'He's here because the police contacted him,' she said. 'Has to be. Someone said he was in Paris – with Percy – then fending off gossip there after the death. That's a bit hard to swallow. For the brief time I knew him before, I'd have said he thrived on gossip – and stirring it up whenever he could.' She would not say that the man was a day earlier than she'd been told he would arrive.

Red hair springing from a central part to curl over his ears, a large black silk handkerchief flopping from the jacket pocket of his pale gray linen suit and a pair of the colorful – leaf green this time – suede shoes Alex remembered him favoring, Wells surveyed the barroom. His narrow face with its memorable bony features was twisted into an expression of anguish – and anger.

His gaze came to rest on Annie Bell. 'You!' More an accusation than a question or greeting. 'You know everything. Of course you're still here. You may fool everyone else with your little girl act, but you don't fool me. I'm going to make sure you don't keep on making mischief.'

Annie didn't answer. She took a deep breath, placed her hands flat on the table and waited.

Alex made to go to Annie, but Hugh stopped her. 'This could be hard on her,' he murmured. 'But we should probably let him have his say in case it's useful.'

'It's a good point,' Alex agreed. 'But it concerns me that she's so vulnerable and I don't think she collapsed from the flu or whatever. I think she was mentally exhausted. Histrionics from Wells Giglio won't help. But I'll try to wait.'

The room had fallen mostly silent although Harvey Peale's leathered companion had moved to rest his hands on Annie's shoulders. And Annie wasn't shrugging him off, or complaining . . .

'Percy Quillam is dead,' Wells announced, as if he were delivering news. 'He came looking for Sonia. Now *I'm* looking for Sonia. Where is she, Annie?'

SEVENTEEN

'I fucking hate this place,' Jillian Miller announced and slammed her black shoulder bag on a metal desktop in Folly-on-Weir's parish hall. 'Isn't there anywhere else in this goddamn place we can set up an incident room . . . guv?'

'Not that I know of,' Bill said, turning his back on her to watch a sergeant work on a whiteboard – one of several attached to a row of screens that cut off line-of-sight from any casual visitor to the hall. 'We've used this place on a number of occasions, Miller. It works just fine. Give the Black Dog a ring and arrange for the usual refreshments, please. They don't deliver.' He stopped short of telling her to pick a couple of officers to help her fetch and carry, but she drove a man to contemplate small-minded retribution. Wishing Jillian Miller on Dan O'Reilly in his new position wasn't kind but Bill would be delighted if she went for a transfer to anywhere that would have her.

Photographs of major and not-so-major players in the case were already displayed together with lists of leads and salient details. Not enough leads – virtually none Bill had much faith in.

He took a folding metal chair into a corner beside a radiator. At least it wasn't winter, so the thing wasn't hissing and popping and broadcasting an aroma of roasting dust. Plenty of dust swirled in a wide shaft of sunshine through the open door. Bill shoved his hands in his pockets and leaned his chair onto its back two legs. Molly Lewis would go over the post-mortem on Percy Quillam in detail late in the afternoon. She was an unpredictable woman but so good at her job that anyone who understood how important she was didn't complain. Too bad she couldn't be ready for him sooner.

Since Hugh Rhys had admitted to seeing Sonia Quillam at Green Friday, they had quickly run through the normal channels trying to find her. They had already established she was not at the Quillams' Hampstead home in London when they tried to make contact following Percy's death. Now the net was flung wider but still no positive word had come in.

Tomorrow her picture would appear in the media along with a request for information about her whereabouts. And throughout, searches continued: the hills and fields, the houses and farms around Folly had been scoured and intensive house-to-house carried out. Nothing. But although the window for finding her alive was technically closed, he had only intensified police efforts.

They had determined she flew into Gatwick less than forty-eight hours before Hugh Rhys, by his own admission, received a telephone call from her. Now the tedious task of trying to track her through rental car agencies had begun in earnest. Sonia could well have used a different name but from photographs, she would be hard not to notice. Getting a definite description of whatever vehicle she'd driven to Folly could be golden, especially since they had no firm leads on that so far.

He went through reports on his desk, flipping pages quickly. The car Hugh was seen driving that night, a BMW Nash, had been picked up the previous evening for forensics to look over. Negative results had come disappointingly quickly.

In a single hurried step, Alex shot into the afternoon sun-spotlight in the doorway and blinked around, shading her eyes. She spotted Bill but immediately searched in all directions.

He knew panic when it confronted him.

Quickly, Bill got up and strode to usher Alex outside again. 'Something going on?' he asked as soon as they were walking toward the back of the parish hall and into the sunshine.

'I'd say so, yes. Is it just me or do you feel anything really weird about this case you're working?' She touched his arm as he would have responded. 'I know it's nothing to do with me, or it shouldn't be, but it's getting pushed at me, Bill. Something's going to blow up anytime soon. I can feel it.'

'That's the disclaimer covered,' Bill said. 'Now let's have what you came for.'

'I've got to put this in context and I don't want to seem as if I'm trying to lead you to think one thing or another.' Alex walked on until they reached the narrow lane that ran behind Pond Street. To their left, St Aldwyn's churchyard, bursting with roses, rested behind a lychgate. On the right, the Burke sisters' tea rooms and gardens backed onto the lane and churchyard.

Alex pulled sunglasses from a pocket in her jeans and pushed them on. 'It's all a mess,' she said. 'You remember talking about Wells Giglio? He was Elyan Quillam's agent and then, apparently, became Percy Quillam's agent?'

'I remember – that was only this morning.' And he wasn't looking forward to dealing with him again. A difficult man who thought his wants came first in all things.

Alex looked sideways at him. 'He was in Paris with Percy. He knew Percy came here and says it was to see Sonia. You said Wells would be here tomorrow.'

'Where are you going with this?' Bill stopped walking and Alex faced him. 'I told you Wells was in Paris and we've been in contact with him. He said he had no intention of getting deeply involved with the Quillams' business again but that he'd come tomorrow to take care of whatever needs to be done for Percy. He was grudging about it but in his words, he'll *talk to us.*' No need to mention that Giglio had been warned to keep in touch – even if there was little the UK police could do about it if he chose to duck out without returning.

Alex jiggled on the balls of her feet. The sunglasses shielded whatever her expressive eyes must show. 'First, Bill, I wanted to say something about Radhika.' She touched his arm again, quickly. 'No, don't say anything yet. I shouldn't interfere, but I care a lot about her and so does Tony. But you know that.'

Did she have any idea how much he cared about Radhika?

'She is upset. She blames herself for not going to you directly and telling you about the woman in the driveway at Green Friday. Radhika feels responsible. If she had made a call immediately she thinks she could have saved whoever it was from disappearing. Worse than that, she's pretty certain she should just have gone right over there to see if she could help.'

'Well she absolutely should not have done so. God knows what might have happened to her.' She might also have been missing by now, Bill thought, and he set his jaw. 'I couldn't talk to you in front of Radhika. There was no point in upsetting her more. But tell me, did what she said about the woman in the driveway sound like Sonia Quillam to you? It did to me.'

'Yes. Absolutely. That's how Sonia would be described by almost anyone under the same conditions. Obviously, you'd have to be a lot closer to describe her face.'

Bill nodded, yes. 'What did you want to tell me? Or is that it?'

'I don't know why Wells told the police he didn't intend to get mixed up with the Quillams again. He came to the Dog today, Bill, at lunch time. He didn't stay long, probably because a customer a lot more imposing to look at than Wells encouraged him to leave, but he made a helluva fuss while he was there.'

Bill screwed up his eyes while he took that in. 'Giglio was at the Black Dog today? How long ago?'

'He left not more than twenty minutes ago. I was floored when I saw him.'

'I've got a feeling you're going to tell me more.' And they shouldn't be chatting away in this lane where someone could be behind a hedge. He frowned, deciding where to go. 'We'd better go back inside the hall. It's not too bad in the balcony and I'll make sure we aren't interrupted unless we have to be.'

Reluctance shadowed Alex's eyes but she nodded and went with him. 'This old parish hall has seen too much action in the past few years,' she said wryly.

Since you returned to the village after your divorce. Better not to voice the thought aloud. 'We could use a decent interview room here, but I wouldn't want to damn Folly by looking for one. It would look too much as if we expected to return.'

Alex gave him a slightly sick grin. 'You interviewed Hugh in Gloucester yesterday.' She let the comment hang.

'You know I can't comment on that.'

She colored faintly and fell in beside him. They crossed from the lane just as a tan Lexus, sunshine turning the very new exterior to gold, swung to a stop in front of the parish hall. LeJuan Harding slid his long body from behind the wheel and rested his crossed arms along the open door. He arched an eyebrow and swept an appreciative look over the vehicle.

Bill laughed. 'Too bad it isn't yours, Balls. Dan get new wheels?'

'Oh, yeah,' LeJuan said, looking crestfallen. 'And I thought I looked so natural standing here, you'd be sure it was mine.' He smiled at Alex and gave her a salute.

'Where's the great man?' Bill asked.

'Dropped him at the Black Dog. He's going to grab a bite and go with you to see Molly. The pesky . . . our psychologist sidekick is with him. I said I'd come over here and catch up with the grunts. In other words, it seemed a good idea to sound a warning and see what you've got that we don't know about – without the interested audience.' He loped away toward the hall and Bill brooded over Dr Wolf's motives.

'Balls?' Alex said, raising both eyebrows.

Bill said, 'As in he's got them. If he's ever been embarrassed, he blushes where no one can see.' He winced. 'To the balcony.'

Treading on eggshells? Alex kept her fingers tightly laced together in her lap. More like stamping on raw eggs if she made a wrong move. Or used the wrong word or gave too much emphasis to the wrong name.

That was what she was really worried about. Who she should or should not mention.

With any slight move she made, the ancient wooden balcony chair whined and creaked. Ringing phones and sharp conversation came from the hall below. She didn't know if she could or should keep Annie's name out of what she had to tell Bill.

His rapid footsteps sounded on the stairs to the balcony. He had asked her to come up alone while he spoke with his team.

With rolled-back shirtsleeves and his tie loose he looked casually masculine and could have been in any white-collar job. When you met his startling light-blue eyes that noticed everything but betrayed little, he didn't look like anyone ordinary. Alex already knew that Bill Lamb could be a hard man and didn't fool herself he wouldn't show that side again whenever he felt the need.

'Sorry about that,' he said, taking a chair beside her and scooting it until they faced each other. 'It's busy and getting busier. Sonia Quillam's disappearance is burning through the news. There'll be a live media announcement before day's end but already the loony or lonely – or both – are coming out of the woodwork with tips.'

'Must be annoying. Do any of them ever pan out?'

'You can't risk brushing anyone off. There can always be that snippet that leads to something useful. We're glad to get calls.' He hiked an ankle on the opposite knee, watching her steadily and letting her feel him waiting.

'Of course.' Alex cleared her throat, still mentally organizing what she would say.

Bill ran a hand through his sandy crewcut and crossed his arms. The hum from below became a saw on Alex's nerves.

No point keeping up the silence. 'Giglio was angry at the Black Dog. Fuming, actually. He announced Percy was dead as if everyone didn't already know.'

'Did he say anything about how Percy died?'

'No. He just talked about Percy coming for Sonia and made a not very subtle accusation . . .' She almost flinched, and waited for the inevitable.

'Who did he accuse, of what?'

And there it was – the inevitable question.

'He was just flailing, Bill. Nothing he said made any sense. You know how melodramatic he is. He wants to find Sonia.'

'Don't we all.' Bill leaned closer. 'Who did he accuse, Alex?'

He asked casually but took a notebook and pen from a pocket and flipped open the book. Alex puffed out a breath and tried to calm down. Bill wouldn't let her get away without telling the whole story.

'It wasn't a direct accusation. Annie was there – of course he knows her from before. He said something ridiculous about it being natural for her to be there because she'd know everything. He asked her where Sonia is.'

Bill sat back again and his gaze moved away from her while he considered.

'It was just silly. He—'

'Who was the customer who took Wells out of the pub?'

'One of the Gentlemen Bikers Club. He's been coming in lately. Seems a decent man and he obviously didn't like Wells picking on Annie.'

'His name?' Bill's pen hovered over the paper.

'Oh . . . Saul. I don't know his other name. He's a friend of Harvey Peale's. The potter – Carrie Peale's husband.'

Bill wrote down the name and tapped the end of his pen against his chin. 'OK. We'll want to talk to him.'

'Wells is out of his depth,' Alex said. 'He doesn't know which way to turn so he's flinging accusations around. He's theatrical.'

'In the snug, when Hugh came down while we were there – why had Annie insisted on going to see Hugh? What was the matter with her? It sounded as if she was sick somehow.'

This wasn't going well. Exactly what she had feared might happen was unfurling – right out of her own mouth. 'She's had a lot of stress and hard times since Elyan was sent away. It's just exhaustion. A break was what she needed and she's getting it.'

'Do you know why she went to Hugh?'

'No, except she knows him and he's been there for Elyan. They both visit him and she knows Hugh cares about him. She doesn't have much, if any, family support anymore.'

Bill ran a forefinger along the crease in a trouser leg. Coming was not a bad idea. She had to remain convinced of that. There would be enough spreading of reports, most of them embellished, from the people who had heard Giglio's outburst at the pub and watched Saul hustle him outside. Since Saul was unlikely to think he should seek out the police, it was her responsibility to make sure the right story reached them.

'Annie must have been with you before the three of you went to the Black Dog. Did she contact you first, Alex? Where were you when she found you? Or did you find her? Bear with me, I'm just trying to get all this clear.'

Of course he was and she didn't blame him – even if she did fervently wish he would simply thank her for coming and move on. She gave him a tight little smile. 'She wasn't really with us.' Bill wouldn't let that go. 'We took her to the Black Dog when she asked to go. It seemed we might as well because she would have gone anyway, and it was late.'

'This is hard for you,' Bill said. 'I know it is, but I do have to find out the whole story. You did the right thing – coming right to me. We will pick up Wells Giglio.'

'For what?'

Bill laughed. 'It's not too late for you to join the force. You don't miss a thing. He can't throw accusations around – or threats, veiled or otherwise. That will do for a start. Where did you, Tony and Annie come from before getting to the Black Dog the other night?'

She sighed. He hadn't trapped her, she had trapped herself even if she had meant well in coming here. 'From Leaves of Comfort. We met up with Annie there. She was upset and we couldn't leave her like that.'

'Granted. Why was she upset?'

'I don't know.' It wasn't a total lie. She didn't have the whole story. At least Bill didn't look incredulous and she was grateful for that.

'Guv!' It was LeJuan, calling up the stairs. He paused at the top. 'Sorry to interrupt. My boss just rang. He'll be over in fifteen.'

'And Wolf will be with him?'

Bill didn't respond to LeJuan's affirmative nod. He waited for the sergeant to clatter away before giving Alex all his attention. 'I'll want to take this up with you again later, but it would help if you could give me a couple of short answers to an outstanding issue.'

'I'll try.'

'Neve and Perry Rhys.'

Her face felt suddenly cold. 'Yes. They're staying at the inn.'

'We know that, and that they are related to Hugh. His cousin and his cousin's wife. Do you have any inkling of why they are here at this particular time?'

'No.' That was true.

'Would you say Hugh and these family members were close?'

Alex looked at Bill and didn't respond.

'I didn't think so,' he said after a pause. 'The three of them have been observed together and it's been suggested there's hostility there.'

'I couldn't say.'

Bill didn't look amused. 'Couldn't or won't?'

'They may not be close.'

'Right. Please chew on this topic for the next few hours. I have appointments until late afternoon but then we should take this discussion up again.' He stood up. 'I am grateful to you for coming.'

'Yes,' she said. 'Thank you,' and got to her feet. She started toward the stairs, desperate to get outside again.

'You've got a dilemma,' Bill said, following her down. 'You think it would be disloyal to tell me everything you know. I want you to think about that, Alex. What does it really mean to be disloyal and that's not really a question.'

EIGHTEEN

For a stocky man, Dr Wolf had an uncanny ability to melt into the background. Bill stood beside Dan in the morgue and tried not to glance in the direction of the motionless psychologist with his tiny voice recorder tucked into the elbow of one of his crossed arms.

Percy Quillam's body was on a slab again, face down with a neck block keeping his forehead tilted to the table. This time all attention was on his head and his scalp, separated and flapped away from the bone at the base of his skull.

Molly wasn't happy but Bill didn't know why. She had hardly spoken since their arrival and looked at Wolf with open dislike. She had barely skirted asking what possible reason he could have for being present but picked up a warning cue from Dan – who didn't look more pleased with the situation.

'There are multiple lacerations and contusions everywhere the body wasn't covered with layers of clothing,' Molly said. 'This isn't news. What appear to be injuries to the head – and other places – they might well have been made by contact with rocks and general rubble. By the pond would be a good guess. But there's this.' She indicated an area low on the back of the head – first on the scalp layers, then by peeling that back to expose the bone.

Leaning closer, Bill studied the areas she indicated.

'He sustained a blow here – a significant blow that we believe was the result of an object being used to hit the head, or a heavy fall onto something, possibly of considerable size.'

'Like what?' Dan asked, looking up from his own close examination. 'Why didn't we see this before?'

'Bruising continues to increase post-mortem.' Molly stood back, a grimace pulling at her lips. 'The blow didn't fracture the skull but there is an indentation. You can see how bruising has blossomed. And if something had not got in the way, we would have identified this at once.'

Bill met Dan's eyes and they both remained silent. She would reveal what was on her mind in good time. At least Wolf still didn't attempt to speak. He kept his heavy lids lowered over rather protruding gray eyes. His blond hair was meticulously slicked down, and his thin lips pursed. Warming to him under any circumstances might have been difficult but given his silent scrutiny, he encouraged antipathy.

'So' – Molly cleared her throat – 'it was the hair – the tail or whatever. With the tissue swollen from being submerged and the knot of hair over it – although it was shaved during the examination – this wasn't immediately obvious.'

Glossing over anything Wolf might feel it was his duty to point out, Bill hurried to say, 'Understandable. Any idea what weapon we should be looking for.'

It was Molly's turn to cross her arms. 'It could be almost anything, a rock even given the grit in the skin. Werner came up with an interesting idea. A golf club, a driver perhaps. But we haven't really identified anything that remotely matches the shape of injury.'

Bill was struck again by the closeness between Molly and the crime scene manager. They ribbed each other cruelly but were obviously also respectful friends.

'There are some pretty strangely shaped clubs these days,' Dan said. 'Some of them look as if they shouldn't be allowed at all.'

'I know, but I don't think that's our answer. If there had been more damage I'd have put in a vote for a hoe, or some garden tool and it could still be that, but we're going to have to think harder. There is a second, smaller wound quite close, but it didn't do much damage.'

'Are you suggesting this blow killed him?' Bill asked.

'No, I haven't changed my mind on a cardiac event. But this is unusual enough it could be a leading clue, Bill. That's what's on my mind. It takes me back to the theory that the killer might not have known when his victim was dead and was still trying to finish the job after it was all over.'

'Doesn't sound like a seasoned killer,' Dan said and was greeted by mumbled agreements.

They thanked Molly and Dan followed Bill out of the morgue. Dr Wolf was close behind.

'Are your observations helping with your project?' Bill asked him, trying for polite interest.

'This study will not be soon over,' Wolf said dismissively. 'There are some years of unsatisfactory resolutions to examine. At least this one is not a closed case so there's room to impact the outcome and reach conclusions about connections that haven't been made between previous cases. I have a meeting but I'll check the schedule for tomorrow. Let me know if anything changes, will you?'

Not waiting for a response, the man walked away and pushed through swinging doors at the end of the corridor.

'And what would we bet that he's on his way to make another report to the chief constable?' Dan said. 'Wolf isn't even pretending we're on the same side anymore.'

Bill looked at the doors that had closed behind the man. 'He behaves as if he's the superior around here. In charge or something. Almost as if he wants to put us on edge. It's difficult to like him.'

'If I were a vindictive man, I'd be considering how to sink the puffed-up tosser,' Dan said.

'But you aren't vindictive?' Bill asked, grinning.

'I'm working on it. How about you?'

'Let's compare progress as we go along. I think we're likely to be vindictive experts in no time.' Bill glanced back over his shoulder. 'I know what the next move has to be in the Quillam case.'

'Surprise me,' Dan said. 'Or are you also thinking that pond they say leads to the middle of the earth must be searched regardless.'

'Great minds,' Bill said.

NINETEEN

His choices were narrowing – fast.

Either he found a way to get Perry and Neve out of the Black Dog, or he would have to make an excuse for living elsewhere and coming there to work only. He didn't want that. He wanted to be rid of the forces messing with his life.

Paperwork threatened to slide from the piles on his desk. Cool, calm and organized Hugh was doing a great imitation of being incompetent.

He threw down his pen and stared from the windows toward the village green. The day was oppressively hot, the sky an eye-watering blue and the sun unyielding in the stillness. Not a branch shifted, not a leaf quivered.

Annie was embroiled in everything. Had to be. Yet she probably didn't completely know she could be courting danger.

He picked up the house phone and called Lily. 'Hello, you,' he said, grateful she couldn't see him. 'We have guest bookings for the Perry and Neve Rhys room. Starting tonight. They weren't here last night – they're just using this as a convenience when they feel like it. Not that we care about things like that usually, but I want them out.' There, he had damn well said it. Let them go to that place they'd rented in Burford, a 'just in case we need a backup' place as Neve had told him.

'Got you,' Lily responded without particular inflection in her voice. 'I'll deal with it, Hugh.' She didn't ask any questions and he heard the click at her end.

Did everyone know how contentious his dealings with his cousin and his wife were? He leaned back hard in his antique swivel chair that creaked with the sudden move.

Getting those two out of here might not completely get rid of them but he wouldn't have to tiptoe around expecting to fall over the pair, or wait for them to get together with Annie and start something.

Annie . . . if she suddenly went out of control, would he still be able to help her?

In a few minutes he had to see Alex. She'd told him she would come up here when she got back from getting Bogie groomed. Why did she want to talk to him?

If he was honest with himself, he had a good idea. Alex and Tony knew much more than they'd ever mentioned to him or, evidently, the police. That meant they had been holding back to support him, to give him a chance to work his way out. But how long would that last, and could he pull the threads together in time.

Just how much did they know, or think they knew?

A single knock on the door made him jump. He got up and went rapidly to let Alex in. Bogie, looking unnaturally tidy, rushed past to find Katie under the desk.

'Is this a bad time?' Alex said.

Will there ever be any other kind of time again? 'No, of course not. Come in.'

Hugh didn't say a word, only sat beside her in his Subaru, one elbow on the window rim, staring ahead at the empty road and the woodlands as he drove.

This was on her head, Alex thought. Successful or total disaster, non-event or . . . she took a deep breath . . . or an ill-conceived dive into a frightening risk, this was entirely her idea. When Hugh had agreed to come with her for an honest discussion she hoped would help them clear the air and try to mend the rift that was widening, she had been delighted. She had been convinced this would be the answer to their problems and return them to the kind of understanding that had made their working relationship so good until recently.

But so far things were not looking good.

The road from Folly up to the Dimple, that then ran in front of Lime Tree Lodge, Alex's own house, and then Tony's place, must have become shorter, or so it felt, certainly since Hugh announced he would like them to go to Green Friday to talk, rather than drive to Naunton and stroll around the quaint village, as she had suggested. They were approaching Trap Lane much too fast.

She hadn't had the courage to ask him why he wanted to go to his house yet, but she'd better do it, and before they got there.

'I'm glad we could get away for a while,' she said. *Not a stellar opening.* 'I've been wanting a chance for us to clear the air.'

'Have you? Why is that?'

He could rile her without apparently trying hard. 'Because we've been barking at one another, ignoring one another, and you've been a bear throughout what we both know have been difficult days. It's not helping a thing, Hugh. Let's get past it.'

'There's nothing I'd like better,' he said, still not looking at her. 'But that would take effort from both of us, not just my saying what you want to hear.'

Alex hit the dash with the heel of a hand. 'That is so unfair, Hugh, and so unlike you.'

'What is like me? Attacking women? Beating up a man years older than I am and throwing him in a bottomless pond?'

'You're not making sense. Have I accused you of anything or done something to make you think I wasn't on your side?'

'If you completely trusted me there wouldn't be any question.'

'That's it. Why bother to try talking? What's the matter with you? I haven't done anything to you, have I?'

Hugh glanced sideways at her, one dark brow arched. 'Temper, temper, Alex. What have you done *for* me? How have you tried to defend me when you know your cop buddies and just about everyone else thinks I'm guilty of who the hell knows what? Let me ask you a question – and I do believe you're an honest woman. I know you saw me at Green Friday on the night you went to visit Radhika. I was walking toward the house according to what was said. I'd parked the Nash facing out of the driveway. I didn't know that was going to be an issue but apparently it is. Was it you who told the police about that?'

He braked, drove onto the verge of the road, applied the brakes again and idled. Careful to keep herself steady, Alex said, 'No.' At some point she was likely to be forced to tell the police a lot more.

'Why didn't you?'

Alex leaned until he was all but forced to meet her eyes. 'That kind of remark is what I'm talking about. You're making things impossible. You know why I didn't tell the police – not that I haven't wondered if I should. Is that straight enough for you?'

He gave a short, mirthless laugh. 'Someone did, so if it wasn't you, you needn't bother now. Conspiracy theories are things I've tried to avoid but I'd be a fool not to think there's an attempt to frame me. For Percy's death, and for whatever's happened to Sonia.'

'Why do you want to go to Green Friday today?'

'I don't even know if I'll be allowed there but I'd like to look around. And I want to know for myself just what you can see from the windows at the back of the house. According to Sam, there was a car parked there when the three of us went up that morning. Then it was gone – or so the police say. Did you see it?'

Alex stared ahead and thought. 'No,' she said finally. 'No, I didn't. Did Sam say he saw it when we were all there together?'

'I don't know now.' Hugh leaned against the headrest. 'How do I ask him? It'll sound as if I either don't believe him or I'm giving him the third degree.'

'Why would it? It seems simple to me. Either the car was still there when we were and we just didn't notice, or it was driven away between Sam's first visit and when we got there with him – and the police got there. Sam could have just assumed it was still parked at the back.'

'Yeah, maybe. What I need to know most is where someone would have to be to see me – or anyone – coming or going from the house. They could have been in the trees or beside the house, but I didn't see anyone. Maybe I've missed the obvious and I want to find out if that's possible.'

Her stomach made an unpleasant revolution. He wouldn't need to be a surveyor to figure out there was a good line of sight from the tower at Radhika's house. But she, Alex thought, would not be revealing anything she knew about what had been said on that.

'When I drove past that evening, you were walking toward the front of Green Friday. That's all I know. As you said, what difference would any of that make now?'

'It's for my own information,' Hugh said. 'I'll drive you to the Black Dog and come back on my own later, if you like.'

'That would be senseless. We're almost there. We're going to Green Friday now, Hugh. Come on. We can be civil, can't we?'

He didn't reply, but drove back onto the street and she was conscious of him keeping his speed down.

At Trap Lane they had to pause and allow a police car and what looked like a SOCO vehicle to turn uphill before them.

'Looks as if I'm likely to be told to bugger off,' Hugh said. 'But not without finding out what they're up to now – if I can.'

He gave the official vehicles a few seconds' head start before following.

'What do we do if they turn in at Green Friday?' Alex asked.

'They will. We follow, and I try to ask some questions. It is my property. You can wait in the car – if you're sure you don't mind going with me, that is.'

Alex didn't answer him, just gritted her teeth when they carried on up the lane. He turned in at the driveway, toward Green Friday. Crime scene tape blocked off the front door but there was no police presence to be seen. Alex opened her mouth to say as much.

'Would you look at that,' Hugh said, leaning forward. 'Isn't that the Mini Annie's driving now? What the hell is she doing here?'

The little red-and-white car turned Alex's stomach. She hated seeing it in the car park lot at the Black Dog because it reminded her of Elyan and the horrible way that whole affair had ended.

'Yep,' she said. 'Elyan's Mini – Annie's now. She must be wandering around up here making herself feel even worse than she already did.' The dirty car was parked at the far left of the turnaround in front of the house.

'She needs to get her life together,' Hugh said. 'She's got too much to offer to throw it all away. She can't stop longing for Elyan, but it's doubtful he's probably ever getting out of that place again.'

It would be so easy to lead into a conversation about his feelings for the girl but the idea terrified Alex. That could easily lead to the end of any hope for mending things with Hugh.

She took a breath and expelled it slowly – and remembered what she couldn't see. 'Hugh' – she put a hand on his arm – 'what happened to that SOCO van and the police car?'

Hugh shrugged. 'Huh . . . Must have been going somewhere else.'

'There's only Radhika's and I don't see anything going on there.'

'Don't forget there's a back route to Derwinter's up the lane, and a way to cut across to the other side of the hill. Let's not buy problems. Come on.'

He got out of the Subaru and looked around. Alex joined him. At first she thought he was trying to locate Annie, but his attention was on checking the surrounding trees and hedges. 'I hadn't realized the tower next door had such a bird's-eye view over here,' he said at last, the corners of his mouth turned down. 'Not really close, but good enough and perfect with a pair of binoculars. Workers have been all over the place for months. They seem to be working entirely on the inside now.'

'They are not there on Sundays,' Alex said, turning away in the hope that Hugh would change subjects.

No luck. 'That top room would have an unobstructed view

of the front of this house. I'll need to walk around to the back to see what would be visible from there.'

Alex swallowed. At least he hadn't mentioned Radhika but he must be thinking about her.

'Annie should be somewhere back there,' Hugh said, after a brief look into the empty Mini. 'I don't see how she could get inside but she spent a lot of time around the pool house with Elyan. She could be there.'

Side by side, they set off along the gravel path surrounding Green Friday. Alex kept glancing this way and that for Annie but there was no sign of her, not there or near outbuildings farther away.

In the area outside the kitchen windows, Hugh stopped. 'I assume Sam was talking about a car being right here, but the extra parking is up there.' He pointed toward the pool house on the far side of the pool – currently covered. 'I've never stayed here but I would expect that area to be used when there are people in residence.'

'I know it was when the Quillams were here,' Alex told him. 'But the car they must think Sonia used would have been down here – outside the kitchen, I would think.'

'That's what I gather.' He glanced toward Radhika's house. 'Otherwise Sam wouldn't have seen it. That tower would have views over the back of the house, too. Before, when it had been empty for years, I don't think anyone thought of the overlook. Radhika owns it now. Has she mentioned being able to see down here?'

Whatever she said was not going to satisfy Hugh but she steeled herself, then said, 'I would ask the police about that. I'm sure they've questioned her – and the people working on the renovation. Why does it matter?'

Hugh gave a short laugh. 'Isn't that obvious? Someone said they saw me leaving on the night I met Sonia here. They had to be looking from up there.'

'You couldn't see farther down the driveway from up there, could you?' Why hadn't she thought of this before. 'You were parked out in the driveway, not by the house. I don't think you could have been seen from that tower.'

Hugh frowned. 'The police talked about my car being parked

facing out from the property. You could be right about the line of sight from up there, but I'd have to take a look myself to be certain. Still, I think someone could have been watching from that tower and feeding assumptions to the police. They took the Nash yesterday, you know.'

'The police will figure out what they should take seriously, Hugh.'

'I hope you're right. Let's find Annie. I wonder if she has a key to the house.'

'Has Sam managed to change the locks now?'

'I'm not sure.' Hugh strode away to the kitchen door, also decorated with crime scene tape, pulled keys from his pocket and tried one. The door opened. 'That answers our question.' He leaned past the tape and shouted Annie's name. No response.

'Depending on where she is, she might not hear,' Alex said.

'True, but we're not breaking the tape and I don't know how easy it would be for her to get in without messing it up, either. She might also have locked the door behind her. That's a bit odd to think about if she was planning on getting out quickly if she had to.'

Mentally tired, Alex bowed her head. 'But she didn't have to be thinking of getting out, did she?'

'No,' Hugh said shortly. 'Why don't we get out of here? It isn't helping a thing.'

'Without finding Annie?'

'Of course not. We need to call her.'

'Darn, why didn't I think of that immediately?' She waited a moment but Hugh made no attempt to use his own mobile. As they walked back around to the front of the house, Alex took out her own phone and found Annie's number.

Five rings and a cut off with no message.

'Nothing. Now what?'

'I don't get it,' Hugh said and started to run. 'Let's check her car again and call the police . . . damn it.'

When they reached the driveway there was no sign of the red-and-white Mini.

Rubbing the back of his neck, Hugh walked to look down the driveway.

'Something's wrong,' Alex called after him. 'Does Annie know you got the Subaru? She'd have recognized it – and she couldn't have driven behind the house or we would have seen her.'

'I don't think she has any reason to know what car I drive – other than the Nash.'

He jogged back, opened her door and ran around to hop into the driver's seat without waiting for her. Alex made it inside the vehicle seconds before he drove away, spitting gravel as she went. 'She can't have gone far.' And to emphasize his hurry, Hugh floored the accelerator. After the slightest slowdown, he shot into the lane and downhill. When they reached the bottom there was no Mini in sight to left or right.

'Let's try her phone again,' Alex said, phone in hand. He turned the corner, pulled over and switched off the engine – and took the phone from her. Alex continued, 'I don't know what we should do or say first. What if she was embarrassed for us to know she'd been at Green Friday? The only reason would be to go over the places where she and Elyan were happy, or she's now convinced herself they were.'

The ringing of the cell phone startled them both.

Hugh held up a hand and answered. 'Annie? It's Hugh. Where are you?' He looked at Alex. 'No, nothing wrong. I haven't seen you today and wondered what you're up to. You know I like to be sure you're all right.' He raised his eyebrows.

For a short while he listened, a frown deepening. 'In Bourton-on-the-Water shopping?' He stuffed the fingers of his free hand into his hair. 'Well that's great. Good for you to get out a bit farther afield. Alex and I took a few hours off to catch our breath, too. Have you given any thought to finding a more permanent place to live?' He grimaced as if he regretted the question. 'OK, we'll talk about it later. Alex will have some ideas.' He put the phone on the console between them.

Alex raised her palms in question. She glanced behind them to make sure they weren't holding up any traffic.

'Supposedly she's shopping in Bourton-on-the-Water. Says she needs new Cotswold threads; whatever that means.'

'But . . .' She shook her head.

'The answer is, I don't know,' Hugh said, cutting her off. 'I'm fond of Annie – you know that – but it doesn't mean I understand her.'

'And I shouldn't wonder what her car was doing at your place? It wasn't a mirage. I don't believe she's where she says she is.'

'Shoot. I'm going to forget it. If she made a getaway while we were looking around the grounds and she doesn't want to talk about it, so what?'

Sirens sounded, growing closer until a fire engine roared and shrieked on the road behind them, lights flashing, and turned up Trap Lane.

Alex watched in the side mirror while two other vehicles screeched past.

'What the hell?' Hugh said, craning to look over his shoulder again.

'We'd better go back and check,' Alex said.

'It's been hot,' Hugh said. 'Everything's very dry. Could be there's a flash fire in the hills.'

Alex drummed her fingers on her knee. Hugh pulled a U-turn and drove back the way they'd come through the still churning dust thrown up by the emergency vehicles. She didn't speak again and neither did Hugh.

Following the rigs, they passed the driveway to Green Friday, pulled up on the verge. 'Oh, no,' Alex said. 'They've gone to Radhika's house. What on earth's happened?' Fire crackled and smoke billowed into the sky. With Hugh, she ran up the driveway in the wake of the emergency trucks. Alex dragged in breaths as she went, her heart beating so hard it hurt.

It was Hugh who stopped her from going all the way to the house. He pulled her back and wrapped his arms around her. 'Hush,' he said. 'Just . . .' But he didn't tell her what she should just do.

'Radhika could be in there?' she said, struggling free. She held her mobile already and called Radhika who answered immediately. 'Where are you?' Alex said, scarcely able to breathe.

'On my way to Trap Lane,' she said. 'My house is on fire.

Don't worry, please. The responders are already there. I will talk to you later. Goodbye.'

Alex massaged her temples and looked at the scene ahead. Flames shot out of an upper window on one side of the house – and they engulfed not only the walls, but the roof of the tower.

TWENTY

oc James stopped Lily from heading for the kitchen and steered her into one of his living-room armchairs. He tugged off his own shoes and tossed them aside. 'Sit down all of you. Let me catch my breath and I'll get us all something to make us feel better.'

That, Tony thought, would have to be some magic elixir. He felt like hell and looking around at Alex and Hugh, he doubted if they had any more faith than he did in anything Doc might have on offer.

'Would that be crack or some good opioids?' Hugh said flatly, surprising Tony.

'I doubt if you've got anything to ameliorate this disaster,' Alex said. She leaned her head back and closed her eyes. 'What a god-awful mess. I'm saying my prayers Bill doesn't show up on the doorstep with a bucket load of fresh questions. And I don't know what to say to Radhika. She was shocked – who wouldn't be?'

'At least no one's been hurt,' Lily said. 'It's a setback, a huge setback, but Radhika will rebuild.'

'I don't get why Bill said you could leave the scene – just like that,' Doc said. 'It's not like him.'

'Don't look at me,' Tony said. 'All I know is what you know. Hugh and Alex showed up at the Black Dog looking as if they'd been to a hanging – or barely escaped going to a hanging.' And he sure as hell wanted to know a whole lot more but knew better than to push until Alex was ready to talk.

'They wouldn't have told us to leave if they'd known—'

'Let's not get ahead of ourselves,' Hugh cut in, shutting off whatever Alex had intended to say.

She looked at him and her tired face hardened. 'That's enough covering up,' she said shortly. 'We couldn't get any more in the way than we already were up there, but we have information the police need – and the fire department come to that. Annie must be brought into this. The sooner the better. Waiting will only make things worse.'

'Agreed.' Tony thought better of adding that he had wanted to go to Bill since yesterday.

Hugh stood up and paced. He shook his head, no, to the whiskey Doc offered him. 'First we have to think it through,' he said. 'I told you what she said on the phone. We can't drop her in it by telling the police her car was at Green Friday.'

'At Green Friday how long before we left – ten minutes max?' Alex said. 'No fire was visible at Radhika's when we got into your car to leave. We were in such a hurry to try and catch up with Annie's Mini, we didn't even look back at the houses again. She couldn't have been where she said she was when you finally got her on the phone. That was no more than another ten minutes before we knew there was a fire at Radhika's.'

'There has to be another explanation,' Hugh said.

Alex got up and stood in front of Hugh. She poked him in the chest. 'I listened to you up there when you asked me to leave it to you to explain to Bill. You didn't say a word, Hugh. What was that about? What aren't you saying?'

'This is all very interesting,' Doc said. 'Would you mind filling us in on what you're talking about? Where does Annie come into this latest disaster?'

Turning away from Hugh, Alex faced the rest of them. 'When we got to Green Friday, the red-and-white Mini Annie drives was parked in the driveway. That's the car Elyan used to drive. There was no sign of Annie. We couldn't find her on the property and when we got ready to leave, the Mini was gone. When we finally got hold of Annie she said she was shopping in Bourton-on-the-Water. She couldn't have been. There was no way she . . .' She met Tony's eyes and he raised his brows. 'We should have asked how she got there. She didn't have to be the one driving the Mini this afternoon.'

'So call her again and ask her,' Tony said. He threw up his hands. 'I don't mean just ask her flat out. We can come up with a way to get to it, can't we? Ask her to pick something up in Bourton-on-the-Water? Ask if she has room for it in the Mini? Hell, I don't know.' He did know they had to do something and fast before a few Folly inhabitants got hauled up on obstruction charges.

'Like what?' Hugh asked. 'A refrigerator? An elephant?'

'Give us a better idea, then,' Tony shot back. He'd had it with Hugh lately. Here they all were talking through theories with the one person who seemed a possible, if not likely, candidate for involvement in serious crimes.

'The police would check CCTV for sightings of her car where she says she's been,' Alex said. Always the down-to-earth one. 'They would already be on it if they knew. I want to call Bill now.'

Hugh produced his phone. 'Let me call Annie first,' he said. 'I know what I'll say.' His mobile rang before he could use it. 'Hello, Annie.'

'Glad you found your mobile,' Alex muttered.

'Be quiet, please,' Hugh said, ignoring Alex. He listened to the mobile for long enough to make Tony expect him to hang up. He half-turned away from them. 'Well, isn't that lovely,' he said, not sounding his usual cool self. 'Enjoy yourself. I wanted to remind you about getting the air in your tires checked? Did you do that? I told you the left rear looked low.'

Alex shook her head with frustration.

'Well, I did mention it,' Hugh said. 'Where are you now?'

Tony tried to signal that he wanted to add something about needing proof. He got no acknowledgement from Hugh who was frowning. 'Still? Well – stop at the petrol station and check your tires. Right, see you whenever you get back.'

'What did she say?' Doc said.

Hugh snapped his fingers and looked at Lily. 'Before I forget. Any problems telling Perry and Neve we don't have room for them anymore?'

'I haven't reached them, but I will,' Lily said, displaying irritation – like the rest of them. 'Annie, Hugh?'

'Says she's still in Bourton – with a friend she met. They're going to have dinner. She'll check the tires on the Mini before driving back. That's likely to be late tonight, if at all.'

TWENTY-ONE

'What do you think Radhika will want to do?' Dan asked Bill. He had given Dr Wolf the slip, or rather he'd called LeJuan with instructions to inform the good doctor that personal business would prevent Dan from returning to work before tomorrow.

Bill had been quiet on the drive from Gloucester to Broadway and the Crown and Trumpet on Church Street. He was still quiet.

'Bill,' Dan prompted him. 'You OK?'

'Sure. Great. If I knew what Radhika was thinking I might really be great.'

'The fire was only today,' Dan said. 'There's a fair amount of damage, true, but it'll all get put back together and it may not take as long as you think once the investigation is completed and they get started.'

Bill looked into his glass and didn't respond.

'Do you feel like expanding on what you're thinking?' Dan persisted.

'She doesn't want to keep staying at Tony's clinic,' Bill said. 'Even though there's a whole unused flat upstairs and Tony's told her it's great to have her there and checking on things. Radhika still thinks she's taking advantage. She's shocked, of course, and probably frightened though she'd never admit that.'

The man was deeply troubled and for once he was letting it show. 'Is she frightened because there's talk of arson?'

'What do you think?' Bill drank some cider and smiled a little. 'Hairy Ferret. With a name like that, it's as well it's damn good cider. She thinks – again she hasn't said it – but she thinks someone wanted to hurt her. I'm sure of that.'

'I don't believe that was it.' Dan thought he knew what was bothering Bill and it wasn't only the manor house damage. 'If it was arson, and I think it was, the fire was set in the tower but it was obvious she wasn't there. All the fire chief has told us is that he thinks it started on that spiral stone staircase.

Probably went slowly at first, then worked upward. There's an attic opening to the rest of the house from those stairs and if it went through there, that's what caused fire to spread across. It was only in the first upper rooms of the house.'

'So you think what they wanted most was to burn down the tower?'

'We'll have to leave that to fire investigators,' Bill said. He sipped his cider. 'Do you want to share what else is on your mind?'

A bartender called out Dan's name and he went to pick up two plates of haddock in deep golden batter, and chips.

The pub was old, seventeenth century, the cozy, open bars running from one to another. Spindle chairs clustered among dark polished tables and high-backed settles with upholstered cushions. The arrangement gave customers intimate spaces although there were only scattered early diners and drinkers on this Sunday evening.

He put down the plates and sat again. They would nurse their drinks. It looked bad when plods got stopped for drink driving.

'Tuck into that,' he told Bill, trying to sound more cheerful than he felt.

They ate in silence for a few moments.

'It's good,' Bill said. 'I've always liked this place.'

'Are you settled in that new flat?' *Not subtle, Dan.* 'I'm thinking of moving but I'll see how Calum reacts to the idea. Kids get attached to homes – not that it is his home now he's in Ireland with his mother.'

Bill put down his knife and fork and tented his hands. 'Do you ever think about marrying again?'

Bingo! He thought about his answer. 'I might like to. Sometimes I'd definitely like to. No prospects on the horizon, though.' These days he tried not to think about Alex too deeply. He couldn't change her feelings, or become the man she wanted to be with.

'I'm damned if I know what I want to do,' Bill said and took a hefty pull on his cider. 'That's a lie. I think I know but I don't want to rock any boats, not now. Not ever.'

'Don't let the boat sail,' Dan said and immediately regretted it. 'I only mean that sometimes you can put something off until it's not possible anymore . . . hell, I hope you know what I mean.'

'Yes, I do. Radhika and I have talked about where we go from here but only around the edges. I know there's love there, and everything else we need to be together, but what if . . .' He shook his head slowly from side to side. 'Timing will be everything. I don't want her to think I'm only interested in getting her to live with me and using the fire as an excuse.' He blushed, not something Dan ever remembered seeing before.

Smart Alec comments were usually a bad idea, definitely at this moment. 'You'll sort it out, Bill. I'm no advertisement for relationship success but I may be wiser than I used to be about some things. Talk to me whenever you feel like it. Just unload. That can help.'

'Right,' Bill said but Dan doubted the man would voluntarily pour out his guts again anytime soon.

'Nothing from the diver up at the pond so far,' he said.

'He'd hardly been in the water when the fire at Radhika's started,' Bill said. 'They heard the calls, and saw smoke, and had the diver come back up. All he'd reached was what they say looks like the first radio made – and fossilized. Junk. The thing is really deep. They knocked off for an hour or so when the fire at Radhika's was reported. Already being so close like that, they wanted to stand by in case they were needed, but they're going back at it. I expect to hear they're either through for the night or just through, period. Looks like they'll have to go back tomorrow. Bloody waste of time and money.'

'Evening, sir – guv.' LeJuan arrived and slid to sit in a chair opposite Dan and Bill. He gave one of his famous grins. 'Thought you might be glad to see me.'

'Do we look that hard up?' Bill said, deadpan.

LeJuan put a manila envelope on the table and turned to look at the counter. 'Can I interest anyone else in a drink – another drink?'

When he got no takers, he went to the bar and returned with a glass of what looked like pale ale, and a bag of crisps. The latter he opened and crunched down rapidly while Bill continued eating and Dan stared at the envelope.

'Interested?' Crumpling the empty crisp bag with one hand, LeJuan pushed the thick packet back and forth on the table with one long forefinger.

Dan shrugged. 'You'll tell us about it if you want to. Won't he, Bill?'

'Get on with it!' Bill made a move toward LeJuan's prize, but he whipped it up.

'If you insist.' LeJuan revealed a sheet of notes and photographs of different sizes kept separated by their own clear sleeves. 'This is all better on a screen but you'll get the idea. The original,' he said, producing the fuzzy photo that had accompanied the one of Hugh found on a bed at Green Friday.

Other shots, some large, some close-ups of details, were soon spread out. Dan moved their plates to a nearby empty table and the three men huddled together to look.

Eventually Bill crossed his arms and said, 'Impressive work with the original, but if this is a big reveal, I'm not getting it.' For which Dan was grateful since he could merely appear impassive.

'Yeah, right,' LeJuan said meaningfully. 'These don't mean a thing to either of you. Look at the wall behind the man. Graffiti art. Brilliant graffiti art.'

'If you say so,' Dan commented.

'Not on my garden walls,' Bill added.

LeJuan only grinned. 'First, you don't have a garden, so no garden walls. Second, these things are worth a chunk by some artists. More than a chunk. People used to pay this man a fortune to do one of these. And he didn't just paint outside walls. He was in art galleries.'

'Not the Louvre,' Bill muttered.

'Does the name Zack in connection with graffiti art – also called urban art or street art – mean anything to you?'

Dan matched Bill's negative shake of the head.

'Well, that's who he is. Zack – one name only. But there's something else he's more famous for. Real name, Scott Zachary Wilson. Ring any bells yet?'

'He's . . .' Bill leaned farther forward and lowered his voice. 'He murdered his parents in the Lake District? Windermere?'

Now Dan remembered. He ought to. The case had been

luridly reported in every gruesome detail, together with the killer's attempt to flee followed by an ambush arrest in which a SWAT team member was badly wounded.

They passed the photos between them and read notes about the process of the examination that had been done, together with a summary of the crime on another sheet of paper.

'The big question is, what was it doing together with a picture of Hugh among our missing woman's possessions – a woman we're presuming is Sonia Quillam?' Bill said.

LeJuan propped his jaw on a hand. 'We don't know, but Zachary Wilson is in the same forensic psych facility as Elyan Quillam.'

TWENTY-TWO

Alex had driven from Folly to Broadway. She parked in the center of the village at Church Close, walked behind the Court Arcade shopping area and around the block to the Crown and Trumpet. Juste Vidal, helping out in the bar at the Black Dog, told her LeJuan had brought in some flyers and said that Bill might be late back to the inn because he was going to the Crown and Trumpet in Broadway.

Each step took her closer until she paused at the path up to the open front door of the pub to take some calming breaths. A happy crowd filled wooden tables and benches in the forecourt – most enjoying an early-evening drink. Striped umbrellas were still up although the bright day had dimmed.

The flyers had shown a good photo of Sonia above a plea for any information concerning her whereabouts. Alex's stomach flipped, and flipped again. She hadn't told any of the others what she was doing, but they had all thought Bill had to be told what they knew – even if it did not turn out to be helpful.

'Hello, there, Alex.' LeJuan startled her, striding from the pub, giving her one of his stunning smiles.

Before she could reply, he added, 'Doing a recce on the competition, or looking for my boss and his former boss?'

Alex stood still, hands on hips. 'And that's why you're a detective. It only took you two tries to solve the question. How are you, LeJuan?' How long, she wondered, would it take to stop remembering the nickname Bill had used for his sergeant?

He gave a so-so waggle of his left hand. 'Good enough, I suppose. We have a fly or two in our ointment right now but I'll save that for another time when we're both really bored. Go straight in then turn left. They're in a settle at the end. Backs to you.'

Alex wasn't surprised to find Dan with Bill. They were exactly where LeJuan had said she would find them. Bent forward, the two men were earnestly talking over several photographs spread on the table in front of them.

Alex walked behind them to approach Bill. 'Forgive me for interrupting,' she said. 'I tracked you down, Bill.'

'Hello, there,' Bill said, standing.

Dan gathered the photos together and slipped them into a manila envelope. 'Sit and join us,' he said. 'What can I get you to drink?'

'Bitter lemon, please. I'm driving. I didn't know you were into graffiti art.'

Bill glanced back at the table. 'Graffiti art?'

'Wasn't that a piece by Zack? He's very distinctive.'

'So LeJuan said. I wouldn't have thought it was your kind of art,' Dan said.

'I was in art school. I became a graphic artist eventually and worked in advertising. That's graphic, not graffiti.' She grinned. 'I can appreciate a lot of forms that are well done.' Alex didn't add that she and her ex-husband had owned a successful advertising business before their divorce.

'You wanted to see me?' Bill said.

Dan left for the counter and Alex sat in a spindle chair with a comfortable tapestry cushion on its seat. 'Yes, I do.' She checked around. People seemed engrossed in their own conversations. 'Perhaps I should wait until you're on your own?'

'You can talk freely with Dan here. He's aware of the case. We talk.'

She smiled again. 'I'm glad you do. You were a great team, weren't you?'

'I like to think so.' He took a swallow from his glass and crossed his arms.

In the midst of a steady hum of voices, the two of them became an island of silence – Bill evidently deeply lost in thought. While he seemed distracted, Alex tried to organize what she should say and how. Somehow it would be easier if they were going to be alone.

'Bitter lemon,' Dan said, placing the glass in front of her and taking his seat again. When he looked at her, she felt a little sad. In a different time and place they might have been much more to one another.

'This isn't easy,' she said. 'You won't be happy with everything I've got to say. I haven't been as forthcoming as I should have been but I haven't forgotten what you told me about the real meaning of loyalty, Bill, when I came to see you at the parish hall. Although I'm still not sure I'm comfortable with the possible answers.'

He was alert now, focused on her – but not saying anything to ease her into the exchange.

'This morning I went out for a drive with Hugh. We needed to clear the air. Up until now we've had a really good working relationship – and we're friends – but it all changed after his cousin and the cousin's wife showed up. And afterwards with what happened at Green Friday . . . and other things.' She was afraid of saying more than was needed.

'I'm glad you came,' Bill said, but his body language let her know he was fully engaged and vigilant. 'I'm going to take notes, but don't let that disturb you.'

It did disturb her, but she said nothing while he took notebook and pen from his inside jacket pocket.

There was nothing she could explain about following Sergeant Miller to Burford and knowing she was after Hugh – nothing that would help.

'In your own time,' Bill said evenly.

'Today. When we left the Black Dog, Hugh wanted to go up to Green Friday. I couldn't understand why and said so. That almost ended the expedition, but he drove on and explained he wanted to check the house – unless it was still being kept off limits. The tapes were up but there wasn't a policeman there.'

Bill grunted and wrote while Dan's face showed no reaction.

'When we got to Green Friday, Annie's Mini was parked on the far side of the turnaround.' She caught her bottom lip between her teeth and waited, gauging how to go on.

Both men looked at her. 'Go on,' Bill said.

Alex drank some of her bitter lemon and coughed. More people were gradually filling tables and she was relieved. The activity blunted a sensation of isolation with the two detectives.

'We checked that Hugh's keys still worked – we wondered if Sam Brock might have changed the locks already. The old keys worked but we didn't go in – not through the front or the back door.' She took a long breath. 'We did call out to see if Annie might be in the house.'

'But she wasn't,' Bill said, noncommittal.

'No. We looked around outside including the pool house and there was no sign of anyone.'

'Despite the Mini being parked at the house?'

'Yes.' She hadn't done anything wrong but felt guilty. 'I've been meaning to tell you I'm just about certain that Mercedes wasn't parked outside the kitchen windows when I went with Sam and Hugh that morning. I kept thinking I must have been too off balance to notice. But now I'm sure that's not the case.' Her own pointless prattling embarrassed her.

Bill nodded sympathetically. 'It can be hard to be certain of some things when you've got a lot on your mind like that. Did you or Hugh look inside Annie's Mini?'

'Yes. Hugh did but there was nothing of interest there.'

'Did he do that before or after you left to go to the back of the house.'

'Before.'

'You didn't see any sign of Annie anywhere?'

'No.'

'Did you take another look after you'd finished searching the area?'

Alex felt a flush climb her neck. 'The Mini was gone by then?'

Without meeting her eyes, Bill set his pen down. Dan did look at her although his expression remained neutral.

'We got in Hugh's Subaru and we drove out to see if we

could see the car but there was no sign. The ring road at the bottom of Trap Lane was empty in both directions.'

'You were at the Manor House when I got there. What made you drive back?' Bill was writing again.

'We pulled over to think and to try to call Annie. A fire engine and police car turned up Trap Lane and we followed. We wanted to see where they were going in case it was Green Friday. Then we found out. You know everything that happened after that.'

Drumming his fingers on the notebook, Bill averted his face. When he turned back his expression was unreadable but it was no longer neutral. 'And where was Annie by the time you called her?'

'She phoned us and said she was at Bourton-on-the-Water shopping.'

For the first time, Bill and Dan looked at each other.

'How did she get there?' Bill asked.

Alex swallowed. 'She said she was in her car. But when we were at Doc's house she told Hugh she'd met an old friend and they were going to have dinner and Annie might not go back to Folly tonight. That was a second call a couple of hours later. She called us.' In fact it had been rather longer than two hours. 'Like I said, we talked to her before that. Then later I was glad to be in touch again to make sure she was all right. I was wondering if she parked her car and forgot where it was. That can take time to work out. Or she could have had a lot of errands . . .'

'You know as well as I do, Alex, that it's impossible to drive from Green Friday to Bourton in a short space of time. That's what you're suggesting she did, isn't it?'

Utter misery squeezed at her. 'Couldn't they look at the CCTV cameras and traffic cameras to try to find out when she got there? Maybe it was another Mini we saw.'

Bill rested his elbows on the table and pushed his fingers into his short, thick hair. 'Do you realize what a difference it might have made if you and Hugh had told us about this during the fire?'

'Yes,' she whispered.

'Have you heard of perversion of justice?'

'Yes.'

TWENTY-THREE

'**B**lues and twos,' Bill snapped.

Dan followed instructions, opening his window and slapping the light on the roof of the car. The siren issued its double wail.

Communications batted back and forth from the radio.

'Right,' Bill said. He was speeding. 'Let's get there and see what's up.'

'Not far to go.' Dan knew better than to warn his ex-partner to slow down. 'This has turned into a hellish night. We need Annie and now, but they're on it. I can't work out the whole Mini, Bourton-on-the-Water story. She lied, but I don't have the faintest why.'

They drove into Folly and took the hill road toward the Dimple.

'Hugh isn't coming clean, either,' Bill said. 'You could say Alex should have told us about the Mini the moment she saw us, but Hugh was doing all the talking. Not a dicky bird. You don't think he's got a thing for the girl, do you?'

Dan braced himself with both hands on the dash and took his time to answer. 'No, she's young enough to be his daughter.'

'When has that stopped some people?' Bill gave a short laugh. 'But I agree it seems unlikely. The difficult part of dealing with Hugh is that the man seems so damned honorable – or so I think.'

'He is or was honorable,' Dan said. 'But somehow he's up to his neck in this.'

'Lamb here,' Bill said, interrupting the brief comments over the radio. 'You think it's important? What does that mean?'

'Diver is using lights, sir. Says he can't get the job done any faster and believe me, we've been pushing.'

'But what does he think he's got and why can't he bring it up? He must have a pretty good idea by now.'

This time a female officer answered. 'There are ledges and

places where the chute narrows. He thinks it's a body caught up. Very deep.'

Bill glanced sideways at Dan. 'Holy shit,' he said with feeling. 'I was expecting Percy's mobile or something we'd have to pray the magicians could do something with. How in hell can there be another body?'

'I think we're both avoiding the obvious,' Dan said, hanging on while Bill cut the corner at Trap Lane and sped upward, bumping madly over dried-out ruts.

Bill's grim silence was all he got as a reply.

'You do think it's her?' Dan pressed.

They passed the entrances to Green Friday and Radhika's house.

'Yeah,' Bill finally said. 'If so, there's a list of people to pick up and get in for questioning. It's a mess. A damned mess. What is it I haven't seen? Is it something so obvious the egg on my face is getting thicker by the second?'

'I feel your pain,' Dan said, and he did. 'I've been there too many times but if you've missed something, that makes two of us.'

'If I thought it was possible, I'd wonder if we're looking at a supposed murder, and a suicide. The Quillam's boy was worse than wrong but both of them played their parts in that. But Sonia couldn't have got Percy into that pond – or chute as the officer rightly called it – not on her own.'

'So,' Dan said, adding up pieces faster than was wise at this point. 'Either Percy did Sonia, then his heart gave out and he hit his head, or we'll be looking at Sonia having a strong helper. If that's the case, it's likely to look as if whoever that was turned on her.'

Lights at the scene grew stronger, lit up the sky. Bill reached the end of the drivable lane and parked behind the investigators' vehicles.

They were out of the car simultaneously and climbing the last distance to the pond, weaving between trees and kicking through scrub toward the spotlights.

Near the pond, Molly Lewis and Werner Berg were an unexpected surprise and one look at Bill told Dan he wasn't thrilled to see the pair. Either of them would prefer to get a first look at a crime scene when possible.

'Molly,' Bill said and nodded at Werner. 'How did you know to come?'

'I have my sources,' Molly said with a small smile. She gave Werner a narrow-eyed stare which clearly didn't trouble him. 'I didn't want a repeat of what happened with Percy Quillam's body.'

'Are you intending to dive this evening, Molly,' Werner asked, straight-faced.

She actually grinned. 'I'm intending to see this body as it comes out of the water, my friend.'

'But the diver will have to move it,' Werner persisted. 'I thought you wanted a body kept *in situ* until you'd seen it.'

Molly slipped her arm through Werner's and they turned back to the pond. Dan didn't see any unsteadiness in her gait this time.

'Those two banter like an old married couple – admittedly with offbeat topics for most,' Bill said. 'I wonder if they see each other when there are no results of a crime around.'

'What would they talk about?' Dan said and they both chuckled.

'I think he's coming up,' an officer called out. He wore a headset with a mic and was in contact with the diver. 'Yes, he is. With a body.'

Werner went directly to kneel beside the water with other members of his SOCO team. A videographer and photographer stood ready to roll.

The diver's slick, wet-suited head broke the surface.

The cameras were instantly in action and instructions shouted.

Molly moved close, bent forward. Once more Werner moved to her side.

Without removing his mask, the diver struggled, and used both arms to haul his burden to face level, then lifted a flaccid, dripping body toward team members at the ready.

'Bloody hell,' Bill muttered. 'I want this tosser in custody. Vicious son-of-a-bitch.'

Stretched on the trampled grass there was no doubt they were looking at the corpse of the victim of a terrible beating.

'Not Sonia,' Dan said, knowing it was an unnecessary comment.

Activity was immediately intense with Molly at the center.

Bill joined her and sat on his haunches, accepting rubber gloves. The scene would be a bear to record and document – especially by the lights that threw the body into sharp focus but tended to flatten shading in the surrounding area.

'Huh,' Molly said. 'I doubt this one's been in the water more than a few hours. Any guesses on identity?' She got a chorus of negatives in response.

'Yeah, I know him, or I believe I do,' Bill said quietly when Dan joined him. 'How about you?'

'It is – or it was – Wells Giglio, poor bastard,' Dan said.

TWENTY-FOUR

The envelope had languished in a pile of unopened post all day. Alex had not found it until she got back from the Crown and Trumpet several hours ago and then she had been busy and stuffed it in her pocket.

Hugh usually made sure she saw anything addressed only to her when it arrived but, again, he was distracted. Each time they interacted she grew more anxious. He was distant and silent. Accepting that there was nothing she could do to change whatever inner battles he was fighting did nothing to soothe her jumpiness.

Finally the pub was empty, the clean-up done and the staff had gone home. Hugh barely said goodnight before disappearing upstairs.

She took a cup of tea and sat where Mary and Harriet had sat that evening. Bogie was still in front of the dwindling fire with Katie, both asleep, their backs pressed together. Tony was dealing with a difficult delivery of a foal on a nearby farm.

The tea, Typhoo with just the right amount of milk, tasted perfect. If it kept her awake, so much the better. This didn't promise to be an early night.

With one thumb, she opened the envelope, leaving the ragged edges Tony rarely failed to mention as he tried to get her to use a paper knife.

Several printed sheets slid out, the top one a letter, the others covered with a bullet-pointed series of numbers and what she hoped were explanations.

With a hand at her throat, she read the letter . . . and dropped the whole sheaf onto her lap.

There was no apparent reason why she couldn't become pregnant again. Fiddle the explanations – that was all she needed to know. Laugh or cry? Both, she thought and laughed while she sniffled and dug out tissues.

The tears subsided to an ache in her throat. Alex was happy! Until this moment, she had swung between wanting this news and fearing how she would feel if it came – or didn't.

There was no wondering about how Tony would feel. She blotted her eyes, drank some tea and tucked letter and envelope back into a pocket.

Tony wanted to get married – even though there wasn't a pregnancy yet and might never be. Taking a deep, calming breath, Alex whispered a mantra: *You will know what to do and when it should be done.* With eyes closed, she nodded firmly.

Once again she was smiling and a shaky, happy sensation bubbled inside her.

The sounds came of someone opening the front door of the inn. She waited to see if footsteps crossed the restaurant and went upstairs.

They didn't.

With Jillian Miller and another detective, Bill Lamb walked through into the bar and gave her a brief nod before taking a seat at the table by the fire. 'Glad to find you still up,' he said. 'Where's Hugh?'

'Upstairs.' She stopped herself from asking why he wanted to know.

'This is Detective Constable Liberty,' Bill said, motioning the tall man into one of the chairs. 'You already know Sergeant Miller. Did Annie show up yet?'

'No.'

'Which room is she in?'

'It doesn't have a number – it's usually mine. Straight ahead at the top of the stairs.' Alex controlled the urge to ask why he wanted to know.

'And Hugh's number?'

'It's at the far end of the corridor. All it says on the door is "Private".'

At Bill's signal, Sergeant Miller left on her tapping, high-heeled pumps. A second inclination of the inspector's head and Detective Constable Liberty followed her.

'Tony?' Bill asked. 'Where is he?' His light and piercing blue eyes had taken on the expressionless quality she remembered so well. In this mood, he disturbed her.

She hadn't answered the last query and he leaned closer over the table, waiting.

'He's at the Drake farm. Emergency delivery out there.'

'How long does something like that take?'

'As long as it takes,' she told him tersely. 'Mares mostly do very well but a birth can be difficult. Why?' she ended with a question this time.

'To find out if I'm likely to be able to talk to you on your own. We can always go to the parish hall – or into Gloucester, if you prefer.'

'Have I done something else wrong since we talked earlier?' This veiled aggression wasn't lost on her. 'You're obviously ticked off with me.'

He leaned back in his chair and stared into space, then got up and took off his jacket. His loosened tie already hung from his unbuttoned shirt collar. 'I'm not ticked off with anyone, Alex. Just doing my job, which isn't always easy around here. We need to talk about when Wells Giglio came in here. Are you up for that?'

'Yes. I came to you of my own accord about that already.'

'Thank you. I'm glad you did. Now there are more questions. Do you remember who was here when Giglio arrived?'

She shifted in her chair and glanced at her cold tea. 'Would you like tea or coffee?' Civility mattered.

He blinked as if his eyes were gritty. 'I think I'll have a Doom Bar,' he said. 'Have something yourself. You're not driving tonight, right?'

'No. And I think it's morning now. Are you going to pinch me for serving after hours?' She smiled.

'Not this time.'

Carrying the cup with her, she went to pull a pint of Doom Bar. She should have asked him if he was driving. Giggling wouldn't help her image. A clear head sounded like a better idea than alcohol.

'Thanks,' Bill said when she brought the beer. 'Are Hugh's relatives still here?'

'I think so. They haven't been mentioned since Hugh brought them up. That was hours ago.'

'Why did he mention it?'

She wasn't cut out for analyzing every word before she spoke. 'I think they're going to leave the Black Dog. I've seen very little of them – the man hardly at all. I'm not sure if they're going home to Scotland or just moving on somewhere.'

'But they've said they're going?'

A flush threatened and she wished she could hide her face. 'Hugh asked them to go,' she said, then had an inspiration. 'We've got prior bookings and we need that room.'

Bill's shrewd look unsettled her – even more. 'You're naturally honest, aren't you?' he said.

'Yes. OK, Hugh doesn't like his cousin and his wife and he would prefer them to stay elsewhere. We haven't discussed it but his feelings are obvious. He told my mum to arrange for them to leave.'

'Good enough.' The notebook appeared again, and the pen. 'Think back to when Giglio came in here. Who do you remember being here?'

'Some of the regulars, of course,' Alex said. 'Harriet and Mary Burke were here which was unusual for the middle of the day, though. Hugh remarked on that – although I'm thinking they've come around that time a bit more frequently of late. Annie was here, but I said that to you before.'

The pen was running out of ink and Bill shook it several times before giving up and finding another. He wrote rapidly. 'Go over it all again for me, please. Sometimes you remember something you'd forgotten before.'

'There were drop-ins that didn't make an impression. I'm sure there were some regulars, too. Mainly it was Harvey and Carrie Peale and his friend, Saul. He's one of the Gentlemen's Biker Club members who hangs out with Harvey a good deal –

he's interested in Harvey's writing. Hugh was working the bar with me.'

'Tell me what happened.'

'I already did.'

'Help me out here, Alex. Go over it again.'

'I don't understand what you think I didn't say.' She didn't, but she was so afraid of being trapped into saying something she'd regret.

Bill took a swallow of his bitter. 'You will in time. It's not you who has me on edge, but others do. We're in dangerous territory. People have died and I don't want to believe I could have stopped others from the same fate, do you?'

She shook her head, no. 'Annie and Carrie were at a table with Carrie's husband, Harvey. Saul was with them. Wells just came walking in and sounding angry. What he said made it seem as if he was accusing Annie of knowing more than she's saying – about Sonia being missing, or wherever she is.'

'OK.' Bill sank into thought.

'Did you find Sonia?'

He raised his eyes, appeared to consider, then said, 'No. I wish we had. You told me Wells threw accusations of a sort at Annie. Was there more?'

'Not really,' Alex said. 'He got hustled outside and that was it.'

'Did Hugh take him out?'

She thought about that. 'No. Saul took him by the arm – Wells isn't the kind to struggle – and Saul hurried him quietly outside. That was it. I got Annie to go back upstairs to her room and relax. She was really upset – shaken. Annie's been through much too much in the last couple of years.'

'She has,' Bill agreed. 'But today you didn't actually speak with her?'

'No. Hugh did. I think Annie relies on him. She sees him as a kind of father figure.'

'Why is that?'

Traps on every side. 'Just because he's an old friend of both hers and Elyan's. I'm sure he tells her about his visits with Elyan.'

'Why would he be close to Elyan?' Bill moved his glass backward and forward on the table, leaving a damp trail.

Alex hadn't expected the question. 'I'm not sure. He knew Sonia before, I'm aware of that. That would be how the Quillams came to rent Green Friday. Hugh only rents to friends or people recommended by friends.'

'Not family?' Bill commented. 'His cousin and his wife weren't offered Green Friday?'

'I have no idea.' These seemingly innocent questions could lead to avenues best left unexplored.

Bill turned a page in his notebook. 'So you think Hugh feels he should visit Elyan because of what? Being cozy with Sonia at one time?'

He looked tired but Alex didn't feel as sympathetic as she might have. 'Ask Hugh these things, Bill. I didn't meet Hugh until long after he was whatever he was to Sonia and I don't know why he considers visiting Elyan something he should do.'

If Bill was chagrined, it didn't show. 'Routine questions, Alex. You're always free to say you can't answer. Back to Wells Giglio. He didn't return to the Black Dog after he was shown the door?'

'He did not.'

'Annie went upstairs. Did the Peales stay?'

Knowing where all this was leading might help. 'They did but I don't recall for how long. I spoke with Carrie again but only briefly. She went back to their table.'

'What did you talk about?'

'Mugs,' she said, deliberately brief and expressionless, and this time she didn't blush at the slight fabrication.

'Mugs?'

'Carrie is a potter. She's going to make Black Dog mugs for us to sell here.' She avoided more comments on Harvey. 'I like to use locally sourced goods of all kinds. Carrie is very good.'

'You're sure you didn't see Wells again after he left the bar?'

'Absolutely sure. And I don't know where he went. Probably drove off in a temper. I won't be surprised to see him back, unfortunately.'

Bill gave her one of his long, silent, unblinking stares.

Miller walked rapidly to join her boss. 'Hugh Rhys isn't here, either, guv. We've looked all over. Longlegs is checking outside one more time, but the only parked cars are ours and Ms Duggins'.'

TWENTY-FIVE

He would have to suggest Annie not call him for a while. If the police questioned him again, which they would, they could decide to ask for his phone and computer. They were welcome to the computer. He would get a new mobile with a new number rather than have Annie's recent messages raise questions.

Hugh drove the dark and winding lanes toward Naunton. Why Naunton? He was damned if he knew why Annie would choose to go and hang out in a car park there – in the middle of the night. At least it was no distance from Folly. And the drive gave him the opportunity to be sure he was alone to think without interruption for a few minutes.

He had seen Neve early in the evening as she tried to slip through the front door of the Black Dog without encountering anyone. Before she could escape, he followed her out and asked when she and Perry would be moving on.

'When we feel like it unless you want to throw us out and make a scene in front of all your sycophants. Give me what I want and I'll go.'

And she'd walked to a dark green Mercedes parked at the curb. She got in, floored the petrol, and drove away too fast.

They must have somewhere else to stay while they kept the room at the inn for whatever purpose they had dreamed up. Hugh had checked on the rental property where he'd gone to meet them that morning in Burford but they were no longer there.

When he reached Naunton, the village was largely in darkness with lights showing at a few windows where night owls burned the late oil. Finding the car park was easy enough but despite Annie's request that he keep his headlights on low, he had to turn them on high to locate the Mini in a far corner and beneath trees.

Once he got close enough, he cut the lights and pulled

alongside. He rolled down his window, letting in the night scents. Annie's outline was clear but she didn't move from behind the wheel.

He got out and climbed in beside her. From the swollen and tear-stained eyes and face he guessed there was a lot on the girl's mind.

'Did you lock your car?' she said.

'Yes.'

'I'm locking this one.' Clicks sounded. 'You know I wouldn't call you like this if I knew what to do next. I don't.'

'Slow down. First, please don't call the number you have again. I'm replacing it and I'll let you know the new number.'

'Why?' Her voice rose and she turned sideways in her seat to look at him. 'What's wrong. Nobody knows anything, do they?'

'What is there to know, Annie? I'm just being cautious. We both know there have been difficult events and so far I've heard nothing to suggest any resolutions. What are you doing out here? You said you were staying with a friend.'

She took his hand and he was aware again of what a thin person she was.

'I didn't tell you everything yet,' she said and he could see the slick of more falling tears. 'Something's wrong with Elyan, it has to be. He's changed . . . toward me.'

Before getting into this, he wanted to know the reason for her being here rather than in her bed at the Black Dog. As yet, he had not had any luck trying to move her elsewhere.

'He hasn't changed toward you,' he said shortly. 'Again, why are you here? Could you tell me what's happened with you today and where exactly you've been?' He couldn't tell her about the fire or his suspicions about where she'd been early that afternoon. She'd take it as an accusation and be devastated. Not that he thought she'd had anything to do with what happened at Radhika's.

'I went shopping in Bourton-on-the-Water,' she said quietly. 'I was there a long time. I met a friend. Then I had trouble finding my car in the car park.'

That had been Alex's suggested reason for Annie's long absence.

'Did the two of you have dinner?'

She cleared her throat and said in an even softer voice, 'Yes.'

'So that's why you came to Naunton?' Giving her the third degree was embarrassing but necessary.

'I ate in Bourton-on-the-Water. At the Kingsbridge by the Windrush. The river makes me feel calm.'

'You ate there. What about your friend?'

'He didn't stay for dinner – I made that bit up. I wasn't ready to come back.'

'OK. Fair enough but you could just have said so.'

Annie swiped at her eyes. 'Everything's a muddle. I thought if I came here where I could talk to you it would all be clearer. It's not you, it's me going to see Sonia that started everything falling apart. I knew I was wrong to do that, I was warned.'

He took a breath. And another. 'When was that? When you saw Sonia?'

'Only about a week ago. It was a couple of nights, or maybe just one, before there was news of Percy Quillam's death in that horrible water. I went to ask Sonia to go and see Elyan. That was the other reason I came.'

She would tell him what she felt the need to say. He waited.

'I didn't think she would go even though she said she'd try. Then I heard stories about someone missing from Green Friday.'

'But you didn't go to the police, Annie?'

'No. I hope Sonia's all right but going to the police wouldn't help Elyan. I don't trust them.' She rested her head against the seat. 'They've only done him harm. I don't mean that what he did wasn't wrong, but he needed to be helped and not the way he's being treated in that place now.'

Hugh didn't think Annie had seen him at Green Friday when Sonia was there or she would have told him. 'When you first came to me at the Black Dog you were very upset. You weren't making a lot of sense. What made you say you believed Elyan didn't want you anymore? What makes you still believe it?'

'I was given a letter from him.' She cried openly again. 'I can't bear to think about it.'

'Elyan loves you even more than he ever has,' Hugh told her, holding back from physically comforting her. 'How did you get the letter? By mail, you mean?'

She shook her head, no. 'He sent it with someone. I promised I'd never say who and if I do, it could be bad for Elyan.'

Now he was vigilant, searching for answers. 'You're saying you were blackmailed not to reveal this?'

For a moment she remained quiet, then she sat up and made an effort to calm herself. 'No, not at all. It wasn't like that. They were trying to be kind and help us both. Please, Hugh, help me decide what I should do. Do I go back and try to see him again? I don't think I can . . . I can't just give up on him.'

As much as he wished Annie could start over, he understood her feelings. 'Follow me back to the Black Dog,' he said. 'A good night's sleep will help and we'll try to work out what to do over the next couple of days.'

'If I go to see Elyan – will you come with me?'

He couldn't say he thought that was a lousy idea, but he did. 'Please tell me who gave you the letter, Annie.'

'I can't!' She made a choking sound. 'Try to understand. I'm not being blackmailed, honestly, I'm not. But I'm afraid I might do something that could cause Elyan to get badly hurt – or die.'

TWENTY-SIX

Tony's arrival in the bar lifted Alex's spirits. He was a solid, logical presence just when she had felt her composure slipping away.

They sat with Bill now, a Courvoisier in front of them both, while Bill had opted for another half of bitter.

Tony kissed the top of her head and she smiled up at him. 'How did it go?'

'Well. Nice little filly, all present and correct. Mom's a champ and very pleased with the new arrival.'

'Good,' Bill said and Alex almost laughed at his blank expression.

'So,' Tony said, 'things were a bit quiet when I arrived. Any news you'd care to share with me?'

Alex kept quiet, waiting for Bill who took a slow, thoughtful swallow from his glass. 'We've been going over the afternoon Wells Giglio came in with his comments to Annie. Anything you'd like to add?'

'I wasn't here. I know what Alex has told me. I remember the man as theatrical in manner and it doesn't sound as if he's changed much.' Tony swirled his Courvoisier and sniffed deep over the rim of the glass.

'You didn't track him down yet?' Tony asked.

Bill looked into the last fading embers of the fire and said nothing.

Tony's raised eyebrows to Alex said it all. Something was definitely bugging Bill Lamb but, at least for now, he intended to keep them in suspense.

Snuffling, sleepy, Katie got up on slightly arthritic hips and rested her head on Tony's thigh. He stroked her gently, his big hand finding all the little places she liked to be touched the most. 'Good girl,' he said.

Her nose suddenly came up and quivered. Tony raised a forefinger in the air in a silent shush, then put the finger to his mouth. Bill was at instant attention and Alex tried to discern what Tony had heard. He looked between them and shook his head, narrowing his eyes and keeping pressure on Katie's neck.

The next sound was a key turning in the kitchen door and Alex frowned at him. Then she remembered Hugh was still out and started to relax. This time it was Bill's hand that went up and she felt both men holding their breath.

The kitchen door swished over stone tile. Rustling followed, but no other sound. Hugh must see the light on in the bar, yet he didn't call out.

Alex's heart beat harder.

There was an unintelligible whisper, then another. Soft foot-falls followed. The kitchen lights went out, then the bar lights. If it was Hugh he must think she'd left lights on for him until he got back.

She could not be the first one to call to him, but they were tricking him, she thought. Why didn't one of them speak out?

They heard no more until the wooden floor in the restaurant creaked.

By the faint glow from the colored outdoor lights that always

burned, Bill got up quietly and swiftly went through the bar
and into the corridor past the snug to the restaurant and inn.

'Hello, there,' Alex heard him say, as the bar lights came
back on. 'Late night for you two.'

Alex met Tony's eyes and they both winced.

'Hugh and Annie,' she said in a low voice. 'I think he went
looking for her.'

'I assumed no one was up,' Hugh said and his voice didn't
waver from its usual assurance. 'Annie rolled in right behind
me. Have a good night, Annie.'

'I'll have to ask you to wait, Annie,' Bill said. 'Hugh, why
don't you join Tony and Alex in the bar. I'll want to speak with
you as soon as I finish with Annie in the snug.'

Bill reminded himself that Annie was an adult and although he
would rather not get tough with her, neither could he show her
any preference if she proved uncooperative.

Her eyes were red and swollen. She was clearly subdued but
he made no comment and chose a table on the far side of the
snug from the wall adjoining the bar. The walls were thick but
caution never hurt. Longlegs and Miller were stationed outside
in a car. He was grateful one of them hadn't interrupted him
by mobile yet. Now he did call the detective constable and ask
him to join them and bring a jug and water and glasses.

'Just make yourself comfortable,' Bill told Annie, turning off
his mobile and slipping it in a pocket. 'One of my officers,
Detective Constable Liberty, will join us in a moment and bring
water for all of us. Having him with us is a formality. Nothing
to worry about.'

Not a word from Annie who sat still, hands in lap, her eyes
lowered.

Longlegs took a blessedly short time to arrive, fill glasses of
water and seat himself on another chair at the table. He took
out his notebook and Bill said, 'I've introduced you to Annie
Bell, Detective Constable Liberty.'

Longlegs gave her a kind smile.

'I know this may be painful for you, Annie,' Bill said. 'But
let's go back to the recent afternoon when Wells Giglio came
into the Black Dog.'

He could see how tired she was already. He had no way of knowing – yet – where she'd been all day, or what she had experienced. Since Alex had thought Hugh went up to bed after closing, it was obvious he'd left the building quietly, quite possibly to find Annie. Long periods of stress wore down the strongest people and he didn't think Annie was one of those.

'Did you think Giglio was suggesting you had something to do with Sonia Quillam's disappearance?'

'He was angry with me. I'm not sure what he was saying but he was horrible.' She reached for her water glass and emptied it. 'He was frightening.'

She would find out about Wells Giglio's death soon enough. 'What do you think he was suggesting?'

'That I knew what had happened to Sonia. I don't. How could I?'

'Is there anything you think – perhaps deep down – that you should share with me.'

After shaking her head, Annie rested her face in her hands and mumbled.

'Excuse me?' Bill said.

Raising her head, she looked directly at him. 'There is something. I went to see Sonia Quillam at Green Friday. I wanted to ask her to visit Elyan, her son, my fiancé, because she's never been and it would help him, I know it would.'

Deliberately, he didn't let time hang. 'That would have been on the 12th?'

'Yes. Once I found out she was there, I drove up to the house and talked to her. She was nice, but she didn't promise to go.'

'And what time was that?' Bill wondered if the visit was before or after Hugh was there.

Annie thought. 'I'm not sure. In the evening, seven thirty or so.'

After Hugh, then. 'Who told you where Sonia was?' He was more than ever convinced that this young woman could be the key to finding the answers to vital unknowns dangling around this case.

She went silent – again.

'Tell me about your conversation with Sonia,' he said.

Her pale cheeks flamed. 'I have. We'd have nothing else to talk about?'

'There was something else, wasn't there?' He almost held his breath.

'I'm so tired,' Annie said and sounded weary. 'Please, may I go upstairs and sleep? I'm not thinking properly. I need a clear head and I don't have one now.'

Longlegs got up and refilled her water glass.

Bill dealt with his own internal war. She wasn't wrong, but experience and protocol said he should push any possible advantage now.

Annie wasn't finished. 'Sometimes when you have others to consider, you can't just . . . jump in to make things easier on yourself. I need to think about other people. Can you understand that, inspector?' She reached a hand toward him.

Bill didn't want to understand but he could no longer pretend he was not human.

'Long day for everyone,' Liberty said quietly, doing nothing useful for Bill.

'All right,' he said, with a sidelong glance at Longlegs. 'We'll resume in the morning. I'll have someone see you get upstairs safely.'

'Thank you,' Annie said, getting up.

Bill rang for Miller to take her and the detective arrived in moments.

Once the door closed behind them, Bill turned to Longlegs. 'I didn't see any point in laying it on her now, but in the morning we'll have her taken to Gloucester and interview her there.'

'Sounds a good idea.'

'And you did a good job. Even if you do find Miss Bell charming.'

Longlegs grinned. 'She's still fairly young and if she's a guilty party in all this – most specifically, a killer – we can all give up on mankind.'

Bill laughed. 'She got to you! Well, join the band of brothers – we can all be susceptible to a lovely, innocent face.'

Laughing with him, Liberty scribbled on his yellow pad. 'Didn't I introduce you to someone?'

'Sorry. Did I forget something important?'

'Yes, you did. At the get together in May I introduced you to Benjamin – my husband.'

'Argh.' Bill grinned. 'Shows you a lot about my retention skills. I remember Benjamin but that's all. Nice guy.'

'The best,' Liberty said, smiling back. 'Guv, I think this girl is on the up-and-up. I don't doubt she's got a lot on her mind and some of it will probably relate to the case, but there's something about her.'

When Hugh had arrived at Alex and Tony's table he had said, 'Why didn't you shout when you heard me coming in? I wouldn't have turned the lights out on you. Sheesh, this hasn't been an easy day.'

Tony responded, 'We thought someone was breaking in for a minute. Good time to have the police at your table.'

Alex hadn't trusted herself to look at him. She smiled and sipped at her drink.

'Damn, I'm bushed,' Hugh said. 'I'm going to have a little Baileys with my coffee.' He sounded breezy, but watching him walk back to find coffee first, Alex wasn't fooled. Even with a smile on his lips, there had been ice not quite hidden in his eyes.

When Hugh returned, he sat in the only spare place at the table and tipped onto the chair's back legs, hands wrapped around his mug. The picture of nonchalance. He sipped coffee and Alex somehow doubted he had added much Baileys.

After twenty minutes, or perhaps more, of pointless banter, they heard the snug door open and close and footsteps on the stairs. A short while later, Bill appeared to join them. The detective constable was still with him. They took two chairs from another table.

Bill pushed his glass of flat bitter aside, abandoning it for silent observation. Cool he might be, but she could feel how sharply he concentrated.

'When I got here, Alex thought you were in your rooms,' Bill said. 'A better offer must have come up.'

'Something like that,' Hugh said calmly. 'I wasn't going to sleep so I went out for a drive. There's been a lot of upheaval in Folly of late. Any news on Sonia Quillam?'

'Not at our end. How about you?'

The cat and mouse game was not fun to watch.

'There's no reason Sonia would be in touch with me,' Hugh said. 'I made my feelings very clear the last time we met.'

'Really?' Bill gave him an unwavering look.

Hugh turned to Alex and Tony. 'What kept you two here so late? Just Bill?'

'I was at the Drake farm,' Tony said. 'Little mare had a difficult delivery but all's well.'

'I was waiting for Tony when Bill came back,' Alex said, feeling like a teenager making an excuse for bad behavior. 'We decided we'd both like a drink. Then Tony arrived and agreed.'

'And now there are five,' Hugh said, so evenly the air crackled.

Suddenly inspired, Alex said, 'Bill came to ask about Wells Giglio's visit. I told him everything I could remember. Can you think of anyone who was here that I might have forgotten. I got the obvious people.'

A door opened and closed – the front door.

'Did you say Harriet and Mary?' Hugh asked.

'Yup.'

'The man who owns the new chippy was here with someone I didn't know.'

Alex smiled. 'The chippy that opened months ago? That's Vince Springer of Springer's. I'd forgotten seeing him. The Peales were here. And Annie, of course.'

'And it was the Peales' friend who took Giglio out of the pub?' Bill said.

Hugh said, 'Yes. Very quietly and efficiently.'

'And the friend came back but Giglio didn't.'

'Giglio didn't.' Hugh tipped his head to one side as if deep in thought. 'I'm not sure about Saul Wilson – Harvey finally introduced me to him when I dropped off the shots they ordered – I don't remember seeing him again.

'It's not easy to notice a whole lot when Wells Giglio's been in the room. He has a way of using up all the air.'

Sergeant Miller hurried into the bar, a definite veneer of excitement on her cool features. She'd swapped her clacking pumps for soft flats and seemed more approachable.

'Well,' she said, 'he isn't using any air now, I hear. They

called from Gloucester to talk to you, guv. Your mobile must have been off. They said it's already on the tele that Giglio's been pulled from the bottom of the same watering hole as Percy Quillam.'

TWENTY-SEVEN

'You're early, Mum,' Alex said. 'I only just got here myself. Bit of a late night for some of us.' She would fill her mother in on the previous night's happenings later, when she felt like facing it all again.

Scoot came through into the kitchen, pointed at the boxes of fresh, fragrant pastries from George's Bakery and mouthed, 'Please?' Alex nodded and he opened the box.

'Take a couple, and for Kyle. Have you got your lunch?' He would be off to school on his bike shortly.

Scoot gave a thumbs-up and grinned at Lily. 'Kyle and I get the best lunches of anyone, don't we, Lily?'

'Off with you,' Lily said, but her smile was pleased. 'Got your homework?'

'Ye-es,' he intoned and left through the back door.

'Alex,' Lily said urgently. 'Do you know about Annie?'

'She's in bed as far as I know,' Alex said. 'What are you talking about?' She checked her watch.

'Mary phoned – about thirty or forty minutes ago. That's odd all on its own. Harriet usually does any phoning, not that it happens often. They're in a state, Alex.'

Bogie and Katie chose that moment to trot into the kitchen, tails wagging, noses raised expectantly. They always took a while to wake up and eat if Tony dropped them all off in the morning.

Alex steered them to their dishes, barely taking her eyes off her mother's taut face. 'What's the matter? Should I go up and wake Annie. Hugh's a bit late this morning, too.'

Lily made a fist and held it over her mouth.

'What?' Alex's insides were jumping around.

'Harriet looked out of the window this morning and saw Annie walking. Just walking, head down with her hands in her pockets. Scuffing along Pond Street as Mary put it.'

Alex thought a moment. 'She must be so tired after yesterday and last night.'

'A car came by – very slowly, Mary said Harriet said. They didn't recognize it but it was light gray. That Sergeant Miller got out and spoke to Annie.'

'Miller on her own? I wonder what that was about?' Alex couldn't stand still.

'Mary said a man came along and stopped. He said something – probably asking if there was a problem and if any help was needed. But he left so it looked as if everything was all right. But then Miller put Annie in the back of the gray car and drove off.'

'To go to Gloucester, do you suppose?' Alex said. She pressed her fingers to her cheeks, trying to decide what to do first. 'Bill's car was already gone when I arrived. He must have left really early.'

'Could we ask Bill about it?' Lily asked with hope. 'About why Miller picked Annie up?'

'I get the impression she only tells us so much about what's going on in her life.' The girl had chosen to be alone, which made her more vulnerable, but Bill knew that. Although Alex had known him for several years as an apparently cold, business-only man, she had learned he had a softer side. If he didn't, Radhika wouldn't love him.

'Bill would make sure she let us know where she is,' Lily said as if reading Alex's mind. 'We'll hear. But we'd better make sure Hugh knows about this immediately. He's good to her, Alex. He cares about her and I think she turns to him the way she would her family if they weren't estranged.'

Alex tried to smile but failed. 'I'll go up,' she said, but Hugh walked into the kitchen at the same time.

He looked at the two of them and frowned. 'Something's up? Tell me.'

'Oh, hell,' he said when Alex finished explaining. 'I wish she hadn't come to Folly at all. But I wonder if she came because of what's been going on – something we don't know about that's behind the deaths and Sonia's disappearance. I'm damned if I can figure it all out.'

His response made Alex feel better somehow. He didn't sound like someone who was involved in two unnatural deaths. 'What do you think we should do?' she asked. 'If she's going to be questioned, she should probably have a solicitor with her.'

'That will be covered, don't worry. I just don't know if she's emotionally in a place to give the right responses for her own good. But then, how do I know exactly what's going on with her?'

'I'm going to phone the police in Gloucester and say I'm coming in there,' Alex said, already in motion.

Hugh shook his head. 'They'll discourage you, Alex. That's a nice way of saying they'll tell you to mind your own business.'

'I'll say I have pertinent information on the case.'

'Such as?' He raked at his hair.

'I'll think of something.'

'I'm coming with you.' Hugh grabbed jackets for both of them from the back of the door. 'Let's just go. No warning phone calls.'

'Mum, call in extra staff, please,' Alex said, smiling this time. 'I don't know how long we'll be gone and you'll probably need help. Carrie Peale is always glad of work and Liz is coming anyway. Have her come earlier. It could get busy. Do what you have to do to cover for us until we get back. I know you'll try to put Harriet and Mary's minds at peace. Or do the best you can.'

Dan O'Reilly joined Bill in the observation area outside an interview room where Annie Bell would be sitting as soon as she arrived with Officer Miller.

'I don't believe this one,' Dan said.

'Neither do I.' Bill didn't need the comment explained. 'Annie's involved. There's no way around that. Could be she's protecting someone – who, I have no idea at this point. If we can get her to open up and give us everything she knows we might be very close to solving the case. I don't think she will, though, and there's going to be an emotional line we can't risk crossing, not unless she accepts representation.'

'What makes you think she won't?' Dan tipped his head to one side. 'What's going on?'

'She told Miller she's going to need time alone to think everything through and she won't want a solicitor. Speaking of Miller, she pulled an asinine stunt last night. I lost my legendary good temper with her once we were alone and she didn't take it well.' He glanced up at the clock. 'She's taking her sweet time to get here this morning. I hope for her sake that she doesn't follow one of her cracked urges and try to get information out of Annie before they come in. Detective Miller likes to try for attention-getting flashy moves. She knows better, but she pushes the limits too often.'

'What did she do last night?'

'Walked into the Black Dog and announced that Wells Giglio's body had been hauled out of that damnable water chute – and she did it in front of Tony and Alex . . . and Hugh.'

'Holy . . .' Dan put his fists on his hips and shook his head slowly. 'Is she going to make it in her job?'

'If she doesn't, I'm not going to be the one left holding the bag for causing her to fail. I'm not going there. But neither am I taking any more crap from her. She argued that news about Giglio's body was already out in the media, but it was obvious no one else there knew about it until she opened her mouth. Then she tried it on by reminding me how the Folly people always find everything out anyway.

'What she has going for her is a good mind and generally good instincts. If she can get it that following those instincts without running them by me could cause one hell of a mess, she might make a damn good detective.'

'Good luck dealing with her,' Dan said. 'Has Annie tried to make any calls yet? To let the Black Dog people know where she is?'

'No. And she doesn't have a mobile on her. Says she didn't take it with her when she went for her walk.' He raised his brows. 'Could be convenient. She's been told she can have a phone if she wants one. And the usual on counsel.'

'Are we sure she was making some sort of getaway from the pub, Bill?'

'Sherlock Miller is. I had her watching for signs that

Annie was up and about before going in to bring her to Gloucester. After she saw Annie leave the pub, she informed me of what our next steps should be. She talks as if she's the one in charge.'

Dan smiled thinly.

'So what's the plan? That's what she asked with Annie already in the car, so I told Miller to be quiet and listen. To say nothing else aloud.'

That brought a more sympathetic grin from Dan. 'And you said?'

'Be businesslike but sympathetic. And don't make up your own rules. She hung up on me!'

Dan laughed aloud. 'You've got your hands full.' His smile dissolved. 'But so do I, or I think I do. Friend Wolf may be making his hand more obvious. Remember how he was there at Quillam's second post-mortem?'

'Of course.' Bill frowned. 'So what?'

'Molly Lewis called me. She's been asked to submit reports on the two Quillam post-mortems. It's been suggested Molly was negligent with the first examination. Know what I'm beginning to think?'

'I think you'll tell me.'

'If you insist,' Dan said, the smile back in his dark eyes. 'I think friend Wolf has a grudge against the police and anyone attached to us – in any way. We may have to defend our honor.'

Before Bill could respond, a raised voice, likely at the booking desk, carried all the way to the observation room.

Dan held up a hand. 'Do I know who that is?'

'Yeah.' Bill drew a long breath. 'Hugh Rhys if I'm not imagining things. I wish I was.' He checked his mobile to make sure he hadn't missed any calls. 'I'm thinking I should call Miller again. She should be here. Come on.' He led the way from the room, closing the door behind them.

'Rhys doesn't raise his voice,' Dan muttered. 'He must be really ticked.'

'There's a special friendship there with Annie. Supposedly she looks on him as some sort of replacement family. She broke with her own. I don't know what to think about that. I'll let you know what goes down with all of this.'

Sure enough, Hugh Rhys stood in the booking hall with Alex Duggins. They both turned to face Bill as he arrived.

'Where is she?' Hugh said, out of character with his Mr Cool reputation. 'Are you questioning her again? She's not a strong person and she's been through too much already.'

'Hugh,' Bill said, 'You know I can't answer questions from the public. Not about an ongoing case. When Annie gets here, we'll take good care of her. That'll have to be enough for now.'

'Why is she being brought here?' Alex said. 'Last night you talked with her and then you were happy to let her go to bed while you sat with Hugh, Tony and me. This morning you pick her up on Pond Street while she's out for a walk. What changed?'

'Again, you know I can't answer your questions, but Annie will not get anything other than appropriate treatment.'

'Is there a solicitor ready for her?' Hugh asked.

Bill recalled clearly how Hugh had been so certain he didn't need, or want, counsel when he was brought in for questioning. 'Just know she's safe and in good hands.'

Alex settled into a chair. 'We'll be here when she comes out. Would you please let her know we're here?'

TWENTY-EIGHT

LeJuan Harding almost collided with Bill outside the observation room door.

'Where's the fire?' Bill grinned and after the tension with Alex and Hugh it felt good.

LeJuan wasn't grinning. 'Miller's been taken to emergency, sir. They say she'll be OK but she's taken a bad blow to the head and was out of it at first. They intend to admit her for observation.'

'I . . . damn . . . I knew it was taking far too long for her to get here. Where was the crash? Annie Bell, is she all right? Did she have to be hospitalized, too?'

'No.' LeJuan looked pained. 'There wasn't a crash. It looks

as if Miller was ambushed. Knocked out by someone. She was found a few feet from her car. We don't know where Annie is.'

When Bill arrived at the hospital, Miller was settled in a room on the second floor. He walked quietly to the side of the bed. With her hair down and in two braids, she looked like a teenager, even with the start of two black eyes and a cut lip.

'Guv?' she whispered. 'Sorry. I messed up.'

'It looks as if you had help,' Bill said and sat by the bed. 'I don't have a full rundown from a doctor yet. How are you feeling?'

'Thumping in here.' She touched her head. 'Sore, but I don't know if I was meant to be alive at all by now. Is Miss Bell OK? I haven't been allowed to talk to anyone but staff and they don't know anything. Or they say they don't.'

Instructions would have been given not to offer any information until the police spoke to her.

'We'll get to Annie. Let's talk about you, first.'

'I'm really sorry, guv.' She sniffed.

'You didn't hit yourself over the head,' he told her. He did know she'd taken a nasty blow to the base of the skull and some body blows – probably from kicks, he'd been informed.

Her eyes lost focus and he was afraid she would pass out again. Bill waited, not prompting, and she looked directly at him again. 'I thought he'd broken down,' she said. 'His car was slewed across the lane and the bonnet was up.'

'So you did what any of us would have done. You stopped to help.'

She nodded, yes, then squeezed her eyes tightly shut.

'Take it slowly,' Bill said. 'Do you need something for the pain?'

'No,' she said clearly. 'I think I called out and a man stood up from behind the bonnet. I flipped out my warrant card. I had turned off Pond Street in Folly to use that little feeder that takes you up to the High Street.'

Bill could see the scene in his mind. 'Got it.'

'The pain was blinding. I don't think that man moved from where he was so someone must have come up behind me.' She gave a weak smile. 'The first thing I remember afterwards is someone telling me I was lucky to have a thick skull.'

What Jillian remembered was everything to the case now.

He wanted her to initiate her own comments. If he led her, he could muddy the waters.

'I saw the car before,' she said, as if a veil were lifting. 'When I stopped Annie. The car pulled up beside us and the driver asked if we needed help. I told him everything was fine and he drove on. An old Passat, I think. Probably red to begin with but rusty and orange in splotches.'

'You're doing really well,' Bill said, starting to jot in his notebook.

Again her expression became faraway. A nurse tapped on the door and came in with a large arrangement of flowers. 'From your mates,' she said, putting it near the window. 'Tall man brought them in. Leggy, I'd call him.'

Bill laughed aloud, joined by Jillian until she closed her mouth and her eyes.

'You keep her quiet, sir,' the nurse said, smiling at her own success as a comedian.

A smile remained on Jillian's face when she opened her eyes. 'I don't think they've ever called me their mate before,' she said, and Bill felt a sliver of guilt. 'Guv, is Annie all right?'

He crossed his arms and let out a long breath. 'We haven't found her, yet. But we will.'

'She was in the car.' The panic on her face approached horror and disbelief. 'She couldn't have hit me like that, could she?'

'We don't know. You and I both know about small people who inflict a lot of damage when there's anger, or fear, behind it.'

TWENTY-NINE

Hours had passed since they talked to Bill. Alex contemplated going to the desk sergeant again but didn't want to annoy the man – more than she already had.

'At last,' Hugh said when Bill came from a corridor behind the front desk. 'Let's try to stay calm.'

Bill stopped to speak to the sergeant, spoke in a low voice and glanced over at them. Alex clasped her hands in her lap.

Hugh got up and went forward, said quietly, 'Annie's had a bad couple of years, Bill. She's been in there for hours. What she needs is some peace and for all this uncertainty to be over.'

'I'm sure,' Bill said. He looked away as if deciding what to say next. 'But you do recognize that we've got two suspicious deaths and a missing woman and Annie has been in the area and closely involved with all these events?'

'No,' Hugh said flatly. 'She hasn't been involved with any of it. Just because Annie was in Folly when both Percy and Wells died, doesn't mean she's involved in any way. Or with Sonia's disappearance.'

Bill waited, then said, 'Just tell me anything you think would help.'

Without further hesitation, Hugh said, 'Annie just opened up about seeing Sonia that night. But so what, she went up to talk to her about visiting Elyan? That was it. Annie loves Elyan – deeply – and tries to ease what's happened to him. Sonia hasn't been to see him but she has sent him messages. She told Annie she would try to go to visit him. Apparently she's very disturbed at the thought of seeing him incarcerated.'

'Right,' Bill said. He didn't seem surprised or very interested.

'That was all she said,' Hugh added.

'Thank you,' Bill said.

Alex went to join Hugh. Their anxiety had to be obvious but she couldn't just sit there anymore.

'There's nothing to worry you too much. This is all routine. I suggest you go home and get some rest. We'll let you know when there's something to report. I'll drive Annie back when that's appropriate.'

'I don't want to go until I see her,' Alex said.

Bill's smile looked forced. 'Of course you don't. But we can't know how long we need Annie here with us.'

Alex snapped, 'You said she wouldn't be here too long. That was hours ago.'

'You will help her the most by being supportive of the important part she's playing in our investigation,' Bill said. 'If you choose to stay, that's your prerogative, but I don't think it will help her to find out you're making scenes out here. But that's up to you.'

Hugh took Alex's arm. 'Let's go home. You'll let us know when we can do something for Annie?' He glanced at Bill who nodded, yes.

'We'll come back when they're ready to release her. Come on, Alex, please.'

She looked to Bill who nodded agreement.

'Inspector,' the desk sergeant said. 'Just an update. Still no sightings. She hasn't been seen on CCTV footage from Folly-on-Weir. They don't have much there—'

Bill swung around and the man stopped talking.

Hugh said, 'Bill?'

'Are you talking about Annie?' Alex asked. She caught at Hugh's arm. 'Are they?'

Bill faced them again and he wasn't hiding his anger as well as usual. 'We have everything under control.'

'That isn't the way it sounds,' Hugh said in level tones. 'Why not be honest with us? Lying doesn't help.'

'Hugh and Alex,' Bill said. 'Please go home and let us do our work. Check back in the morning.'

'And ask what?' Alex said. 'If you know where Annie is yet? Bill, we're her close friends and we feel responsible. How can we just go away and sleep?'

He sighed. 'If you think I feel any better than you do, you're wrong. I suppose, despite going against official protocol, I've got to say we're all very worried.'

'She's left this building?' Alex said. 'She ran away from you and you don't know where she is?'

'We're wasting time,' Bill said.

'Can't we start searching?' Hugh asked. 'The more eyes, the better, and we know who we're looking for.'

Bill sighed. 'We have ways of conducting this kind of search – we're pretty good at it and I don't think she'll have got very far. We're already on it.

'No one will get any sleep here, but please, go home and get some sleep yourselves tonight so you can be at your best for Annie. Will you do that?'

Hugh and Alex looked at each other and nodded faintly. 'Yes,' Alex said.

'We'll do our best,' Hugh responded. 'We're in this for as long as it takes.'

'Good,' Bill said. 'That's great. We're pulling out all the stops. Probably best not to raise alarm in Folly. Our people there already know and they're on the lookout. If Annie is heading there, we don't want to put her off with an agitated welcoming committee.'

THIRTY

Tony and Alex sat staring into the glowing fireplace at what Tony regarded as their home. He thought Alex probably did, too.

She only seemed lovelier to him. Simple in the way she presented herself, her hair dark and curly, her eyes greenish and curved upward at the outer corners, like Lily's, her mouth soft in repose, everything about her natural, compact and perfect for him. How plain would she have to be not to be perfect for him? He almost grinned but controlled the urge. He loved this woman.

'You doing OK?' he asked, knowing she couldn't be but that she would not give in to fear.

She sat beside him on the couch in the breakfast room and shifted closer beneath his arm. 'I am for now. Horribly worried about Annie, yes, but doing OK.' She turned her face up to his. 'Look at us. How could I not be?'

'That's how I always feel with you, but I have to be careful not to get soppy or you're likely to slap me down.'

She rewarded him with a sharp elbow to the ribs. 'We should probably get some sleep. It's late and tomorrow isn't going to be easier than today. Nasty thought.'

'We'll both be OK. I believe in Annie.'

'So do I,' she said. 'But I'm also a realist, Tony. I could never have expected her to decide to escape from the police. It's unbelievable. Sometimes the people we trust the most shock us.'

'Just keep on trusting,' he told her, although he was more than nervous about what they would confront. 'Wells Giglio was something I never expected, but it sounds as if he was murdered.'

'I feel guilty for being happy like this, but not letting myself take the moment won't solve anything.' Alex just kept her face tipped up to him. He smiled and rested his mouth against her forehead.

She pulled his hand down, opened his palm, his fingers, and placed a piece of paper there.

Tony frowned slightly. 'What's this?'

She pressed a finger to his mouth and he started unfolding the sheet.

'You can keep that for later,' she said, her lashes lowered. 'Just pop it away for now. I don't want to keep it to myself anymore, that's all. I'll be relieved when we get Annie back. She's too tense already. Hugh was obviously strung pretty tightly, too.'

He smiled and brushed her hair away from her forehead. 'And you aren't one bit upset, hm?'

'Of course, I am but . . . why pretend, I'm very worried. This thing with Annie frightens me. But I'm even more worried thinking about what's behind all this and whether we're going to face more . . . well, you know what I'm thinking. Is someone else going to die. It's horrible, Tony.'

'Please relax.' He pulled her even closer. 'We'll do whatever we need to do. And I trust the police to do the same. Most of all I'd like to hear they've found Annie. How the hell did she get away without anyone noticing? Was she snatched? What?'

'I don't think Bill and his people have any of the answers to that. I don't have any idea why or how she left the police station, but she wouldn't go if she didn't want to – unless, well, unless she was forced. That's something I believe. I'm trying not to think of her hurt and in danger.'

'Tomorrow is another day,' Tony said, and laughed. 'Not original, especially when it's already tomorrow. But it is true. And in the morning we'll be better able to see all this more clearly. Or I hope so.'

She settled against him, thinking, and trying not to consider what she'd given him. The sound of him unfolding the piece of paper and shaking it out put any idea of waiting a little longer aside, but it wasn't right to keep it from him.

Alex closed her eyes while she knew he was reading.

He was quiet for longer than it would take for him to absorb what the letter said.

'Alex,' he said softly.

'Mm.'

'Whether we do or don't have children – biological children – makes no difference to how much I want to be part of your life. For as long as possible.'

She held onto him.

'You know how I feel. I've told you often enough. Thank you for this – this report. It would never have made any difference, but I'd really like us to have children if you want them, too. Alex, can we get married? I'd really . . . damn it, girl, I'm fed up with trying to be so carefully unromantic. I want us to marry because I'm in love with you. I have been for longer than you can imagine. What do you say?'

'Hmm.' She smiled against his chest. 'That's all a bit soppy but I liked it. I say yes. Yes! But we do have some problems to deal with first.'

'Right.' It wasn't easy to sit still and be cool.

THIRTY-ONE

The phone had awakened them both before six in the morning. Bill called to tell them he was at the Black Dog and there was no news of Annie.

Alex stood in the kitchen, watching Tony make coffee. He had put bread in the toaster, pulled butter from the refrigerator and placed a carton of milk on the table. Neither of them had started a conversation since they came downstairs.

She poured some of the milk into a jug and set a knife on the counter.

All business, habit, to avoid talking about what really mattered.

Tony took travel mugs from a cupboard and poured coffee. 'Sit down while I do this, Alex. I'll get the toast, too. Do you want marmalade?'

Ordinary. Or trying to be ordinary when they were both so worried about what the day would bring – and enmeshed in their decision of the night before.

He poured coffee for them both. And ducked to kiss her cheek before putting the pot back. 'We're ready, Alex. Bill has let us know what they're doing. If we don't hear anything else very soon, I think we should contact some folks when we get to the Black Dog and let them know what we're planning for the day. Or at least for the morning. Hugh deserves that, too. He's as worried as we are. What I want most is to hear they've found Annie.'

'Tony,' she said, 'why doesn't she just show up? She's been gone all night. I don't know what we'll do if they haven't heard from her.'

'They hadn't when Bill phoned,' Tony pointed out. 'I don't expect him to be there when we arrive but we'll hear as soon as they get news, though.'

Carrying toast and coffee, they took the dogs and left for the Black Dog. Driving down the hill in Tony's Land Rover, Alex felt tighter and tighter. The sun rose, promising a clear, bright day but she felt a deep turbulence, a sickening premonition that the best of this day was behind them.

Tony pulled out his mobile and gave it to her. 'Could you get Radhika on the phone, please? No clinic this morning but she'll be there.' He picked up his coffee. 'She's got the house fire to deal with. I haven't done enough to help.'

When Radhika answered, Alex handed over the mobile and stared out the window, inhaling the scent of her coffee rather than drinking from the mug. She recalled asking Bill what he thought about finding people who were missing within a certain number of hours? Twenty-four and the chances of a good outcome got slimmer?

Sonia Quillam hadn't been seen in days, despite media appeals and search efforts. What about her car? If she had driven away intending to lose herself, she would surely have been noticed somewhere by now. Alex knew that a rental car had not shown up, or she hadn't heard about it if it had.

'That woman is something else,' Tony said, breaking into Alex's racing thoughts. 'Radhika takes things in her stride, some things that would stop a lot of people in their tracks.'

'I know.'

'Are you trying to fall asleep on me?'

She caught his little smile and patted his thigh. 'No. Afraid not. We're going to have another body show up, aren't we? Sonia Quillam isn't coming back.'

'I understand why you say that. It's impossible not to think the worst. But we must try to be hopeful – or, it would be easier if we could.'

'It would. So we get squared away in Folly and then start driving to every place we're aware of Annie going with Elyan. I keep hoping the police will find her Mini on CCTV from the day before yesterday. I tried to ask Bill about it but he cut me off.'

'We'll ask again,' Tony said, turning at the driveway to the Black Dog car park. 'A tow truck's coming out,' he said and backed onto the road again, parked to one side.

'Who would call a tow truck?' Alex said. She opened her door and jumped out. 'That's not even a tow truck. They've lifted it onto a flatbed.'

Her waving arms stopped the truck and she ran to the driver's window. 'What are you doing?' she cried. 'You can't do that.'

'Talk to the man inside,' he told her, indicating the pub. 'This is official business.'

And he drove on, carefully turning the vehicle onto the High Street.

Tony joined Alex and they watched, stunned, as Annie's Mini was hauled away.

Breakfast was served as usual at the Black Dog. Bill had almost decided to go to his flat in Gloucester the night before, but he had wanted to see Radhika and remain at the center of what was unfolding in Folly-on-Weir. He still had to think most of the answers were here.

He had barely slept and appreciated solitary quiet in the

restaurant, drinking the excellent coffee Lily had served and waiting for his full English.

He had no doubt that the parish hall was getting more frenetic by the hour and, no doubt either, fielding a stream of mostly useless tip-off calls.

He also knew he would hear the moment there was something useful. So far, nothing. What he wanted more than anything was word of Annie Bell.

He didn't look forward to dealing with the superintendent about her disappearance while under police supervision, but it was the fate of the girl herself that troubled him more. Her Mini was to be taken in for forensic examination this morning. Bill couldn't get his mind off the car being at Green Friday around the time Radhika's house had been torched. If Hugh and Alex had followed up on what had to seem odd, at once, and informed him the moment they saw him . . . If? If a lot of things on this one.

Voices reached him from the direction of the bar – growing closer. And hurrying footsteps. Alex preceded Tony into the restaurant and Bill prepared for whatever was making her search for and find him at his corner table, with anger radiating from her every rapid gesture.

'Did you arrange that?' She pointed toward one of the front windows, then looked out at the forecourt. 'It's gone now. You know things you're not telling us. That's your right but not when we're desperate to find Annie.'

Doc James, coffee carafe in hand, was an unexpected arrival. He took two cups from another table and poured for Tony and Alex.

Damn, he didn't need more complications now, Bill thought. This time they needed to let him do his job, not distract him.

'Sit and drink that.' Doc wasn't issuing an invitation. 'And keep your voices down. Hugh's using efficiency to pretend he's not losing more control by the second, and Lily's trying to appease everyone.'

Tony smiled at his father and Bill knew gratitude when he saw it, but Alex wasn't smiling as she slid into a chair opposite Bill and leaned toward him. 'OK, this is quiet now. Why has Annie's car been taken away?'

'I couldn't say.' As if that would buy him any space.

'Breakfast,' Lily said, carrying in two plates. 'One for you, Bill, and doughnuts for the table.' She dislodged a wad of serviettes from beneath an arm and set them down.

'Can I keep this on topic, please, people?' Alex took a bite out of a doughnut, rested her elbows on the table, chewed, and stared Bill in the eye. When she had swallowed, she added, 'That wasn't an answer and I'm not taking much more of this.'

The bacon was losing its appeal. 'Alex, I cannot share that information with you.'

'But—'

'I can't. We don't have Annie yet. We're going at her disappearance and at this case with everything we've got. I know you're upset – and scared – but I also have a detective sergeant in the hospital and I need you behind me, not blocking my path.'

'That's awful,' Alex said. 'But what does that have to do with Annie?'

He narrowed his eyes. 'I'm letting you know I've got a lot on my plate.'

She put her face in her hands and mumbled, 'Sorry.'

Tony stood behind her and squeezed her shoulder. 'What can you tell us, Bill?'

What he wouldn't and couldn't tell them was that Annie Bell could move into the suspects' circle, if she wasn't already there.

All eyes were on him. No pressure here. 'We have priorities – a plan with numbered bullet points. Joint top of the list: Sonia Quillam and Annie Bell.' *Not necessarily in that order.* He looked at his congealing eggs and picked up a piece of toast.

Doc James refilled the coffee cups, and Lily turned to leave the restaurant. The atmosphere did not get any lighter, but Bill would take any break he could get from the questions he couldn't answer, or not with what they wanted to hear.

His mobile, vibrating in his pocket, was a welcome diversion. 'Lamb,' he said when he answered. 'Yes. One moment.' He stood, holding up an apologetic hand to the rest of them, and withdrawing to stand by the reception desk. 'Go on, Legs. What have you got for me?'

'They're going to feed the CCTV footage to you down there, guv,' the detective constable said. 'They say it's not as good as they'd like it. They're still working on it. Three sightings so far and one of them is promising. They think all three show the Mini.'

THIRTY-TWO

There was no way to turn the light off from inside the room.

The fixture, high on a wall, had a metal mesh cover over a dim yellow bulb. By now it must be morning but there were no windows to help her know.

Her shoes were gone. Or had she lost them before? Her head felt wooly. It ached. When she touched her forehead she felt a lump there, bruised and sore, and flakes of dried blood came away on her fingers. Her body was heavy, the muscles tight. More bruises. Bruises everywhere.

This was a different room.

Again, she touched her head and wanted to cry. Would anyone hear? They had to hear. They had to come for her. They said they would.

Didn't they? When she was picked up?

The mattress on the floor had no pillow and her neck hurt, but she must stay there.

The light went out.

Screaming again. It had been screaming that woke her.

Screaming, or laughing?

Had she screamed?

I'm sorry. I didn't mean to make any noise, but you frightened me. Don't leave me here any longer, please, please. All I did was love him. All I have ever done for so long is love him. I never thought anyone would be hurt – would die.

No one will know. Believe me, please. You never have to fear me or be angry with me again. If you let me out, I will keep the secrets forever.

I fell. I remember now going down, pushed down, but I didn't do what you think. I didn't tell anyone. I kept you safe.

If you're not safe, I'm not safe. I told you no one had found out.

Under the door, a line of bright light showed. Morning – or later. Daylight, but not in here. Even while she was sucked away – again and again, she had heard him talk. He said he had to decide, but he wasn't going to let her . . .

Pain seeped back in behind her eyes, exploded inside her skull.

He was saying what he would not let her do, but she couldn't hear the words anymore.

THIRTY-THREE

'**B**ill's afraid we'll do something stupid,' Alex said while they watched him swing his car out of the car park. When they had closed the front door of the Black Dog behind them, they walked directly into Bill's path. Their mistake for assuming when he quit the restaurant he had driven away immediately. He was standing beside the Optima, just finishing a call on his mobile. Bill asked what she and Tony intended to do next and she told him. And he came as close to losing his temper as she had ever seen. As the tirade went on about interference, risking hurting rather than helping those who were in trouble, or worse yet, in danger, only once he'd said his piece did he slip back into Bill Lamb mode and lose the flush in his face and the jut of his chin.

He had said what he expected of them and walked away.

Tony shrugged. 'Shall we walk to the parish hall as ordered?'

'Of course,' she replied. 'What is he going to do? Stand us in a corner with a police guard?'

'I think we've stepped in it this time,' Tony said, setting off briskly. 'But you're right in what you've been thinking and saying – the police have more information than we realized, and they're determined to head off any interference.'

Alex hurried to catch up and took his hand. 'I want to know what they think they might find on Annie's car? Fingerprints – should be plenty of those – fibers, or blood?' She hunched her shoulders.

Harriet Burke's white handkerchief flapped from the window in their flat above Leaves of Comfort. 'Don't answer any questions,' Tony said. 'If anything gets passed on and Bill finds out, well, I think we'll be careful, won't we?'

She smiled a little. 'And that was your attempt to back away from telling me the obvious, I suppose. Work on it in case there's a next time.'

'Hi, Harriet,' he called, waving. 'Can't stop now. Get you later.'

'Just tell me if you've heard anything about Annie?'

Harriet leaned farther out and Alex pulled Tony to a stop. 'Let's not cause her to fall out of the window.' She raised her voice. 'Nothing yet. We'll let you know as soon as there's any news.'

'Did you hear that poor Mr Giglio was . . . well, he was beaten to death?'

They hadn't. 'No, who told you?' *And no doubt Annie's disappearance was all over the village by now.*

Harriet wafted a hand vaguely. 'It's fact. Coming from the post-mortem, we've been told.'

'By whom?' Tony asked, firmly enough to make it clear he intended to find out.

'Who do they think the killer may be?' Harriet persisted. 'Have they arrested anyone?'

Tony held firm. 'We don't know. Where did you hear about Giglio's death?'

'You come and see us later,' Harriet said, and closed the window.

'It's already getting hot and I'm already tired,' Alex said. 'Next those two will be telling us they can't reveal their sources. If they had a tele I'd accuse them of watching too many crime shows. And no, I won't be telling Bill what was just said. As it is, he's on the warpath about Folly gossip.'

The air was still and seemed tinted by the intense blue of the sky. Even the few cotton wool blobs of cloud hung still. Alex longed for a breeze.

'This walk is too short when you don't want to get where you're going,' Tony said and laughed. 'I wonder if Bill's told Hugh not to do any searching of his own.'

'He will anyway – if he wants to,' Alex said. 'I suppose searching might be pretty pointless, but you feel you have to do something.'

The parish hall door stood open – on hot days it soon got stuffy in there. Alex heard the constant sounds of ringing phones and waves of conversation. Not too many laughs. She and Tony gave one another a significant look and went inside.

Officers filled a phone bank on a row of metal desks facing the door in front of the tall screens that were now too familiar. Behind them, Alex knew, was the important stuff, the action center. Charts and photographs. Maps, whiteboards covered with briefing notes, sometimes more pictures taped there, and plans of attack on the current case together with names of detectives assigned to different tasks. And there would be that bullet-pointed master list, Bill had mentioned. She had caught sight of the 'private' area on two previous occasions.

'Now what?' Tony said. 'I almost think we should wait outside. The last thing Bill wants is for us to hear anything useful.'

'Useful how?' The man himself had approached behind them and Alex saw that he'd moved his desk under the windows, facing the hall and putting more distance between himself and the general clamor.

'Caught – again,' Alex said. She didn't feel like smiling. 'You know what we'd find useful. Anything that started pulling all this apart and showing us what's really happening – what you're thinking and which direction you're taking.'

He didn't use a snappy comeback and he certainly could have come up with several. 'I moved my desk,' he said, unnecessarily. 'More air around me. Come and grab a couple of chairs.'

Bill took two folding metal chairs from a stack against a wall.

'I never thought about getting in your way by looking for Annie,' Tony said.

'We wouldn't have,' Alex chimed in to be sure Tony didn't get too apologetic for being human. 'It's a helpless feeling to just wait. Every horrible scenario crowds your mind. Did Annie run away, or was she taken? If she ran away, where would she go? We don't even know if we should try to track down her family and find out if she went to them.'

'Already done,' Bill said. 'Coffee?'

Alex already felt vaguely sick from having too much coffee. 'No, thank you.'

'Not right now,' Tony added. 'Alex's questions are good ones. They're basic.'

Bill tipped his chair onto its back legs and rocked slightly. He clasped his hands behind his head and even though his startlingly light-blue eyes were veiled, she knew he was making decisions – about whether there was anything he would share with them.

Despite the noise in the hall, she felt separated from it, closed off with Tony and Bill.

'Would you have contacted the Bell family if you'd located them?' Bill said.

So, there was to be a test. 'No,' Tony said before Alex could give the wrong answer. 'It's not our place but when we don't know what you've thought of, we're bound to search for answers.'

'You would have brought their information to us to follow up?' The chair slapped back down onto all legs. 'Yes, I suppose you're telling me you would. But that's now, after the fact. Your history doesn't help your case. You've both put yourselves in danger before. OK, OK, let me say this much. Unless the Bells are hiding her somewhere and lying to us, Annie didn't go to them. We don't know for certain how she left – whether it was under her own steam or not – but we have theories I can't share with you.'

'No information, then,' Tony said flatly.

'Do you think she's alive or dead?' She hadn't intended to ask that.

Bill didn't immediately answer. He shifted a pen on the desk and watched the action.

You think she's been killed. The next breath she took shuddered. Tony didn't move at all.

'You must see the position this puts me in.' They got the blue stare. 'We assume life until we find out otherwise. Yes, the chances go down with every hour, but it hasn't been twenty-four yet, and we don't know – as I've already said – how or why she got away.'

A uniformed officer came to put a printout on the desk and Bill picked it up to read. He lowered the paper slowly. 'I can tell you something since it'll be on the news before we know it. There is footage of Annie's car in Bourton the day before yesterday. In several locations. We don't have a clear image yet, but we believe someone else was driving the Mini, possibly a man.'

'That can't be,' Alex said. 'She talked to Hugh from the car. She drove it back to Folly.'

Bill didn't comment. He straightened in his chair and stared past their shoulders. Not turning around was too much to ask. Alex looked and so did Tony.

The Burke sisters were on their way to the front desks.

'I'll get them,' Bill said, getting up and crossing the floor rapidly.

'Oh, dear,' Alex said. 'Since we didn't give them any extra information, they're likely to be here to ask for more from Bill.'

'I wish them luck,' Tony said, unsmiling. He got up. 'Could be they're going to spring us. We won't be learning anything else here and Bill will want to talk to them on his own.'

Alex stood also.

'Stay where you are,' Bill said, getting closer. The ladies were not fast walkers.

Tony and Alex situated two more chairs, automatically placing Harriet and Mary in the center. 'Easier if we can watch from the wings,' Alex murmured.

When they were seated, Alex turned to Harriet and Mary and decided not to say anything. They were agitated, fidgety, staring at Bill as he sat down. Instead, she looked at Tony who raised his brows.

'Nice to see you, ladies,' Bill said. 'May we offer you some Black Dog coffee?'

'No,' Harriet said, uncharacteristically short. 'We mustn't be long. Our boys and Lillie Belle are on their own.'

Bill made an understanding noise, impressing Alex.

'It's about yesterday morning,' Harriet said.

'It's about my not being a reliable witness,' Mary cut in. She pressed her hands flat on her skirt, deliberately making them still. 'I don't think I said everything to Lily. Lily did tell you about our phone call, inspector?'

His expression didn't alter. 'Why don't you tell me about it.'

'It's my fault,' Harriet said. 'I shouldn't have become so agitated and had Mary make the phone call instead of doing it myself.'

'Not at all,' Mary said – the sisters looked at one another now – 'I'm the one who screwed up.' She put fingers to her lips.

Harriet broke the strain by giving a short laugh.

Both women became quiet, Mary with a faint blush on her cheeks.

After a moment, Harriet went on, 'I'm sorry, inspector, but I was anxious about calling you directly. Not like me, I know, but in case – good gracious, listen to me babble. We decided to call Lily to see what she thought, and she said she would report what we'd seen. Lily is always so sensible.'

'Mum told me,' Alex said, unable to let them suffer on alone, 'and I rushed off to Gloucester to do things my way. Since I thought you knew the whole thing, Bill, I didn't say a word about what Harriet saw.' *Idiot.*

'Well,' Tony said. 'I can't miss this moment for joint confession. Alex and Lily told me, and I didn't say anything, either, for the same reason.'

'This is the thing,' Harriet said, with a reassuring pat to Mary's arm. 'We left out the bit about the other car.'

Bill leaned forward.

'The man you were told about, stopping to speak to Annie and Sergeant Miller was in a car. It probably doesn't mean a thing and we're wasting valuable time, but we had to make sure you knew about it.'

'My fault,' Mary said. 'I left it out when I told Lily.'

'I don't think I said anything about a car,' Harriet insisted. 'It's my fault.'

'Ladies, ladies,' Bill said. 'This is important, very important. Take a breath and tell me what you saw, Harriet.'

Harriet blew out through pursed lips. 'I was watching Annie with Sergeant Miller. The car came along behind them, slowly, of course. I actually thought there were two people in it at first, but my eyes aren't what they used to be, either.' She gave Mary a quick smile.

'Go on,' Bill said.

'The driver spoke to them and then he drove on. I was mostly watching Annie and the sergeant, but I do think it crossed my mind that I'd been wrong about the two people in the second car – unless the other person was short. That's all there was. The gray car drove away, too.'

Harriet paused, a hand slightly raised. 'There were two people, at least when I first saw the car coming. I don't know why I thought otherwise when it left.'

Bill smiled but he looked as if he wanted the interview completely over. 'Wonderful,' he said. 'That's extremely helpful.'

'Yes,' Mary said. 'Once we heard about Sergeant Miller being in hospital from a road accident yesterday, we knew we must come. Was Annie with her? Is she all right?'

'Inspector Lamb! May I speak to you, please? It's really important. I'm so worried.' Carrie Peale rushed beside the desk without acknowledging the rest of them.

Alex realized she'd been swallowing air since Mary's last revelation and closed her mouth. It was Sergeant Miller in the hospital.

'Sit here,' Tony said to Carrie Peale, giving up his chair.

Carrie seemed to notice she wasn't alone with Bill for the first time. 'Have you seen Harvey?' she asked all of them. 'I've tried to stay calm, but I can't any longer. There's so much whispering going on in Folly. He's missing. I'm afraid he's been hurt.'

'Thank you for coming. Carrie Peale, is it?' Bill's voice was gentle. 'Harvey is your husband?'

'Yes.'

'Where did you last see him – was it at your home?'

'Yes. I was in the pottery behind our cottage. I heard him start the car – it's difficult sometimes because it's old – so I ran to ask where he was going.' She turned rosy at that. 'I just like to know in case he needs me for something. That was early morning yesterday. I've got such a lot of work to do, I had started before dawn.'

'It's unusual for him to leave for work early?' Bill asked.

'He works at home,' Carrie said.

Alex made herself concentrate on what was being said.

'Was there someone with him?'

Alex held her breath.

'I don't think so,' Carrie said. 'I didn't get close to the car. Harvey got out when he saw me coming. He was angry, I think. He doesn't like me to ask questions.' She squeezed the bridge of her nose.

'Could you describe your car to me, please?' Bill said.

'Yes.' Carrie nodded. 'We rarely drive it. That's another reason I was surprised to hear the engine. It's a Passat. I'm not sure what year – about 1996, I think, or 97. It was red, but it's been parked outside for years and it's rusting, so it's more orange than red in places.'

Harriet said, 'Oh, my goodness! That's the car I saw. That's it.'

THIRTY-FOUR

'We're doing exactly what the police are doing,' Tony said. 'Driving around looking for this mythical red turning orange Passat. Old Passat.'

'It's not mythical,' Alex responded. 'It belongs to the Peales. And the police have technology and manpower on their side.'

'You know what I mean. I never heard of it before and I've certainly never seen it. I thought they walked everywhere.'

'I know. Harvey hangs out with the motorcycle club a lot, but that's mostly around here, I think, at the Black Dog. I don't think he owns a motorcycle.'

They had driven for two hours, almost following the Land Rover's nose through villages surrounding Folly.

'Do you want to risk calling Bill?' asked Tony, who was driving. He leaned to look up the driveway to a stone building on Kingcombe Lane after leaving Chipping Campden behind. 'I'll talk to him if you get him. If you'd rather, that is.'

'You don't think he'd call if they found Annie?'

'I don't know anymore,' Tony said. 'Let's hope Hugh never caught up with him. I understand the police not wanting to publicize what happened to Sergeant Miller, but I don't know how Bill could stand there in Gloucester and not tell the two of you that Annie never arrived. When Hugh found out he was so angry, he couldn't speak.'

The day continued to bake everything in sight. They had to stop for a tractor to leave a field. Unfortunately, it turned in front of them and traveled on slowly in the same direction.

Alex got her mobile but held it on her leg. 'I think I understand Bill not telling us. He must be under horrible pressure about losing Annie. And now it would be best if Harvey, or whoever was driving that car, didn't find out the vehicle has been identified. If he's got Annie and does a runner, it could be a total disaster. It may already be a total disaster. And Harvey is involved somehow.' She thought about it. 'It is. It's all horrible. When Bill decided to talk, he said Sergeant Miller was really bruised as well as having a blow to the head. Do you think it's the same person? With Percy and Wells – and now, Miller?'

'Because of the way he attacks? Yes, I do. I'm going to drive closer to Folly again. We went through Naunton, but let's do it again. Hugh said Annie likes Naunton.'

'That doesn't mean whoever she's with likes it,' Alex said, and picked up her mobile. 'Let's go there, though. All we can do is try.'

Bill finally answered. 'Hello, Alex. No, we don't have Annie.'

'Has anyone seen that car?' She no longer cared if she irritated him.

'We put out a description. Had to. Several potential sightings – each one in an unlikely place and a long way from one another. Oh, might as well tell you it was definitely a man driving Annie's Mini on the day of the fire. Forensics did their work on the images. No identification to share.' He hung up.

Alex started searching again while she thought about what Bill had said.

'Are you going to share?' Tony asked.

She told him what had been said and turned toward him. 'Who could this man driving the Mini be?'

'No ideas here, unless it was Harvey – which doesn't make any sense.'

'Even if the forensic people are right, a man couldn't be driving Annie's Mini without her knowing about it? Not when she drove it away and she drove it back?'

'That brings on the biggest question about this, doesn't it? If Annie did know, she's been complicit in a lot of lies – why?'

'And was he the one who drove it to Green Friday?'

Questions but no answers.

No luck in or around Naunton. They carried on toward Upper Slaughter and Lower Slaughter, twin villages.

With the River Eye in sight, Tony slowed the Land Rover. 'You have to go in by foot,' he said. 'Can you imagine them leaving the car and walking in? Why would they do that?'

'I don't think they would.' Alex flopped back in her seat and stared out the window. 'We're just filling up time pretending we're doing something that might be useful.' She sat straight again and peered down a bank toward a track through a stand of trees. Below was a stone barn, in need of attention, with the driveway leading past it to a limestone farmhouse in poor condition. A dark green car arrived and drove behind the barn. Within moments a woman walked from the direction the car had taken, toward the farmhouse.

'You've seen something,' Tony said. 'Tell me.'

'Between that barn down there and the farmhouse behind it, there's a gap that's hidden by the barn. Look, Tony, at the woman walking to the door. Quick. Is that who I think it is?'

He watched until the woman let herself into the house and closed the door.

'You go first,' he said.

'Neve Rhys! Tell me I wasn't seeing things. How could you miss how tall she is and all those black clothes?' She went for her mobile and Hugh picked up immediately with a barked, 'Yes.'

'Do you know if Neve has been, or could be staying at an old farmhouse near Lower Slaughter?' She could hear him breathing, feel him thinking, so went ahead and told him exactly where it was. 'They must have somewhere else to stay when they're not bugging you at the Black Dog. Neve does, I should say. I don't see Perry.'

'No,' Hugh said flatly. 'I don't know anything about this farmhouse. I have wondered if Neve had any connection to Annie. It seems vague, but I think they go out of their way not to acknowledge one another. I'm not sure they've ever spoken.'

'I've wondered about them running into each other but I haven't noticed what you're talking about,' Alex said. 'That would be strange.'

'I thought the same thing,' Tony said when he had her attention again and she told him what she and Hugh had discussed. 'I'm going to park and go down to see what I can see. She was very comfortable going to that house so it isn't the first time. We can't afford to miss a lead of any kind, even if I can't figure out the connections.'

'Neve and Perry sought out Annie at the tea rooms,' Alex said. 'She was very upset afterwards, remember. I don't think the Burke sisters thought those two were there by accident although it was Neve, not Perry, who did all the talking.'

He gave a tuneless whistle. 'Do we drive around and go up to the place? I don't think so. If it is what it might be and Annie's there, willingly or unwillingly, we don't want them to see us coming. If it isn't, I don't want to call Bill in, then try to save face if it's nothing.'

'Neither do I.' Suddenly, Alex's breathing was shallow. 'So let's decide how to do this. We need a closer look at the car she was in first. I know the one she was driving the last time I saw her and the one down there looked like it.'

Tony made a U-turn, drove up a footpath that was definitely not meant for vehicles, pulled off to one side beneath some trees, and they got out. 'You stay here,' he said. 'It won't take two of us to find out what we're seeing.'

Without arguing, Alex followed him across the road and started looking for a way to get closer.

'Don't run ahead or do anything on your own,' Tony said, without surprise that she had ignored his request. 'Please.'

'What's the worst that can happen? We say something silly

about thinking we saw Neve and wanting to look at the farm-house. Maybe we're thinking of buying one.'

Tony shook his head. 'Maybe you should leave this to me.'

At that, she left the conversation.

An overgrown track from the road quickly disappeared between trees. It was easy to veer right, staying under thick branches, and approach the barn. It seemed the trees grew right up to the ramshackle building on one side.

Stepping fast but carefully, Alex followed Tony, who must know she was still there, but made no further comment. She smiled at his broad back.

By unspoken agreement they made no attempt to leave the cover of mostly beech trees and made their way, with as little noise as possible, to where they could eventually see the barn. It was very close, its stones covered with moss where the trees shaded them.

At that wall, Tony edged along toward what was the front. They could see the driveway.

Voices, a man's and a woman's reached them and Tony pressed Alex close to the rough stones, flattening himself at the same time. He looked back at her, frowning, and held a finger to his lips. Alex's scalp started its prickling act and she grimaced. She didn't need a reminder that danger could be ahead of them.

'You sure you didn't hear anything?' the man said. 'Or read anything?'

'I told you, no,' the woman said. Alex was afraid she was already persuading herself this was Neve for sure. 'I'm driving back – now – and I'll check on the way.'

'No, I don't want you to leave. I need your help. You can't pay me enough for all the extra trouble you've dropped on me.'

Tony reached for Alex, found her shoulder and pressed. What the man said sounded odd, but it didn't have to be.

'I've paid you plenty.' The woman's voice was hard and almost a snarl. 'If you had just killed Sonia that night as we agreed *we* wouldn't be in this mess. All you were told to do was deal with her and then the girl – when I said the time was right. It was too bad Percy Quillam showed up like that and we couldn't expect it, but you didn't think it through. Look what you've done. Look what has to be cleaned up because you had no control.'

'Don't start with me,' the man was close to shouting, 'I already told you that disposing of two bodies at once was impossible. It isn't easy dragging a body to that pond. It wasn't my fault the husband had turned up and attacked her. After that we needed Sonia alive for a few days so that – damn it, I didn't want anyone saying the two of them had died at the same time! If Hugh is going to take the fall for Sonia, it couldn't be that way.'

'What is it with you and disposing of bodies in water?' The woman sounded genuinely mystified . . . and mean. 'You've got quite the history with watery graves. Now I know your secrets, and you'd better not push me any farther. Tell me about Wells? You still haven't explained that one. And more water, you fool. Where's your imagination? Tell me, did you have a good reason for what you did to Wells, too?'

'Apart from my hating the dramatic tosser, you mean? Yes, he was upsetting Annie and at that point you and I hadn't made a final decision what to do about her. Not for sure. But we didn't want her going to Hugh with the truth about the letter. That would've given it all away, wouldn't it?' The man phrased that last comment as a question but it was more a statement. 'Now, stop with the questions and come back inside with me.'

'Don't tell me you want sex again.' The woman, Neve – Alex was sure of it now, didn't sound completely opposed to the idea. 'The first time I saw you, at that hellhole psych place, I didn't have you pegged as a sex addict. I thought it was kind of fate that we found each other then.'

'You have some good ideas, when you aren't spouting your fantasies,' he said, 'but no, thanks anyway. We'll save it for later. You need me and I need you – just as we decided months ago. We set it all up – partly thanks to Annie – and Sonia. Now, you know what needs to be done, and there's more of it. It's time.'

If only she recognized the man's voice, Alex thought. It sounded familiar but she couldn't place it.

'And that,' the woman said, 'is all your fault for not making sure you'd done your job properly and then losing your head. And the police officer – I couldn't believe it when I heard. How many more do you intend to kill and still think you'll get away without consequences?'

'Don't start that again. I'm running out of patience with this, and with you.' The man's voice had become ominous. There was no reply this time.

Footfalls crunched on gravel, rushed footfalls.

'They don't know Miller's not fatally wounded,' Tony whispered and started moving forward and Alex followed – all the way to the corner of the building where he very carefully extended as little as possible of his head to see around.

His face jerked toward her and he offered his hand, which she held tightly. Quickly and quietly they moved around the corner and Alex saw that a door on the front of the building, the one nearest the farmhouse, was wide open, screening off any view of the approach to the front door.

They slipped inside the barn and Tony put an eye close to a door hinge and almost leaped back. He pushed her in front of him beside one of two cars parked inside. 'I'm texting Bill,' he said against her ear, and his thumbs probably moved over the keys faster than they ever had.

The passenger door on the car in front of them was slightly open, the failing light inside struggling to keep casting a thin veneer of yellow light.

An old Passat. Alex didn't need to make sure it was the right color, but she thought it was some shade of red.

A stench all but overwhelmed her.

She looked at the empty passenger seat, only it wasn't empty. Jean-clad legs, twisted sideways, were part of the man who had slid sideways in his seat.

Tony ducked his head in time with Alex.

The man's face was streaked with thin rivulets of blood turned near black.

She didn't need to get closer to know the glassy eyes had belonged to Harvey Peale.

THIRTY-FIVE

The pace at the parish hall had not let up. All around Bill he felt a fresh determination to break the case. This had been intensifying since news of the attack on Jillian Miller worked its way around.

He had eventually called them all together and emphasized the importance of trying to evade any questions on the subject from the media. Once the attacker knew Miller wasn't dead, she would be in danger again. She was being guarded at the hospital.

One of the contacts had been substantial and, if it checked out as he thought it would, it cleared up some queries. Percy Quillam's solicitor had called, asking for Bill. He told a fragmented story of Quillam calling him the night Sonia went missing. Percy said he was in the house with her – hidden, listening to a conversation with a female he didn't recognize. Who knew what part the man had played in Sonia's disappearance? The solicitor said Percy told him he probably needed to change his will, that Sonia told the other woman he wasn't Elyan's father. Apparently, he'd been distraught. Bill was almost certain the person with Sonia had been Annie making the visit she now admitted to.

'What do you think, guv?' Longlegs asked, coming to Bill's desk and pointing at photos spread there.

'Sergeant Miller has seen these and she doesn't know if they're of her attacker because she didn't see him – or her. Neither do we but we'll identify this man one way or another. He was driving Annie's car.'

His mobile rang and he saw Hugh's name. 'What?' he said as he picked up. 'Have you got anything? And where are you?'

'Outside,' Hugh said. 'I heard something that's probably nothing, but it could be deadly serious.'

As he cut off, a text came in. Bill glanced at the time it was sent. 'Five minutes ago. Mobile service is so slow out here.' He read the text from Tony and spun around. 'Armed response. Now. Going to Lower Slaughter. They'll get right there. I want you four' – he counted off the first four officers at the desks – 'follow us in two cars. No lights. No sirens. Listen to your radios.'

THIRTY-SIX

The quiet inside and outside the barn made Alex's eardrums prickle. 'Poor Carrie,' she whispered, but Tony touched her lips and glanced around.

He looked toward the other parked car and leaned across the Passat's bonnet to see better, moved behind her and back to see the rear. 'Mercedes,' he mouthed. 'Rental.'

'Sonia's.' She almost forgot to keep her voice very low. Dear God, what had happened here? What was going on inside that farmhouse?

A front door to the barn swung open with force.

Framed there, the sunlight behind them, were Neve Rhys – and Saul Wilson – from the Gentlemen Bikers Club – as Hugh had told them he was called. Their faces were shadowed.

Neve stepped inside, just inside, a gun in her hand and trained on them. 'You two,' she said, her voice clear and higher than normal. 'I might have known it would be you sneaking around. What do you want?'

Neither of them answered.

'It doesn't matter. You've interfered, and you've signed your own death warrants. All Hugh had to do was sign the intent letter to sell the distillery, but he wouldn't do it. For months I asked him, but he kept on refusing. I came to this nowhere place to give him one more chance. Now he's going to pay more than I could hope for. He's got everyone here fooled.' A sneer entered her tone. 'You don't know him. I deserve that business for what he did to my father.'

'Neve,' Saul said, and Alex didn't miss that he kept a hand in a windbreaker pocket. 'Neve, let's get this done.'

She waved the gun back and forth between Tony and Alex. 'Has he ever said he was engaged to be married? Of course not. Well, he was – to me – and I should have gone ahead with the marriage as planned. It would have been easier than being with his useless cousin. At least Hugh had the control.'

'We've got our own plans,' Saul said. He put a hand on Neve's shoulder but she shrugged him off. 'Listen to me. Keep the gun on them and wait. The timing will be everything. If the two in the house hear more gunshots, they won't buy my excuses this time and getting them out here will be more difficult. If Perry happens to be coming around from the last shot you gave him, he could be trouble, too. Let me go get them and I'll be right back.' Looking at her for seconds first, he left the barn and his running footsteps seemed loud.

'This will work. Don't move,' she snapped when Tony shifted a foot. The gun settled in his direction. 'As we leave, we'll text Hugh from your phone. Something vague like you've found Sonia and Annie and figured everything out. Tell him where you are. Perfect. A bit later, not too much later, we'll alert the police. Very neat. You see, Hugh has a vicious side you never knew about. Really vicious. He won't be able to talk his way out of this mess and Birnam Bricht will finally be mine once Perry follows all of you to hell.'

The woman could make a credible insanity plea, Tony thought. He'd never understood how killers who planned their crimes could be considered unfit to stand trial – for any reason.

He wanted to look at Alex but kept his eyes on Neve and his expression nervous enough to please her.

'They've found him, guv,' Longlegs said beside him. He glanced behind Bill at Hugh who was riding with them because he knew the area best. Bill nodded for Longlegs to continue.

He read from his phone. 'Saul Wilson, brother of Scott Zachary Wilson. Juvenile record. Nothing in recent years that we know. Early teens he had a penchant for setting fires. Liked to pick on sleeping homeless people. Give them a turn, a hot turn. Never got more than probation. No significant injuries. No deaths. Too hard to prove. They tried to get him for helping his brother chuck their dead parents into the water from a bridge.

Didn't stick because big brother wouldn't budge. Baby brother had nothing to do with it, according to him.'

Bill drove faster. 'And he was driving Annie's Mini on the day of the fire.'

'That makes sense,' Hugh put in. 'He wouldn't know it was my vehicle at Green Friday that day. And he could have set the fire at Radhika's. But, why? As a diversion? This is the turn for Lower Slaughter coming up.'

Various pieces started to fit together in Bill's mind. Looking at Longlegs he clarified, 'Saul and Zack's parents' bodies were dumped in water and over the past week we have pulled two bodies from that chute. I don't think that's a coincidence.' Meeting Hugh's eyes in the rear-view mirror, he said, 'I think Saul was hoping to distract the SOCO team from diving that afternoon. Perhaps hoping Wells would sink so far into the chute he wouldn't be found.'

The sounds of sobbing preceded Saul's return into the barn. Holding his hand, it was Annie who cried and held back as he pulled her along. His other arm was around Sonia Quillam's waist, half-dragging her with them.

'Shut up,' Neve all but screamed and Alex felt her own eyes sting. She was useless, she couldn't help Annie and there was obviously something wrong with her.

Barely conscious, Sonia sagged in Saul's arm. Barefoot, she wore a filthy pair of men's pajamas. If her greasy hair weren't scraped back from her bruised and scratched face, Alex wasn't certain she would recognize her.

'Still not saying anything?' Neve said, waggling the gun again. 'Isn't Sonia one of your friends? And Annie?'

'They are,' Tony said. Alex screwed up her eyes and waited for the impact of bullets.

Neve laughed. 'Sonia doesn't hold her drugs well,' she said.

Saul pulled Annie beside Sonia. 'Hold her up,' he told her. 'Shake her and she'll walk – more or less. Take her over there with them. I've got to help Neve here.'

By the time Annie had urged and dragged the shuffling Sonia close to Tony and Alex, the two women were practically crawling, and Alex tensed, expecting Tony to help them. But he knew what that would bring as well as Alex did and held his ground. Their only hope was that Bill had received Tony's text and was on his way; she hoped with others. They might be shot anyway. The certainty turned Alex cold to her bones. Her skin was crawling and clammy.

With Sonia at her feet, Annie got up to walk back and Saul said, his voice without inflection, 'Stay where you are, Annie.' She didn't protest, or cry out, just let her arms fall to her sides.

'Stupid, stupid, Annie,' Neve said.

'Not now, Neve.' Saul took out his own gun.

Neve seemed determined to spew all the hate she had stored up, and make sure they could see how brilliant she was. 'You did everything you were told to do for your pet convict lover,' she said. 'Saul told you his mad brother would keep Elyan safe from all the other big bad wolves in that sickening place and you were running out of money to pay him when you met me. Lucky you, I took over dealing with Saul.' She giggled. 'I'd already been there several times when you met me, you know. Sonia arranged it because the poor little woman couldn't go herself.

'Guess how I found my helper and lover boy?' She waved toward Saul. 'His brother was taking piano lessons from Elyan. Can you believe that? They came up with the notion to hit you up for protection money – for mad Artist Zack to protect Elyan from those nasty guards, or whatever they call them, and you swallowed it. I wrote the letter to you, Annie. But I'm sure Elyan would have done it himself in time. He's sick of you turning up and crying on him.'

Annie crumpled to the ground, wrapped her arms around herself, and started sobbing and rocking back and forth.

'For Chrissakes, Neve. Stop and let's get out of here.'

Neve's volume increased and she looked maniacal. 'You thought Saul was a friend and you let him use your car that day. Did you know he used it to get rid of Giglio's body? Would you have cared? After all, that man was drawing attention to you and the letter warned you not to bring any more unwanted attention to Elyan. Up the hill. Down the hill. Whatever the hill. Saul did it all for you and me – and himself.'

Annie's rocking brought her close to hitting her head on the floor. She repeatedly doubled over and then threw herself back, wailing loudly now.

'Saul was clever, too. When he saw the police and the diver going up to the watering hole – Saul's favorite dumping place – he didn't panic. There's nothing like a fire to divert attention. Not everything went exactly to my plan' – Neve cast a glare at Saul before continuing – 'I planned it all and I'll still get what's coming to me in the end. But I was the one who planned it all. I paid Saul to frame Hugh.'

A shot rang out.

Neve screamed and fell to her knees. Blood welled at her left shoulder.

'You're coming apart,' Saul said and took a single step backward. 'I told you to shut up! I looked forward to sharing your whiskey money, but I've made a pile already. You're too much of a liability. Throw me your keys. They don't know your car.'

Instead, Neve pointed her weapon at him, but it slipped through her fingers and she slid, moaning, all the way to the filthy floorboards.

Saul went to pick up the gun but before he could stand again, a figure in black crossed the space from the open door and took him in a headlock.

No more shots were fired.

THIRTY-SEVEN

We're alive and we're here and there are no other people I'd rather be with or any place I would rather be.

Alex looked around the quiet group gathered in the snug. Tony beside her, probably feeling as dirty as she did. Hugh studying his untouched coffee but managing frequent sips of his brandy. Lily and Doc James sat on the banquette, but Alex felt Lily hovering, barely able to hold back from the questions she wanted to ask – again.

'Anyone else expect to be questioned again at any moment?' Tony asked. He let Bogie nuzzle his fingers. 'Intuition tells me Bill Lamb will come back to us, and soon. Questions and more questions. But he gave us more information than I expected.'

Hugh emptied his glass and reached for the bottle. 'I'm the fool here. Charges will probably come my way. Fortunately, I don't know enough to work out how many or exactly what they'll be for. It's easier this way.'

'Don't get ahead of yourself,' Doc said. 'None of you took bullets. That's what counts.'

Hugh offered the open bottle around and poured for everyone. 'True, Doc, but I'm going down as an obstructionist and a liar.'

'You didn't hurt anyone, and you tried to help,' Alex said. 'You were trying to protect other people. And you haven't been arrested yet.' She slapped her hands over her face.

Laughing with the others, Tony said, 'That was a reassuring thing to say, love. Very kind.'

She took her hands from her glowing cheeks and laughed, too.

'You're not going down for anything,' Lily said. 'Don't think about prison.'

More chuckles followed.

Tony muttered, 'Gallows humor.'

All they had left for that were smiles.

'They won't let Saul out on bail, will they?' Lily asked.

'No,' Doc said at once. 'He's never getting out. Neve Rhys won't see daylight for a long time, either. She's in for some surgery first and from what I've been told, Saul did a lot of damage to her clavicle and the shoulder is a mess.'

'And Perry's a mess,' Hugh said. 'He was almost in a coma when they found him in that farmhouse. He was quiet and getting quieter while he was here after they arrived, then I didn't see him at all. I should have tried to find out why but I think he was being systematically drugged. I believe Neve was only keeping him alive so he could take over Birnam Bricht – in name anyway – after I took the fall for her. I don't see how she would pull off selling, but I don't have her mind.'

Alex thought about, but didn't mention aloud, Hugh being engaged to marry Neve. It was unimaginable.

'You all need food,' Lily said. She went to the bar window and leaned through. Liz Hadley was working tonight, with curate Juste Vidal.

The hum of noise from the saloon bar was noticeably tamped down – a sign that people knew who was in the snug. How they would love to hear what was being said!

'Neve must have given those two photographs to Sonia to make some point,' Hugh said quietly. 'Neve took the one of me – in another lifetime. So true that love and hate are close neighbors. I didn't guess how close. What she did for hate . . .' He picked up his glass and watched the brandy swirl slowly.

What Alex felt for him wasn't pity, it was closer to grief for the loss of his youthful optimism.

They were avoiding talking about Annie. First, she would have to get well and nothing had been said about what charges she might face if and when that happened.

With a large plate of golden chips and serviettes in hand, Lily came back to the table. 'Sausage rolls being heated,' she said. 'I'd rather not discuss Annie tonight if that's all right.'

Alex blew her a kiss. 'Sonia's puzzle will have to wait, too. The poor woman has been through so much and I don't think she intended anyone harm.'

Hugh grunted. He was making a sizeable dent in the chips.

'I want to ask Tony and Alex to do something for me,' Lily said. 'Today was horrible. Worse than almost anything I can imagine.'

'I was terrified,' Alex said quietly, and reached for her brandy.

'Ditto,' was Tony's response.

Alex turned to him. 'I've never been so scared.'

'Yes, that too.'

Lily put her elbows on the table and said, 'So will you promise me nothing like this will happen again?'

Placing a hand firmly on top of Alex's, Tony said, 'Alex and I—'

Scoot tapped the door and came in. 'You're not answering

your phones,' he said. 'Inspector Lamb says for you to stay
here until he comes and he'll soon be on his way from
Gloucester.'

Tony turned to Alex and shook his head, a wry smile on his
lips. If he was planning an announcement, it had been thwarted,
at least for now.

Bill waited while Dan finished putting on his coat. 'You on
your way home now?'

'Unless I get a better offer.' Dan cocked his head toward the
door of his office. 'I'll walk you out and you can fill me in on
any grisly details I've missed. Don't let me forget to tell you
the latest on Dr Leon Wolf.'

'Tell me now. That man gives me hives.'

'Yeah?' Dan said. 'I think he'd like to give me worse than
that. He's working hard on proving I'm incompetent, while
suggesting my ongoing cases might be saved with a lot of
help from him. He's scuttling back and forth to the chief
constable. The walls have ears around here and the doctor
doesn't realize the old guard, and some of the not so old, stick
together. I hear things.'

'Rat,' Bill said and when Dan raised his eyebrows in question
explained, 'I'm cleaning up my language for Radhika.'

'Oh, well Wolf hasn't allowed for Balls and Dan, intrepid
investigators. It may take time to blow him out of the water
and if we fail . . . we won't fail. And we're watching him, and
listening. We have the Force on our side.'

Bill grinned. 'Heaven help him.' He hoped he was right.
They pushed open the door to the car park. 'I'm going to Folly
to make sure there isn't anything the Black Dog crew have
forgotten to tell us.'

'Be kind if you can,' Dan said. He rubbed at his jaw where
the old scar still irritated him, and pulled his ever-present
bag of sticky sherbet lemons from a pocket. 'Will you have
one.'

'I'll pass, thanks. I've saved the best for last tonight and I'll
be giving them a shortened version of this. You know Molly
confirmed that Percy Quillam was dead before he went into the
water?'

'Right,' Dan nodded.

'It's now certain he died from cardiac arrest and was most probably dead when Saul Wilson got to the scene. Saul didn't know that and still doesn't. He will. He's running his mouth, by the way. Can't tell enough tales fast enough.

'The irony is that if Percy hadn't come along, Wilson – if he kept with the plan he and Neve Rhys hatched – would have murdered Sonia. By falling and dying on top of her, Percy saved Sonia's life.'